To Becky,

Revolutionary
Messages

f ... it

means to fall in love again,

yours forever,

Ted x

To find out about other titles in the Theatre Makers series,
please visit:

https://www.bloomsbury.com/uk/series/theatre-makers/

Revolutionary Messages

Antonin Artaud

Translated by Joel White

methuen | drama

LONDON • NEW YORK • OXFORD • NEW DELHI • SYDNEY

METHUEN DRAMA
Bloomsbury Publishing Plc
50 Bedford Square, London, WC1B 3DP, UK
1385 Broadway, New York, NY 10018, USA
29 Earlsfort Terrace, Dublin 2, Ireland

BLOOMSBURY, METHUEN DRAMA and the Methuen Drama logo are
trademarks of Bloomsbury Publishing Plc

This translation first published in 2024
Translation copyright © Joel White

Cover image © Pawel Czerwinski / Unsplash

Bloomsbury Publishing Plc does not have any control over, or responsibility for,
any third-party websites referred to or in this book. All internet addresses given
in this book were correct at the time of going to press. The author and publisher
regret any inconvenience caused if addresses have changed or sites have ceased
to exist, but can accept no responsibility for any such changes.

A catalogue record for this book is available from the British Library.

ISBN: HB: 978-1-3501-7902-8
        PB: 978-1-3501-7901-1
        ePDF: 978-1-3501-7903-5
        eBook: 978-1-3501-7904-2

Series: Theatre Makers

Typeset by RefineCatch Limited, Bungay, Suffolk
Printed and bound in Great Britain

To find out more about our authors and books visit www.bloomsbury.com
and sign up for our newsletters.

For Mads, for their support and love

CONTENTS

FOREWORD

Antonin Artaud's force and intense focus as a thinker of revolution has until now been lost in translation for his English-language readers. The arrival of *Le Théâtre et son Double* at Black Mountain College, North Carolina, in the baggage of John Cage in the late 1940s would situate Artaud's work for almost half a century in the exclusively aesthetic context of Happenings, chance and Experimental Music. The emergence of Mary Caroline Richards' translation from the matrix of reading and discussion groups at Black Mountain College accompanied by Maurice Saillet's 'In Memorium: Antonin Artaud' sealed its avant-garde but apolitical fate. Moreover, Saillet's widely shared fascination with Artaud's descent into and return from madness also shaped the later translated selections from his works, above all Susan Sontag's collection of shards from the mirror that Artaud, in André Breton's words, 'went right through'. Not only is the political dimension of Artaud's work almost lost, but the focus on his psychopathology and aesthetics has encouraged serious misunderstandings of his political stances during the 1930s.

The welcome publication of *Revolutionary Messages* in Joel White's forceful translation makes available in English an important series of documents connected with Artaud's visit to Mexico in 1936. They testify to the lucidity of Artaud's political judgement and to its inseparability from a sustained reflection on the question of revolution, extending back to his expulsion from the Surrealists. The testimony of *Revolutionary Messages* unequivocally distances Artaud from any enthusiasm for the Fascist movements gaining power in Europe at that time and shows him as a shrewd analyst of the limits of the Mexican Revolution. White's invaluable introduction traces the origins of some of the limits of Artaud's political understanding, especially around the questions of colonialism and race and offers an irresistible invitation to follow Artaud in elaborating his views on European and Mexican art and politics through the lectures and newspaper articles that accompanied his journeys through Mexico.

The translation of *Revolutionary Messages* joins the recent complete translation of *Heliogabus or, the Crowned Anarchist* in providing the material for a fundamental reassessment of Artaud's revolutionary politics as it emerged during the critical years of the mid-1930s. It provides the setting for a reconsideration of *Le Théâtre et son Double* and another direction from which to approach the perplexities of *The New Revelations of Being*.

Yet, White's translation offers far more than a mere act of scholarly restitution. White believes we still have much to learn from Artaud, not only from his reflections on the energetics of revolution and solar politics that are of glaring contemporary relevance but also from his style of thinking the political as a 'logomachy'. This translation subjects us to the test not only of reading Artaud differently but also of heeding his messages when confronting our own emergent fascisms.

Howard Caygill

INTRODUCTION

Artaud's 'Messages'

On face value, Antonin Artaud's *Revolutionary Messages* is an English translation of the French *Messages révolutionnaires*, first published posthumously in 1971 as a major part of *Tome VIII* of the completed works of Antonin Artaud, edited by Paule Thévenin and published by Gallimard, the title of which remains *De quelques problems d'actualité aux messages révolutionnaires*. The book, itself envisioned by Artaud, collects a set of lectures, articles, reviews, notes and catalogue texts that Artaud mostly wrote while in Mexico in 1936 between 7 February, the date of his arrival at Ver Cruz, and 31 October, the eventual date of his departure. Since 1976, *Messages révolutionnaires* has been published by Gallimard outside of the collected works in the collections 'Ideés' and now 'Folio essais' under this singular title.

However, to leave it at such face value would do an injustice to the palimpsestuous history of Artaud's *Messages révolutionnaires*.[i] The present translation into English, for the most part, is based on the posthumously published French translation or 'retranscription' conducted by Thévenin under the name Marie Dézon (due to the ongoing dispute between her and Artaud's family over the manuscripts) and Philippe Sollers. This retranscription was based on Spanish translations of the 'original' French, which is now mostly lost. As Thévenin confirms in the notes to *Messages révolutionnaires* and the 'Préface' to *Les Tarahumaras* (Artaud's other 'Mexican' text), many of these originals were either written on scraps of paper or serviettes picked up at the Café de Paris where Artaud would spend most days in Mexico City, or they were interpreted directly from a dictated French – as Artaud was apt to do – into Castilian.[1] The Spanish versions were mostly published in the Mexican newspaper *El Nacional Revolucionario* and translated by several of Artaud's friends and acquaintances in Mexico: Alberto Ruz Lhuillier, Samuel Ramos, José Ferrel, José Gorostiza, Xavier Villaurrita, Enrique O. Henriquez and, lastly, Luis Cardosa y Aragón, Guatemalan writer, poet and diplomat, who collected the Spanish translations, publishing the first edition of this text under the title *México* in 1962.[2] Often the French was, therefore, *originally* ephemeral. Thus, no trace of it would exist. Cardosa y Aragón writes this beautiful passage about Artaud and the way he would dictate his texts in Mexico City:

> I see him with the cigarette butt stuck to the corner of his mouth, a handkerchief tied around his head, writing his despair to get rid of it. His eyes, blue and reddish, open with the frantic brilliance of the tension of his spirit. Gnarled hands, roots that want to grab hold of the air. Suddenly, he takes the pages, his magnificent voice unravelling the hidden meanings in his words.[3]

While Artaud is entirely responsible for the book's concept and its French title, *Messages révolutionnaires*, as stated in a letter dated 21 May 1936, to his friend and editor Jean Paulhan, to which three dactylographic copies of the lectures delivered at the University of Mexico were attached, Artaud did not compile any of the other articles for the book.[4] As per the posthumous nature of the publication, they were initially collected and ordered chronologically by Cardosa y Aragón, an order that Thévenin and Sollers mostly

---

[1] For example, 'I Came to Mexico to Flee European Civilization' was entirely dictated to Alberto Ruz Lhuillier. See n. lii.

[2] Antonin Artaud, *México*, ed. by Luis Cardosa y Aragón, coll. 'Poemas y ensayos' (Mexíco: Universidad nacional autónoma de México, 1962).

[3] Luis Cardosa y Aragón, 'Prologo', in Artaud, *Mexíco*, ed. by Cardosa y Aragón, coll. 'Poemas y ensayos', 7. All translations from Spanish and French, unless indicated otherwise through the citation of a particular translation, are my own.

[4] V, 205. References to Antonin Artaud's work will be to the 26 tomes of the *Œuvres complètes* and to the two volumes of the *Cahiers d'Ivry*, published by Éditions Gallimard (1984–2011) and edited by Paule Thévein and Évelyene Grossman, respectively. I will refer to successive volumes of the *Œuvres complètes* using the roman numerals I, II, etc, and to the *Cahiers d'Ivry* with the abbreviation CdI. The symbol * will indicate the volume number of different tomes.

followed. There are, nonetheless, several important distinctions. First, unlike Cardosa y Aragón's *México*, *Messages révolutionnaires* is split into three parts by Thévenin; the first, 'I', now translated as 'Three Lectures Delivered at The University Of Mexico', collects the three lectures given at the Mexican University on 26, 27 and 29 February; the second, 'II', 'Mexico', collects the articles written for *El Nacional* that do not explicitly refer to the Tarahumaras plus the article 'Post-War Theatre in Paris', a conference published in the journal of the University of Mexico (UNAM); lastly 'III', 'Franz Hals. Ortiz Monasterio. Maria Izquiero', collects the articles, also published in Mexico, that concern Artaud's review of two Mexican artists, Maria Izquierdo and Ortiz Monasterio, as well as a text on the Dutch painter Franz Hals. This last text was strangely published in the *Boletin menusel Carta Blanca* at the request of the Mexican brewery Cuahtemoc, which still runs today, albeit now owned by Heineken.

Since the aforementioned first three lectures of the book exist in their French original as manuscripts – the first of which, 'Surrealism and Revolution', was not published in Spanish – parts of the present translation constitute direct translations from French that were sent to Paulhan at *La Nouvelle Revue Française (N.R.F.)*. Thévenin and Sollers likewise used these originals alongside letters that Artaud wrote at the time to retranscribe the French from the Spanish. This produced the retranscribed version that approximated the original French, and these texts were indicated as such at the end of each article. For the present translation, I have likewise consulted the Spanish, when needed, as collected and published in Cardosa y Aragón's *México*, as well as the notes that Paule Thévinin and Philippe Sollers left regarding their choices, notes provided in the augmented version of *Tome VIII*.[5] Cardosa y Aragón also prefaces *México* with an especially useful 'Prologue' that has supplied this translation and introduction a great deal of extra information about Artaud's trip to Mexico.

As one might expect, the convoluted nature and retranscription of these articles were subject to some scandal in France. This has

---

[5] I tried at length to contact Phillipe Sollers, who sadly passed away while this translation was in preparation.

often been the case for texts published in Artaud's name and stems from the feud that existed between Thévenin and Artaud's own family over who should be in control of Artaud's legacy. Before his death, and as a part of the initial research for the present translation, Sylvère Lotringer assured me via personal correspondence of their authenticity:

> There is no question about the authenticity of the *Messages révolutionnaires*. There was a small scandal in France when it was discovered that a text that Artaud wrote in French, and that he got his Mexican friends in Mexico to publish in Spanish in a Mexican magazine (he was broke) had been translated back into French (the original was lost). Besides that, Artaud's style and obsessions are definitely his. I personally met a Surrealist Mexican poet in Mexico City, and he had these articles turned into a book in Spanish.[6]

The Mexican poet here is most likely the Guatemalan Cardosa y Aragón, who should be recognized as the hero of this book's survival. Mexican poet and Nobel Prize winner Octavio Paz describes Cardoza's importance for Mexican poetry, 'We heard Cardoza defend poetry, not as an activity at the service of the Revolution, but as the expression of perpetual human subversion. Cardoza was the bridge between the avant-garde and the poets of my age.'[7] This is certainly the case for *Messages révolutionnaires*; Cardosa y Aragón was the bridge that made this present translation, or any other translation of *Messages révolutionnaires*, possible.

Parts 'I', 'II' and 'III' of the present translation hence constitute an English translation of Thévenin and Sollers' division and retranscription of the texts taken from Cardosa y Aragón's *México*. Deciding that four articles from *México* were more at home in *Les Tarahumaras*, they were placed into this edition by Thévenin, 'La montagne des signes' ('La montaña de los signos'), having already been published in 1945 by Henri Parisot in *Au Pays des Tarahumaras*, a year before Artaud's release from Rodez. Artaud's intention to

---

[6]Private correspondence, November 2017.
[7]Luis Cardosa y Aragón, *Luna Park*, trans. Anthony Seidman (Phoenix, AZ: Phoenix Cardboard House Press, 2016).

publish a book about the Tarahumaras as separate from *Messages révolutionnaires* is made patent by this publication. There is also the letter to Paulhan, where the title *Messages révolutionnaires* was first mentioned.[8] Here, Artaud writes: 'a Mexican editor has just proposed to collect all my texts on the indigenous culture of Mexico into one book, and to add diverse texts on the theatre, "Affective Athleticism and the letters on language", among others'.[9] Stressing 'all my texts', Italian translator, Marcello Gallucci, whose 2021 translation of *Messages révolutionnaires* includes a very detailed overview of all the articles' histories, argues that there are grounds to include into *Messages révolutionnaires* all texts on Mexican culture, including those about the Tarahumaras.[10] Given that Artaud published a book called *Au Pays des Tarahumaras* in his lifetime, that the existent 'Messages' mentioned in the letter have already been collected into *Messages révolutionnaires* and that Artaud's writings on the Tarahumaras have remained separate since 1974 (the publication date of *Tome IX* of the collected works), different to Gallucci, I find there is no reason to integrate all Mexican texts into the present translation of Artaud's *Revolutionary Messages*. If one were to undertake such a project, collecting everything under an all-encompassing heading such as *Mexico* would make more sense, following Cardosa y Aragón's initial title.

However, the complexity of *Revolutionary Messages* does not end here. Due to a series of discoveries after the initial publication in 1971, eight other texts from this period can now be included in *Messages révolutionnaires*. These eight texts include three texts that appear in *Tome VIII* of the completed works: 'Mexico and Civilization', which remains in note form and likely served as a draft for one of Artaud's three conferences at the Mexican university; 'Awakening of the Thunderbird', written in 1935 for the journal *La Bête noire*, no. 6, and which now appears as an addendum to *Tome VIII*; and 'The Eternal Betrayal of White People', which was originally published in the Cuban journal *Carteles*, November 1936. Indeed, on 30 January, before Artaud arrived in Mexico, five

---

[8]V, 205.
[9]V, 205.
[10]Antonin Artaud, *Messaggi rivoluzionari*, trans. Marcello Galluci (Milan: Jaca Books, 2021).

texts were given to different editors in Havana. This last text, now also belongs alongside four more recently discovered articles published in Havana in 1936 (June to December) for the Cuban journal *Grafos*. These four articles include: 'Theatre in Mexico', '*La Corrida* and Human Sacrifices', 'Red Paint' and 'Indians and Metaphysics'. Poet Laurine Rousselet discovered these texts in 2009 at the Biblioteca Nacional de Cuba José Martí while on a writing residency at the Stendhal Institute. They were translated back into French by Vincent Ozanam and included as an annex to the *Correspondance avec Bernard Noël* by Rousselet, published in 2021.[11] Finally, there is also 'The Force of Mexico', which, like 'Mexico and Civilization', remains in note form. This was published in the *N.R.F.*, no. 254–5 (July–August 1982). While these constitute the entirety of the texts so far rediscovered, according to letters sent between Thévenin and Cardosa y Aragon, 1971 to 1978, Artaud also sent at least one article to the Argentinian conservative newspaper *La Nación* in Buenos Aires – this has yet to be found despite Artaud scholar Illios Chailly and myself contacting archivists at *La Nación*.[12]

The translation of Artaud's *Revolutionary Messages*, similar to Galluci's newly published Italian translation, has chosen to incorporate these eight texts, as Gaulluci chose to incorporate the five published in the Cuban journals as well as 'Le Rite des Rois de L'Atlantide' (which is usually published in *Tarahumaras*). Since there is no reason that the other four texts mentioned above should not be included, I chose to include all eight.

This makes the present translation of *Revolutionary Messages* the first English translation of these texts and the most comprehensive collection of his Mexican revolutionary texts yet published. Using Thévenin and Sollers' divisions as inspiration, part four, 'IV', has been named 'Havana' and collects the five texts written for the Cuban journals. As Artaud scholar François Audouy writes, 'These texts would undoubtedly have found a place in *Messages révolutionnaires* [. . .] Besides, they would have undoubtedly been included if Paule Thévenin – who was aware of their existence –

[11]Laurine Rousselet, *Correspondance avec Bernard Noël Artaud à La Havane* (Paris: L'Harmattan, 2021).
[12]See Fabienne Bradu, *Artaud, Todavia* (Mexico City: Fondo de Cultura Económica, 2008).

had been able to locate them.'[13] Already having the idea for an English version, the four recently discovered Havana articles were translated in collaboration with Audouy and Professor Paul Allain from the University of Kent in the UK. I likewise collaborated and ensured stylistic similarity was kept with the other texts. They kindly agreed to include these texts in the present translation.

The last part, 'V', 'Three Texts on Mexico', includes the three texts, 'Awakening of the Thunderbird', 'Mexico and Civilization' and 'The Force of Mexico'. While these last texts may well have been placed elsewhere by Artaud or Thévenin, I have decided not to disrupt the order of the texts established by Cardosa y Aragón's *México* and maintained by Thévenin and Sollers. Even though Artaud frequently incorporated letters into his published works, it is hard to predict which ones would have been included in *Messages révolutionnaires*. For this reason, none have been included.

Mostly published during 1936, Artaud's 'Messages', so termed in the letter to Paulhan, should be classified as part of a so-called middle era alongside major works such as the books *Heliogabalus or, The Crowned Anarchist* (1934), *On the New Revelations of Being* (1937) and *The Theatre and Its Double* (1938). Artaud's trip to Mexico and the 'Messages' chronologically follow his attempts at practically establishing the Theatre of Cruelty in Paris and the disappointment after the lack of success of his adaptation of *The Cenci* (1935). As many biographers have pointed out, Artaud spent much of the year before his departure attempting to secure financial aid and state cultural support for his stay and research in Mexico; the text written for the Mexican Brewery highlights Artaud's need for money during this period. As Lotringer writes, 'he was broke'. 'Awakening of the Thunderbird', the earliest text included in this translation, was written as a research programme that Artaud wanted to conduct once in Mexico. In a letter to Jean Ballard, dated 15 December 1935,[14] Artaud outlines that he has procured 'an Official Mission from the Ministry of Public Instruction'. The 'Awakening of the Thunderbird' constitutes a 'paper programme' of what Artaud intended for Mexico. This alongside many letters and especially the notebooks dedicated to Oriental, Greek and Indian

[13]François Audouy quoted in Clément Solym, 'Des textes inédits d'Antonin Artaud, publiés à Cuba en 1936', *Actualitté*, 2 November, 2022.
[14]XIII, 416.

culture, attests to the intended rigour of Artaud's scholarly research conducted before his departure. Artaud had previously performed such a feat for *Heliogabalus*, the only published work for which a bibliography exists. *Heliogabablus* provides the strongest example of Artaud's metaphysical system, which does not significantly alter until the later writings, where instead of a matter/spirit monism, Artaud much more zealously attacks the spirit.

Artaud's 'Messages', therefore, precede his nine-year internment and post-internment writings and publications such as *Van Gogh, the Man Suicided by Society* and *To Have Done with the Judgment of God*. Indeed, the closest equivalent of the 'Messages' in this period is *The Theatre and Its Double*. As the letters of this period evidence, including the letter to Paulhan where the title is found, Artaud was trying to expedite the publication of the *Theatre and Its Double* while in and on his way to Mexico. Although the precise date of its redaction is unknown, the eventual 'Preface' to the *Theatre and Its Double* refers to the Mexican civilization multiple times. It includes many of the same themes, such as European cultural decadence and the *energy* of the Mexican civilization.[15] Moreover, performed in 1934 at the house of Lise Deharme, *The Conquest of Mexico*, of which a rather detailed scenario still exists, was supposed to be the first work of the Theatre of Cruelty as per the second manifesto and constitutes Artaud's first piece of writing on Mexico.[16] Many overlapping conceptual concerns deal with the purpose and intention of the theatre, especially what could be called Artaud's metaphysics of space and his criticism of Jacques Copeau and the reduction of the theatre to the text. The purpose of translating Artaud's 'Messages' into English, besides offering English readers the opportunity to read and study new texts, is to enlighten the theoretical theatre texts with more explicit political texts. To follow an Artaudian figure of speech, if the *Theatre and Its Double* constitute the theoretical side – spirit – then Artaud's *Revolutionary Messages* constitute the practical side – matter – each being the Double of the other.

---

[15]IV, 12.
[16]V, 137.

What is revealed by reading Artaud's 'Messages' is the historical context in which many of his once seemingly obscure ideas concerning theatre, culture, metaphysics and politics are laid out. This most prominently includes Artaud revisiting his dispute with the Surrealists concerning what constitutes 'Revolution', situating his theatre theory as a response to other interbellum theatrical movements and offering political and cultural responses to the accelerating disorder of Europe and the rise of fascism.

The present translation of *Revolutionary Messages* is, among other things, then, an attempt to draw attention back to Artaud's ideas and away from simply focusing on Artaud's life as an oft-anthologized avant-garde *poète maudit* and untranslatable schizophrenic.[17] This is not to downplay the suffering that Artaud experienced during psychotic phases of severe mental illness, such as those on his return from Mexico, in Ireland and, most famously, at Doctor Gaston Ferdière's Rodez, *but to say* that Artaud is more than just a psychiatric case study. *Revolutionary Messages* places Artaud, and his ideas, into a much more intimate relationship with his historical moment. While saying such a thing is tantamount to a biographical reading, what is important about this contextualization of Artaud is that his ideas concerning the theatre, metaphysics and revolution no longer appear as the musing of an ascetic.

Indeed, one of the other major tasks of this translation is to offer readers explicit statements in English about Artaud's politics. Since the publication of *Artaud and His Doubles* by Kimberly Jannarone, no tangible scholarly response has been undertaken to counter her accusation that Artaud's theatre and politics are indistinguishable from those of a fascist.[18] I hope that the last section of the Introduction, 'Artaud's *Révolution*', which offers an overall reading of the book and an interpretation of Artaud's metaphysics and his politics, will provide some answer to this accusation with the prudence that it deserves, especially concentrating on Artaud's use of 'race' and his 'anti-Marxism'. Before that, however, I would like to say a few words and add some notes concerning my own translations.

---

[17]See Pierre Seghers, ed., *Poètes maudits d'aujourd'hui: 1946–1970* (Paris: Seghers, 1972).
[18]Kimberly Jannarone, *Artaud and His Doubles* (Ann Arbor, MI: University of Michigan Press, 2012).

Translating *Revolutionary Messages*

As mentioned, *Revolutionary Messages* constitutes the first full translation of the abovementioned texts. Only three text and two letter translations by Helen Weaver were included in the *Antonin Artaud: Selected Writings* edited by Susan Sontag: 'Man against Destiny', 'First Contact with the Mexican Revolution', 'What I Came to Mexico to Do' and two letters, one to Paulhan and another to Barrault.[19] These are fine translations and were a crucial basis for the present work. These texts have been newly translated to maintain stylistic consistency with the other chapters. Lastly, as per the '*In Preparation*' advertisement of the *Collected Works* published by John Calder, while Victor Corti was preparing the translation of Volume 6 to include 'Revolutionary Statements', this was never published, and no manuscript has been found.

Since one of the major aims of this translation was to showcase the rigour of Artaud's own philosophical studies, I have tried to be as conceptually continuous as possible. This has often been at the expense of a more 'English'-sounding translation. The goal was to aid a reader without access to the original French the means with which to connect certain notions and concepts internal to Artaud's work (for example, '*race*' remains 'race' not 'ethnicity', since it is conceptually operative throughout Artaud's work). The same goes for those influenced by Artaud. For example, French avant-garde writers, who might have drawn on Artaud's concepts after his death (for instance, the slightly awkward 'the youth' for '*la jeunesse*'; this was a crucial term for the Lettrists and Situationists around May '68). This has also meant avoiding the poetics of synonyms where the same word was used in the French and other perhaps odd choices such as finding the same Latin equivalents for words in English (a translation *faux pas*), especially where words were as rare in French as they are in English (for example, 'sybaritism' instead of 'wantonness').

I have, of course, attempted to avoid claque – that other translation no-no – wherever possible so that Artaud's singular

---

[19] *Antonin Artaud: Selected Writings*, ed. and with notes and introduction by Susan Sontag and trans. Helen Weaver (Berkeley and Los Angeles, CA: University of California Press, 1976).

voice in French finds its home in English without loss of force. Other brilliant translators of Artaud such as Jake Hirschman and Clayton Eshleman (both of whom sadly died during the translation period in 2021) as well as Peter Valente more than surpass me in this regard. And some of my abovementioned translation choices meant that some calque probably became unavoidable. I only hope that this will enrich the English language and not distract the reader too much insofar as the translation draws attention to its own status as a translation.

Lastly, I have, on occasion, put into square brackets the French word that was translated. This was chosen, for instance, where it would greatly help the reader to know what the French was, for example, when '*moi*' was translated as 'self' or '*élite*' as 'intellectual'.

The journey of completing this translation has been rather long; the global pandemic and the precarity of early career academia did not help. While it perhaps began when Howard Caygill first introduced me to Artaud in Paris in 2014, the translation itself started between London and Paris during the completion of my PhD at King's College London under the supervision of Professor Patrick ffrench. It was finished in Marseille, Artaud's place of birth and now his final resting place. Much of the translation was, nonetheless, completed in Switzerland at La Becque in 2022. I have had much help along the way. My tireless friend and colleague Nathaniel Wooding deserves first mention since the initial attempts at translating Artaud's 'The Social Anarchy of Art' and 'I Came to Mexico to Flee European Civilization, . . .' were conducted with him in a small flat in London. As always, his influence is ever-present.

The discovery (both by Rousselet in 2009 and my own in 2023 of Rousselet's book published in 2021) of new texts to be potentially added to *Revolutionary Messages* was of course exciting to say the least, but it also required a last-minute decision to augment the size of the book. Here, I would like to thank my editors, Anna Brewer and Aanchil Vij at Bloomsbury for their patience and willingness to do what was best for the book. Through the discovery of these Havana texts, I likewise met Illios Chailly, François Audouy and Paul Allain, the last two of whom were already working on English translations of the discovered Havana texts. I would like to thank them for their help and enthusiasm toward the end of the project.

Lastly, I would also like to thank the reviewer of the manuscript who offered many crucial comments about the translation prior to publication. Having read and reread the French what feels like over a hundred times, the difference between the target and source language started to blur. If it was not for the reviewer, many obvious mistakes would have remained. The translation is much stronger thanks to their review and comments. All mistakes that do, however, remain are my own.

Artaud's *Révolution*

Realism or Surrealism

The answer to what Artaud means by *Révolution* in its political distinctions and similarities to other revolutions, whether Surrealist, Marxist, anarchist, reactionary or conservative, first requires returning to the period of the Surrealist movement between 1924 and 1926. During this period, Artaud moved from being the director and principal editor of the Surrealist journal *La Révolution surréaliste* (*R.S.*) no.3, which is also to say the writer of some of its most ardent revolutionary texts, to being exiled by the Surrealist Politburo (what Artaud called the 'The French branch of the Third International of Moscow'),[20] for not adhering to the party line concerning whatever it was that the Surrealists meant by an 'economic and social revolution'.[21] What was at stake at the meeting of the Surrealists on 23 November 1926 was not necessarily concerned with the revolution itself, nor really its definition. Although this was certainly the pretense. Over the previous year, as the Surrealists slowly adhered to the *Parti Communiste Français* (*P.C.F.*), their definition of 'Revolution' became less and less 'Surrealist' and more and more 'realist'. Instead, the meeting focused on identifying whether or not those in attendance, including Phillipe Soupault and Artaud, were or were not 'counter-revolutionary'.[22]

---

[20]Marguerite Bonnet, ed., *Archives du surréalisme 3, 'Adhérer au Parti communiste?'* (Paris: Gallimard, 1992), 24.

[21]Bonnet, ed.,Bonnet, ed., *Archives du surréalisme 3*, 24.

[22]Bonnet, ed., *Archives du surréalisme 3*, 24.

The main criteria used to determine counter-revolutionary action was whether or not their intellectual activities could be considered 'literary', an accusation that the *P.C.F.* had also levelled at the Surrealists and to which they were trying to prove otherwise.

One cannot help but smile at the absolute seriousness with which each Surrealist member plays the role of the revolutionary as well as the often sarcastic lucidity with which Artaud confronts them. Having been invited to the meeting by André Breton, who admittedly takes on a more sombre role, Artaud was accused of being counter-revolutionary for writing in journals such as *Cahier du sud*, for attempting to establish closer ties with the *N.R.F.* (who continued to sell and advertise in the *R.S.* after Artaud's exclusion), for starting a theatre project, The Alfred Jarry Theatre, with already exiled members Roger Vitrac and Robert Aron and lastly for having 'personal thoughts'. In response to these accusations, Artaud contends that, for the most part, he agrees with Rolland Tual's introductory speech concerning what revolution means. He then suggests that for two years there had been little revolutionary action from the Surrealists that a mutual understanding between the members no longer existed since the collusion between the Surrealists and the journal *Clarté* and, finally, that one cannot simply force someone to think something about social and economic factors that one has no clarity about. As this last point is being made my Artaud Paul Eluard chips in that 'Artaud speaks about exercising thought for himself; this is a counter-revolutionary attitude since thought is for everyone!' To this, Artaud mockingly counters, given the absurdity of the occasion, 'I deny it.'[23]

As comes across from Artaud's 'defence', which is reluctant at best, Artaud argues that his counter-revolutionary activities, such as participating in the theatre, were, while imbecilic, in part necessitated by the revolutionary inaction of the group, inaction that followed Artaud's *action*. As Pierre Naville writes in *La Révolution et les intellectuels*, it was, after all, Artaud who first significantly oriented the Surrealist movement toward something that was more than just an extension of Dadaism, toward an all-out attack on political and cultural institutions, toward something that was not just 'literary' but precisely 'revolutionary'.[24] As Artaud proclaimed on 27 January

---

[23]Bonnet, *Archives du surréalisme 3*, 24.
[24]Pierre Naville, *La Révolution et les intellectuels* (Paris: Gallimard, 1975), 14.

1925 at the Cèrta bar, while taking charge of the *Bureau de recherches surréalistes* and editorship of the *R.S.*, 'Are you really revolutionaries, are you really disinterested? Do you place things of the Mind before the menagerie of all literary ideas? . . . Are you at the centre of the Revolution?'[25] Indeed, Artaud then proceeds to read out the revolutionary 'Declaration', written by himself and signed by all Surrealists and, in which, among declarations such as, 'Surrealism has nothing to do with literature', it is written:

> We do not pretend to change the desires of men, but we nonetheless believe that we can demonstrate the fragility of their thoughts; and on which moving chairs, and in which caves they have built their trembling houses.[26]

Along similar lines, though written with more precision, is Artaud's pronouncement published in no. 3 of *R.S.* under the title 'Activity of the Surrealists Bureau of Research':

> This revolution aims at the general de-valorization of values, the depreciation of the mind, the demineralization of evidence, an absolute confusion and renewal of language, and the delayering of thought.[27]

Arguably the clearest of all pronouncements of what Artaud, and the Surrealists, meant by a Surrealist Revolution from this period comes from a document written around 30 March 1925, the date of the Surrealists' 'Ideological Committee'. In this 'Second Document', Artaud writes, 'the idea of any Surrealist revolution is to target the deep substance and order of thought'.[28]

For Artaud and the Surrealists, before 23 November 1926, what was meant by Revolution was a quasi-Nietzschean attack on value itself, an attack that was to revolutionize thought, language and the mind. It is, therefore, not surprising that when asked by Phillipe Bernier a year later whether he 'didn't give a damn' about the

---

[25]Paule Thévenin ed., *Archives du surréalisme* 1, '*Cahier de la perméance*' (Paris: Gallimard, 1988), 116.
[26]Thévenin, *Archives du surréalisme* 1, 119.
[27]I**, 219.
[28]I**, 219.

Revolution, Artaud replied: 'No ... Obviously. ... I care about it, but if I am forced to understand by revolution ... a revolution as you understand it, then yes, I don't give a damn.'[29] After Artaud clarifies this, there is then some attempt to force his hand further by getting him to agree that what he 'doesn't give a damn about' is precisely a communist revolution. Artaud continues to argue that he cannot simply improvise a definition of Revolution and that the 'Revolution' he 'does for himself'.[30] After this, which is taken as a clear indication of 'personal thoughts', Breton declares Artaud a counter-revolutionary and a vote to exclude him is brought forward. At this, Artaud declares that he has nothing more to say. '*He leaves.*'[31]

The history of Artaud and Surrealism and the question of the Revolution does not end there. Although, at Breton's suggestion, the Surrealists had agreed never to shake the hand of those excluded again, Artaud continued to publish texts in the *R.S.* up to no. 12 and participated in the 'inquiry into sexuality' of 1928. Before this 'reconciliation', however, which begins with the Surrealists' defence of Artaud's clandestine staging of Paul Claudel's *Partage du midi* (Claudel had not yet given permission for the play to be staged), and in response to the rather insulting *Au grand jour*, the text published by the Surrealists that publicly announced the exclusion of Artaud and Soupault, Artaud writes the self-published *In Total Darkness, or the Surrealist Bluff* and *Final Point*. Both of these texts are not only enlightening regarding the history of Surrealism and Artaud's involvement, exclusion and reaction against it, but they also offer insights into Artaud's 'revolution' that is useful in their comparison and radical distinction to certain points made in his *Revolutionary Messages* written almost exactly a decade later in Mexico.

Although Artaud writes in the first long footnote to the *Total Darkness* that 'all the substance, all the expressions of our quarrel revolve around the word Revolution', one might want to add to that the word 'spirit/mind [*esprit*]' since what was at stake for Artaud was not just a question of the meaning of revolution but where such a revolution was to take place, as indicated in the 'Declaration' of 1925.[32]

---

[29]Bonnet, *Archives du surréalisme* 3, 24.
[30]Thévenin, *Archives du surréalisme* 1, 24.
[31]Thévenin, *Archives du surréalisme* 1, 24–25.
[32]I**, 59.

Indeed, what becomes evident from these two 1927 texts is that Artaud fundamentally questioned, perhaps rightly so, how the Surrealists' understanding of historical materialism (which in its more orthodox conception viewed *reality* as a historical material effect caused by the social and political struggle between the bourgeoisie and the proletariat over the economic base), might coexist with a philosophy that, at its inception, was concerned not with the relationship between *matter and reality* but with the *mind/spirit and sur-reality*. As Artaud writes:

> Is there still a Surrealist adventure, was Surrealism not dead the day Breton and his adepts believed that it was their duty to rally to communism and to search in the domain of facts and in the immediacy of matter the conclusion of an action, which should only be able to take place in the intimate frame of the brain.[33]

For Artaud, the struggle for the passage of power from the bourgeois to the proletariat would have been an excusable goal for the Surrealists, 'if not banal and restricted', had this been their only goal. But, in so doing, they would no longer be Surrealists but realists.

Whether political aesthetics should be realist or Surrealist, whether it should be based on the externality of facts or the internality of the mind, forms the subject of György Lukács's 1938 *Realism in the Balance*, who, different to Bertolt Brecht, for example, sides firmly against the latter.[34] For Artaud, the revolutionary *action* of Surrealism was precisely to *alter* the facts of reality and not search there for historical truths and, in these truths, become descriptively complacent. As he writes in *Total Darkness*, Surrealism's purpose was to 'liberate the unconscious'; it aimed at the 'revalorization of value', the transformation of the depths of signification where the 'virtuality' of the mind's forms, where the 'value of appearances', could themselves be changed. For Artaud, Surrealism was a form of 'idealism', but a *concrete idealism* that distinguished itself from 'pure metaphysics' by the fact that the

---

[33]I**, 60.
[34]See Georg Lukacs, 'Realism in the Balance', in *Aesthetics and Politics*, trans. Rodney Livingstone (London: Verso, 2007).

abstract itself is said to have a 'body' and that this body was possible to denature and deform.

While Artaud does not misconstrue the 'advantages of the collective suggestion', revolution, in this text, is explicitly said to be 'truly an individual affair'.[35] The question of individual freedom is expressed most clearly in the closing lines of the second to last paragraph of *Total Darkness*:

> I know that in the current debate, I have with me all free men, all true revolutionaries who think that individual freedom is a superior good, no matter what conquest is obtained on a relative plane.[36]

If this was Artaud's definitive political pronouncement, in that case, one might want to agree with Eluard that beyond Artaud's literary endeavours, what is most counter-revolutionary about Artaud's Revolution is the alignment of 'individual freedom' to a Revolution that takes place at the individual level, one that does not take into consideration the energetic, social, political and cultural reproduction of the 'body' that sustains the virtual forms of the 'soul' that Artaud so desperately wants to destroy. One might want to ask Artaud, where precisely does this *concrete idealism* lie if it is not supposed to be pure metaphysics? Where is this body? One might want likewise to counter Artaud's quasi-Freudian–Nietzschean tropes by asking what differentiates Artaud's 'individual freedom' from bourgeois freedom. Is it not precisely the individual as a free agent who occupies the mind and desires of bourgeois liberalism? Insults aside, Artaud might reply that bourgeois individualism is structured through idolatrous unfreedoms and ideas such as the family, the nation and the state; these ideas and values are precisely what he intends to undermine or destroy in his Revolution.

Is Artaud's individual freedom, then, one that attacks bourgeois values *as and from within these values*? Is it an anarchist individualism one similar to that of Max Stirner or perhaps closest

---

[35]I**, 74.
[36]I**, 65.

to the Nietzschean psychoanalyst and anarchist Otto Gross, who likewise aims at the total liberation of the unconscious? Certainly, Artaud's turn to the notion of anarchy as underpinning his metaphysics throughout the 1930s indicates at least philosophical affinity, the publication and importance of *Heliogabalus* (1934) being the culmination of this turn.

While there is not the space here to undergo a rigorous assessment of the relation between Artaud's metaphysical or 'Formal' anarchism – that of the monistic doubled origin – and that of political anarchism, individual or collective, it is nonetheless worth giving an overview of some of the points that arise in the last section of *Heliogabalus*, 'Anarchy', since they demonstrate why Heliogabalus was himself an 'anarchist-born' and the importance of Heliogabalus's actions for Artaud, political or otherwise. For what is certain, is that Artaud sees himself in this fourteen-year-old Syrian Roman emperor.

In one of the last sections of 'Anarchy', Artaud reproduces the famous anarchist *devise*, adding a second line to it, 'No God, no master, myself alone.'[37] Used to describe the action of Heliogabalus, Artaud writes that Heliogabalus accepts no law, making the law for themselves. Instead of human law, Heliogabalus raises law to the level of the 'divine'.[38] As always, it is difficult to know what divinity means for Artaud, other than perhaps that Heliogabalus, as Artaud will say of the Indigenous people of Mexico, is somewhat closer to the Double.

The Double, though signifying several things in Artaud, including life, should be understood more or less as an entwined mixture of spirit and matter (a '*duité*'),[39] as is outlined via a citation to Antoine Fabre d'Olivet's *L'Histoire philosophique du genre humain* in an appendix to *Heliogablus*. Here it is written, 'If the origin of sound is double, then all is double.'[40] Just as music requires both an instrument to emit sound and the 'matter' of air to receive this emission (the relation between signal and its carrier medium), mind and matter were required to be simultaneously united and separated for there to be what Fabre d'Olivet calls 'creation'.[41]

[37]VII, 95.
[38]VII, 95.
[39]Antoine Fabre d'Olivet, *L'Histoire philosophique du genre humain* I (Paris: Éditions Tranditionelles, 1989), 247.
[40]VII, 111.
[41]Fabre d'Olivet, *L'Histoire philosophique du genre humain* I, 183, 247.

Artaud insists that Heliogabalus should, therefore, not be regarded as a madman but a 'rebel' whose actions revolted against Roman religion and the 'Roman monarchy'.[42] Scorning the 'cowardness' of the previous 'monarchs', Heliogabalus is said to have placed a dancer as the head of the police, replaced all senators with women, prostituted himself on the streets of Rome, chosen his ministers by the size of their penis, castrated himself and celebrated endless festivals.[43] These actions, for Artaud, constitute what he calls a 'courageous anarchism', one which considers 'weakness: strength' and 'the theatre: reality'. In other words, the anarchic political actions of Heliogabalus are those which overthrow 'received order, ideas and the ordinary notions of things'.[44]

While Artaud praises this revolt, it is hard to extract from this any alignment to a type of anarchism as a political or social structure – if this would be at all possible. What is clear is that Heliogabalus's actions practice the theoretical and theatrical desires that Artaud outlines for Surrealism and the Theatre of Cruelty. That is, Artaud sees in Heliogabalus a historical figure who attacks moral values *as and in these* values. Indeed, Heliogabalus, the crowned anarchist, is a born paradox, a contradiction that abolishes monarchy through monarchy. He represents the living Double of spirit and matter who, born from the excrement of the sun, is sent to Earth to *work* and returns to the cosmos via the sewers of Rome. If anything, *this* is perhaps the divine cosmic *law*, a negative dialectic where the Spirit starts and ends in 'shit', the 'ka–ka', the Ka being the Ancient Egyptian word for Double, the spirit of man that is itself sustained by food even after death.

Putting this metaphysical individualist anarchism to one side, besides *Heliogabalus*, one of the only statements concerning political anarchism that exists in Artaud's work is from a letter to Anne Manson dated 13 September 1937, written while Artaud was in Galway, Ireland, and severely suffering from psychosis. Here Artaud writes that while what the 'Spanish Anarchists' are doing in Spain is unheard of, they are nonetheless trying to 'fix the absolute of the earth' in an evil manner and that 'anarchists' in general were

---

[42]VII, 99.
[43]VII, 100.
[44]VII, 100.

'repugnant property owners' whose maps of 'love and bread' were the 'consecration of inhuman disorder'.[45] From a biographical, which, for Artaud, is also often to say clinical, but especially from a critical point of view, it is difficult to determine what this might indicate for Artaud's revolution, especially since, according to Manson, the response itself was provoked by some relations Artaud had with a 'young communist woman' before Ireland.[46]

Before turning to Artaud's Mexican revolutionary messages, where, as mentioned, a much more explicit politics is expressed, it is perhaps opportune to finish this section by questioning and opening the possibility that Artaud's Revolution, especially as he lays it out after his exclusion from the Surrealists, is perhaps more of a reactionary or conservative revolution (I shall also return to this in more detail later, especially the accusations of connection to fascism by Jannarone).

In what is probably Artaud's most anti-communist piece of writing, dating to the January after his expulsion from the Surrealists, and what is in content most likely a precursor to the *Total Darkness*, Artaud adds as a 'P.S.' to a piece of text called 'Manifesto for an Aborted Theatre' where he writes that among all the manners of understanding what a revolution is, the 'Communist' is by far the 'worst' and the most 'reductive'.[47] For Artaud, the revolution cannot constitute the simple passage of power to the proletariat and their control over the modes of 'production' for the main reason that this does not constitute a critique of power itself – a common anarchist criticism of communism, for example, see *Statism and Anarchy* by Mikhail Bakunin.[48]

Radically different to Bakunin, however, Artaud argues that the only revolution 'worth speaking about' achieves a 'regression in time', one that takes us back to the 'Middle Ages' in both mentality and the habits of life.[49] Although this does not constitute support for a return to Feudalism as such, Artaud's alignment of Revolution to a 'regression in time', while being anti-progressive insofar as it is highly critical of 'mechanism' (an ideology that Artaud will align

---

[45]VII, 214.

[46]VII, 449 n. 3.

[47]II, 25.

[48]Mikhail Bakunin, *Statism and Anarchy*, trans. Marshall S. Shatz (Cambridge: Cambridge University Press, 1990).

[49]II, 25.

with European cartesian dualism and whiteness in the Mexican
'Messages') and the 'multiplication' of its 'force' at all levels of
society, nonetheless constitutes a conservative reaction against it,
one that was common among reactionary so-called degeneration
thinkers.[50]

One might want to ask Artaud to what extent this regression to
medieval mentalities and life habits includes reinstating social
hierarchies based on class or caste; are we to see the return of kings,
noblemen and peasants? If Artaud's identification with Heliogabalus
as the crowned anarchist, 'enemy of public order', 'who cannot
tolerate his crown' and who paid the price of being a monarch by
practicing his anarchy on himself, indicates anything about Artaud's
opinions concerning monarchy, then one would either have to
search for a medieval equivalent to Heliogabalus (a Christina of
Sweden perhaps, who forced her court to dress as men and whose
hair, hoarse voice and refusal to marry caused scandal and mayhem
in the court of Sweden),[51] or, indeed, conclude that this 'regression'
does not signify a return to Feudal structures of power.

By the end of *P.S.*, it also becomes slightly clearer that the desire
to regress in time is motivated by the sacred theatrical structures of
previous eras, where, to use a Benjaminian concept, the spiritual
aura has yet to be industrially extracted from theatrical
representation.[52] Indeed, Artaud's Mexican 'Post-War Theatre in
Paris' makes clear what Artaud appreciated from the Middle Ages
were the '*compagnons*', 'those travelling companies where the actor
was at once a craftsman, poet, author, beggar, and adventurer'.[53]
However, as Benjamin also makes clear, a desire for the return of
aura is not without its political implications. The aesthetic search for
purity or authenticity in the past always, at the same time, announces
an impurity of the present, projecting a resolute purity of the future;
it damns those not deemed worthy of the return to authenticity.

---

[50]II, 25.

[51]See Lindsay Ivan, *The History of Loot and Stolen Art: From Antiquity until the
Present Day* (Luton: Andrews UK Limited, 2014).

[52]See Walter Benjamin, 'The Work of Art in the Age of Mechanical Reproduction', in
Illuminations, ed. by Hannah Arendt, trans. by Harry Zohn (New York: Schocken
Books, 1969).

[53]Antonin Artaud, *Revolutionary Messages*, trans. by Joel White (London:
Bloomsbury, 2024), 91. Hereafter, RM.

In *Revolutionary Messages*, the question of purity is certainly at stake, even racial purity. However, as in *Heliogabalus*, the return to the origin for Artaud is never just a simple return to some form of self-presence. Not only is the origin Double, but the principles that derive from it are not determined transcendently. Instead, they partake of a unified energetic magmatic continuity, Artaud's Bergson-inspired magmatism.

The Double and the Race-principle

Before turning to the Mexican 'Messages' it is worth looking at what could be considered a bridging text between Artaud of the Surrealist period and Artaud of the Mexican 'Messages': the 1934 *The Conquest of Mexico*. Not only does this text highlight what is politically at stake in the 'Messages', but it also raises the question of the metaphysical system that underpins it.

As mentioned, *The Conquest of Mexico* was intended to be the first scenario staged in Artaud's Theatre of Cruelty. Written around the same time as the publication of *Heliogabalus*, it reveals some of the major political aspirations for the Theatre of Cruelty in their relation to Artaud's later political convictions for Mexico. It also raises other more sensitive questions, such as what Artaud means by 'race' and its connection to Artaud's idea of a cultural revolution, a notion that, although present in *Heliogabalus*, takes on a much more prominent role in the Mexican 'Messages' as it also does in the *Tarahumaras* book.

Artaud begins *The Conquest of Mexico* by outlining two intentions for it as a scenario. The first is indicative of what one might call the anti-colonial or decolonial purpose of the play:

1 . . . From a historical point of view, *The Conquest of Mexico* poses the question of colonization. In a brutal, ruthless, and bloody manner, it brings to life the still-existent self-importance of Europe. It will attempt to deflate the preponderant idea of its superiority. It opposes Christianism to much older religions. It will give justice to the false conceptions that the Occident has formed of paganism and certain natural religions and underline in a sympathetic but burning manner the splendour and poetry

that still exists of the old metaphysical depths on which these religions were built.[54]

Notwithstanding Artaud's adamant stance against Eurocentric superiority, a point that he also labours throughout the 'Messages', the second purpose of the play also deserves citing and commenting on since it reveals what could be called Artaud's *racism*:

> 2 . . . By asking such a terribly current question about colonization and the right that one continent believes that it has to help itself to another, it asks the question concerning the real superiority of certain races over others and demonstrates the internal filiation that connects the genius of a race to precise forms of civilization.[55]

Alongside Artaud's pertinent critique of European imperialism is, what appears on paper to be an affirmation that racial superiority is 'real', or at least, the play *The Conquest of Mexico* is to question the 'real superiority of certain races over others' and to demonstrate the 'internal filiation' that connects 'race' to 'civilization'. The first problems that arise, assuming that Artaud believes in racial hierarchy, are what he means by 'race', 'superiority' and, crucially, whose 'race' is considered superior. What is certain and evidenced by a large number of 'Messages' – even the above first intention – is that Artaud's racism, insofar as what is at stake is racial superiority, racial distinction and hierarchy, does not assert *white* racial superiority. Inverting the white supremacist idea that the white race is somehow contaminated or degenerated by interracial mixing, in 'Awakening of the Thunderbird', a text written before Artaud arrived in Mexico, Artaud writes that, 'In Mexico, like elsewhere, it is the White man that perverts the race.'[56] Said with even more vehemence in 'Indians and Metaphysics', Artaud pathologizes the white race, writing that 'very few have escaped the utterly utilitarian and self-serving virus of today's world'.[57] The idea that 'whiteness' contaminates or infects the racial purity of the Mexican indigenous

---

[54]V, 18.
[55]V, 18.
[56]RM, 194.
[57]RM, 187.

community is a constant trope in the 'Messages' and one that goes hand in hand with Artaud's damnation of European culture.

There is, therefore, in Artaud not only an idea of racial superiority but also racial purity. As again evidenced in 'Awakening of the Thunderbird', Artaud blames the 'five million Spanish métis' for what is perceived in Europe as a country in 'perpetual upheaval', auguring that, 'As long as the government does not belong to the true Indian race, Mexico will remain in revolution.'[58] The 'true' Indian or Mexican race for Artaud is, therefore, the 'pure' Indian race, the indigenous people of Mexico, and its purity is determined through what he calls 'blood' and 'Culture'.

As Artaud writes in 'Surrealism and Revolution', the first lecture given in Mexico, 'All true culture is based on race and blood.'[59] As per *The Conquest of Mexico*, for Artaud, the 'genius of a race' connects directly 'to precise forms of civilization'.[60] The question of what Artaud means by 'race' is either complicated or answered by these citations, especially that of 'Surrealism and Revolution'. On the one hand, there appears to be a form of cultural determinism that relates 'race' and 'blood' to 'culture', which, in the case of the Mexican 'métis' or 'the mestizos of the cities',[61] is mixed with Spanish European blood and is, as such, compromised through what scientific racism might call 'miscegenation'. On the other hand, 'race', 'blood', 'culture' and 'civilization' function as quasi-synonyms for what we might call the cultural or spiritual specificity of the Mexican indigenous people, not only in its historical distinction to European culture but as the last remaining civilization that has not yet been – hence 'pure' – entirely colonized in its mind and body by a self-important notion of whiteness that values itself as the indication of true 'culture'.

This inversion of cultural supremacy is particularly visible in Artaud's art criticism of contemporary Mexican artists. His aesthetic evaluations are based on an aesthetic principle that determines what is good or bad art: how closely does the artwork adhere to indigenous versus European, particularly, Parisian, ideals. As Artaud writes of the Mexican sculptor Luis Ortiz Monasterio:

---

[58]RM, 194.
[59]RM, 67.
[60]V, 18.
[61]RM, 167.

The young sculptor Monasterio demonstrates through his carved stones that he has felt the intellectual oppression of Mexico, and certainly, one feels that something is in gestation in his stone. However, Parisian sculpture's fashionable fine art styles and speculations still taint the *form*.[62]

The same can be said of Maria Izquierdo's artwork, which Artaud organized an exhibition for upon his return to Paris, and whom Artaud saw as the greatest promise for the cultural rebirth of Mexican indigenous art, as well as art in general:

> Maria Izquierdo's pictorial practice is becoming increasingly influenced by modern European techniques and, in some paintings, even by its spirit. And this is all the more regrettable.[63]

It is regrettable for Artaud, not only because European techniques taint the purity of her practice, but because with an increase in imitation comes a 'disappearing' of the 'Indian spirit', which means that European standards are replacing it, and it risks dying. Indeed, Artaud portrays Mexico's political and revolutionary struggle as one where 'the mestizos 'are determined to destroy in themselves whatever remains of the red spirit, if they do not kill their red blood first.' [64] The politico-cultural struggle for Mexico is, thus, represented as a 'struggle between two bloods'.[65]

'Blood' and 'race' are thus spoken of as indicators of cultural or societal specificities mostly devoid of any discussion of phenotypical or biological differences, except, of course, from the obvious fact that Europeans are considered 'white' or 'white people' and the Mexican indigenous people are referred to as 'red-faced'.[66] Furthermore, in 'La Corrida and Human Sacrifices', Artaud also comments on his Creole interlocutor's 'blue eyes' and 'dazzling European brain', both indicators that Artaud's notion of race was not entirely cultural or spiritual.[67] Moreover, Artaud was fully

---

[62]RM, 153.
[63]RM, 157.
[64]RM, 167.
[65]RM, 167.
[66]RM, 159.
[67]RM, 181.

aware of and had read texts on contemporary scientific racism. For example, Artaud cites the French surgeon and fascist eugenicist Alexis Carrel's *Man, the Unknown* in 'What I Came to Mexico to Do', a book in which Carrel advocates for voluntary eugenics, the extermination of 'defectives and criminals' and the creation of a biotechnical society led by elites as a remedy to the degeneration of civilization.[68] Artaud writes:

> Dr Alexis Carrel, who also recognizes the defects of the mechanized civilization of Europe, does not fail, in his book *Man, the Unknown*, to advocate the need for a revolution and even suggests ways of carrying it out.[69]

Although the book was incredibly popular worldwide, especially in America, where eugenics was supported by institutions such as the Carnegie Foundation, this so-called 'revolution' and the 'ways of carrying it out' mentioned by Artaud constitute nothing less than the theoretical and practical basis for the racial genocides carried out by National Socialism.[70] While Artaud agrees with Carrel that civilization is in decline, it is critical to emphasize that no support for eugenics can be found in Artaud's published works, notes or letters. What is more, in April of 1936, while in Mexico, Artaud wrote a letter to Alexis Carrel in which he strongly criticized his scientific 'remedy' to civilizational decline. As Artaud writes, 'You have identified the evil [*mal*], but your remedy is a bad remedy; it stems from the same spirit as this evil [*mal*].'[71] For Artaud, the source of civilizational decadence stems from the expansion of the scientific mechanical spirit, which, as he writes in the letter, analytically divides the world into 'Species'.[72] In the letter, it is precisely this spirit, this 'criminal superstition', that Artaud accuses Carrel of being 'infected with'.[73] Indeed, by the end of the letter,

---

[68]See Alexis Carrel, *Man, the Unknown* (Harper and Brothers, 1935).
[69]RM, 120.
[70]More recently, in the 1990s, Carrel's ideas were revived by Jean-Marie le Pen in France in support of the Front National's anti-immigration policies.
[71]Antonin Artaud to Alexis Carrel, 15 April 1936, GULLACC, box 70, section 18–5, file 11–1.
[72]Antonin Artaud to Alexis Carrel.
[73]Antonin Artaud to Alexis Carrel.

Artaud essentially tells Carrel to shut up and stop writing. In a wonderfully Artaudian rhythm, he writes: 'This is why I repeat to you: Silence now about Science.'[74] Instead of being strictly scientific, Artaud's idea and use of race metaphysically relates to what Artaud calls the 'race-principle', a notion whose two conceptual halves require close analysis. In 'Indians and Metaphysics', Artaud gives a rather succinct definition: 'a race-principle is a race which is closer to certain mixtures, to some physical sources from which the life of Nature began'.[75] Artaud continues in this article to state that 'Nature' should be understood as a combination of Male and Female forces; that is, Nature should be understood as a doubled or 'mixed origin' between spirit and matter – the same doubled origin that Artaud champions Heliogabalus for embodying.[76] Artaud's pure metaphysical origin is, therefore, originally *im-pure*. Instead of a monism of the Absoluteness of the One, or spiritual unity, this monism also includes the Dyad, or material indeterminacy, as co-original.

Artaud is, as such, a Platonist of the unwritten doctrines. Indeed, Artaud's support for Platonic esotericism is made patent in *Heliogabalus*, where Artaud writes that we should understand Plato 'as he should be understood' by following the 'ancient esoteric path'.[77] The Platonism of the unwritten doctrines, whose accuracy was famously later supported by the Tübingen school of Platonism, places the One and the Dyad as co-original.[78] The Dyad, understood as chaos or indeterminacy, interacts with the unity and order of the One as the cosmos, and this interaction constitutes the cause of all principles and things.[79] If the Tarahumaras and other Indigenous people are pure, then it is because they are closer to Nature qua the chaosmos. For Artaud, the ancient and current Mexican Indigenous people's racial superiority stems from their proximity to this metaphysical system. Thus, their purity is not connected to a

---

[74]Antonin Artaud to Alexis Carrel.
[75]RM, 188.
[76]RM, 188.
[77]VII, 53.
[78]See Hans Joachim Kräme, *Arete bei Platon und Aristoteles* (Heidelberg: C. Winter, 1959). This was the first major publication from the school.
[79]VII, 53.

common moral notion of purity, where purity would be the antimony of dirty or unclean. As Artaud writes, 'To clean is to dull. Everything pure smells bad.'[80] Artaud's purity places the Tarahumras as closest to this productive fetid impure co-origin.

Whether purity is metaphysical impurity, the origin a non-origin, Artaud appears to affirm, nonetheless, a form of racial–cultural essentialism. In other words, race is not explicitly understood as a historical notion invented, developed via pseudo-scientific means, and conceptually sustained to systematically justify the imperial and colonial pursuits of one 'race' over another.[81] If we suppose race is a 'principle' in the exoteric Platonic sense, a Form (*eidos*), then, it would be hard to see how there could be any political abolition of race or escape from its determining factors.

To rigorously assess whether Artaud holds this view, whether this is, indeed, Artaud's notion of 'race' and 'principle', it is important to turn to the two tomes of Fabre d'Olivet's *L'Histoire philosophique du genre humain*, since these books, alongside Artaud's engament with other French Traditionalists such as Joseph Alexandre Saint-Yves d'Alveydre and René Geueon, from the basis for many of the references that Artaud cites throughout the 1930s and explicitly deal with 'race'. [82] Although there is no space to offer an in-depth analysis of Fabre d'Olivet's notion of 'race' or the relation that Occultism and Traditionalism have to Artaud's entire oeuvre, it is important to note the major similarities and, chiefly, differences.

For Fabre d'Olivet, humanity or 'l'Homme', is the bridge between the divine and the mundane. Although humans are one 'kind [*genre*]', they are divided into four 'races' whose interrelated history is driven by supposedly inevitable falls into racial war.[83] For Fabre d'Olivet, as Artaud admits in the notes to *Heliogablus*, the white race is considered 'primary' and 'anterior' to the others, the white

---

[80]RM, 209.
[81]See Denise Ferreira da Silva, *Toward a Global Idea of Race* Minneapolis, MN: University of Minnesota Press, 2007).
[82]See Joseph Alexandre Saint-Yves d'Alveydre, *Les Clefs de l'Orient* (Paris: Librairie académique, Didier et Cie, éditeurs, 1877).
[83]Fabre d'Olivet, *L'Histoire philosophique du genre humain* I–II.

Hyperborean or Aryan race that descends into India from the North.[84] Despite Fabre d'Olivet's equal treatment of each race, it is clear that the white race remains superior. The book finishes, for instance, in a proto-fascist flurry where world peace is achieved through the racial domination of a united white Europe over other races, where all linguistic, religious and political differences (differences that Fabre d'Olivet just spent two tomes outlining) is effaced.[85] Saint-Yves d'Alveydre, who is directly cited in the Mexican 'Messages', follows Fabre d'Olivet's racial-politico-historical structure, this time arguing for the unification of the world and Europe via the installation of a Judeo-Christian dictator who ultimately takes direction from a cult of initiated priests, the 'Authority'.[86] In *La France Vraie*, this political structure is named 'synarchy', a term that continued to have a rather strange history, one that even ended up being used by pro-Catholic clerico-fascist Mexican political parties such as the *National Synarchist Union*.[87]

In 'The Universal Bases of Culture', Artaud has the following to say regarding a United Europe:

> For two or three years now, there have been grotesque talks of a United States of Europe. It would have been more profitable to talk about the total imbalance of European culture since the lamentable state of this dust of a culture that today represents Europe would have been proof to everyone that the United States of Europe was already an obsolete buffoonery.[88]

There would have been nothing more 'grotesque' for Artaud than the realization of the domination of the world by European white culture. Indeed, in 'I Came to Mexico to Flee European Civilization. . .' Artaud writes explicitly that 'there is no revolution without a revolution against the culture of Europe' and that he does not 'distinguish the white mind from the forms of white civilization'.

---

[84]VII, 270.

[85]Fabre d'Olivet, *L'Histoire philosophique du genre humain* I, 47.

[86]Michael Pym, 'Saint-Yves d'Alveydre', *Advocate of Peace through Justice* 88, no. 11 (November, 1926): 609–614.

[87]'Manifiesto   Sinarquista'   (1937),   https://www.memoriapoliticademexico.org/ Textos/6Revolucion/1937MCO.html.

[88]RM, 103.

[89] What is clear is that Artaud's cultural or spiritual 'racial' revolution does not share Fabre d'Olivet's desire for white European domination or Saint-Yves d'Alveydre's theocratic Judaeo-Christian Synarchy.

One should not mistake, therefore, the convictions of Artaud's sources for Artaud. Artaud is not Julius Evola, the Italian far-right and *superfascist* Traditionalist who, through the work of Aleksandr Dugin, continues to this day to inspire neofascism in Europe, the US and Russia, even if Evola held a comparable notion of 'spiritual racism' and developed his ideas from out of many of the same sources as Artaud.[90] Where Evola and Italian fascism idolizes the patriarchal strength of Roman monarchy, the power and heroism of Caesar, Artaud, in 1934, the same year Evola published *Revolt Against the Modern World*, crowned a fourteen-year-old Syrian transexual anarchist as Roman Emperor.

When reading Fabre d'Olivet and Saint-Yves d'Alveydre alongside Artaud, as well as Evola's elitism, one often gets the idea that while certain concepts are repeated, such as the unitary nature of 'Man', the monistic but doubled and mixed origin of matter and spirit, even to a certain extent, the concept of race, it becomes clear that Artaud often perverts these writers' notions, not only inverting their logic but an-archaically destroying it from its root. Guénon, being contemporary to Artaud, and who, although Evola's teacher was no fascist, notices how Artaud completely invents a quote of his cited in *The Theatre and Its Double*.[91]

Despite these influences, then, the question still remains, what does Artaud mean by race-principle if not by some pseudo-scientific or anthropological determining idea. If a race-principle determines the race–culture relation, one would expect that the racial–cultural expression of this principle would be static and immutable, which is to say, that culture participates in or is subsumed under the race-principle qua the unconditioned concept. However, a closer look at what Artaud means by culture, and indeed principle, reveals that instead of being something immutable or eternally fixed by the race-principle, culture is, in contrast, that which 'lives' and 'moves'.

---

[89]RM, 146.
[90]See Julius Evola, *Revolt against the Modern World*, trans. Guido Stucco (Rochester, VT: Inner Traditions International, 1995), 265.
[91]IV, 290.

Different to the European conception of culture as a 'veneer' expressed in material objects such as those one might find in museums, culture for Artaud, as he writes in 'The Universal Bases of Culture', is 'related to the integral modification, one might even say, magical, not just of man but the being in man, for the truly cultured man carries his spirit in his body. It is his body that he works through culture, which is equivalent to saying that he likewise works his spirit.'[92]

Culture, then, is productive and dynamic, not immutable, and constitutes not only the material production of works of art or literature but, in a quasi-Hegelian manner, the very transformation of the being of man's body and mind through life qua *work*. In other words, culture is precisely that which is mutable, and to think otherwise falls into the European trap of considering the production of *things of value* – what a Bordieuan might call 'cultural capital' – as the *telos* of culture:

> Because I have a unitary idea of culture, I say that thinking, sleeping, dreaming, eating are all but one and the same thing. All of this is life. But this same taste for collecting, which accumulates pictures and books and amasses stones in museums, is nothing but the impulsion to hoard the bare necessities of life. It asphyxiates the world's production and appropriates for the benefit of a few individuals an entire collection of material riches, the enjoyment of which belongs to all.[93]

Artaud's notion of culture could be understood as allegorically following the eruptive flows of volcanic molten lava, whereas European art seeks to set, mould and carve stone effigies.

These images of molten lava are the same Artaud uses to describe what he means by 'principle' and the relation that 'principles' have to what could be called their energetic continuity, or as Araud writes, referring here to Bergson, '*pure duration* [*la durée pure*]'.[94] As with many of the more metaphysical concepts in Artaud's work, one must turn to *Heliogabalus* for a clearer idea of what 'principle'

[92]RM, 102.
[93]RM, 147.
[94]VII, 54.

means. In the section 'War of Principles', through a sort of auto-elenctic method, Artaud refutes by question and answer that principles exist outside the mind or that there is any *real* separation between them other than what can be named or termed as such through Number. Inspired by Pythagoras's notion of a number-principle, principles and or any 'Being' should be understood as particular degrees of vibration arising from the 'Will in Energy'.[95] Principles, Artaud writes, are therefore more like 'determined organisms' insofar as they form through a 'creative energy'.[96] This is similar way to how different organisms arise by 'channeling' the energy of the sun in Bergson's 'creative evolution'.[97] Thus, as Artaud writes in the notes to this section of *Heliogabalus*, there is no real separation between things or principles, they are more like different 'breaths' in the '*durée*', momentarily set rocks that were once part of the same matter–spirit molten 'magma'.[98] To think otherwise, that principles are separate, is to make idols of them, effigies that need to be burnt. Indeed, such a magmatism, which views things and principles as moving between states of solidity and fluidity, is expressed by Artaud in the following alchemical way:

and to mercury corresponds movement
to sulphur   >>   energy
to salt   >>   stable mass,[99]

Principles are thus 'emanations' of the mercurial movement of energy, 'energy differentiated' stabilized, or metastabilized saline crystals that may fall back into the movement of sulphur.[100] If principles are metastabilized ideas that arise from and feed off the unity of matter–spirit understood as energy, then precisely like the Ka, they live through consuming this energy. Principles, though, in, and of the mind alone, require the sustenance of matter to survive. This is why, for Artaud, such an idealism is, in fact, always a concrete

---

[95]VII, 55.
[96]VII, 54.
[97]Henri Bergson, *L'Évolution créatrice* (Paris: Presses Universitaires de France, 1941).
[98]VII, 265.
[99]RM, xx.
[100]VII, 265.

idealism. Artaud writes: 'Culture is eating, but it is also knowing how we eat, and for me, when I think I eat, I devour and assimilate thoughts.'[101] Here the entangled doubled unity of Artaud's magmatism appears with more clarity. Eating and thinking are the same.

If this is Artaud's notion of the principle, it is far from an exoteric Platonism where Form transcendently determines the particular. This answers, to a certain extent, what could be meant by the race-principle. There would be no *real* separation between the races like there is no *real* separation between things and thoughts. Race and the difference between races arise from this magmatism the same way organisms arrive through creative evolution. Race determines only insofar as it is a metastabilized principle, one that is maintained through 'devouring' energy. Thus, since race is not scientific, historical or metaphysical in a strong sense of the term, it is not all-determining. Indeed, one could reinterpret the domination of Whiteness as the overfeeding or engorgement of the white-principle. In the same way, European colonial expansion fed the capitalistic machine, always hungry for new sources of extraction and exploitation, it also fed the white-principle. This is precisely what Artaud argues in *Heliogabalus*, adding patriarchy to the mixture of dominant principles, that the history of the modern world is a history of the white-male-principle's domination over all other principles. For Artaud, there will only be 'harmony' once the reign of this domination ends. Where Heliogabalus represented an *individual* balancing of these principles, the indigenous people of Mexico represent a *collective* harmony. To achieve such harmony, however, we must wage a war of principles, a logo-machy, capturing back the energy from this overfed effigy.

The Void and Life-Death

Though arguably more mystic than esoteric, the metaphysical *an-arche* that grounds the living mutability of such *magmatism*, functioning as its efficient cause that sets 'creative energy' into motion, is not some divine monotheistic God as it is for Fabre d'Olivet, Saint-

---

[101]RM, 144.

Yves d'Alveydre's 'Father', or some other male unmoved mover, but precisely the ignorance of the origin or the origin *as* ignorance: 'to affirm the flowering in man of an eternal spirit of culture is to affirm man's ignorance regarding the sources of true life'.[102] For Artaud, this original ignorance, which should be grasped and acted upon with humility, stimulates culture or *is* culture qua the ground on which life and principles emerge. Scientific knowledge stifles and stagnates, occupying itself with dead reason, whereas 'not knowing where he comes from, man can use his ignorance, this kind of *original* ignorance, to know exactly where he must go'.[103] Artaud is, here, following the *via negativa* of negative theology, the same method that he argues inspired Surrealism: since like the 'Unknown God of the Cabeiri Mysteries, as Ein Sof, as the animated hollow of the abysses in the Kabbalah, Nothing, the Void [. . .] we can say what Surrealism is not, but to say what it is, it is necessary to employ approximations and images, and Surrealism is a movement clothed in images.'[104]

One may even argue that, for Artaud, culture itself is apophatic, that the consistent cultural production of aesthetic images and forms results from the sublimation of the energy directed by this original ignorance. This apophatic method is compared to the Daoist notion of the void by Artaud, who argues that this void is a productive emptiness that 'science will never fill' but that nonetheless inspires 'poetry'.[105] As per the Daoist example that Artaud cites several times, 'Though thirty spokes may be joined in one hub,' writes the *Tao Te Ching* of Lao Tzu, 'the utility of the carriage lies in what is not there.'[106] The carriage's function, its efficient cause, is made possible only because of the empty space that allows the wheels to connect to the axles. The carriage moves because of this nothingness. Comparing the Christian cross to the Mexican cross, Artaud likewise argues that while in the Christian religion, the cross symbolized the anthropomorphic death of Christ, 'The Mexican cross, emerging from the void, shows us how life enters space. It shows how the void of space might provide an opening for life.'[107] This quantum

---

[102]RM, 133.
[103]RM, 133.
[104]RM, 61.
[105]RM, 134.
[106]RM, 81.
[107]RM, 148.

metaphysics of the void, that the emptiness of space conditions the emergence of life and culture, is one of the very Ideas that underpin the Theatre of Cruelty, as especially depicted and described in Artaud's 'Staging and Metaphysics' from the *Theatre and Its Double*.[108]

While there are many aspects to Artaud's theatrical project, ranging from the concentration on breath, the contempt for psychological drama and the creation of a pure theatrical hieroglyphic language, to name but a few, one that often stands out is Artaud's distaste for the reduction of theatre to the text, especially written and spoken dialogue, at the expense of the stage or staging. As Artaud writes in 'Staging and Metaphysics': 'I say that the stage is a physical and concrete space that demands to be filled and that we make its language speak.'[109] The theatre is, above all, for Artaud, a type of writing, a physical space that distinguishes itself as an art form from literature precisely because of this fact. For theatre to be theatre, it must be staged. As Artaud writes in 'The Theatre and the Gods,'' '[t]here is a movement which wishes to withdraw the theatre from everything that is not space, to send textual language back to the books from where it should never have left.'[110] Indeed, in this text, which was given as the third lecture at the University of Mexico, Artaud connects this apophatic theatre to the Mexican Codex, saying that the Gods depicted in this historical pictorial document 'were before anything, Gods that were *in space*' and that the 'Mythology of the Codex was hiding a science of space.'[111] It is precisely Artaud's metaphysics of space and the fact that he championed the written language of the stage over written textual language that troubles Jacques Derrida's interpretation of Artaud. Indeed, as Derrida admits in his 1968 to 1969 unpublished seminar given at Johns Hopkins University, 'L'Écriture et le théâtre: Mallarmé/ Artaud', such a fact troubles the Derridean claim that the living voice has always been metaphysically privileged over the written word. In the theatre, the voice, acting and staging supplement the authority and presence of the text.[112]

---

[108]See the new translation of *The Theatre and Its Double*: Antonin Artaud, 'Metaphysics and Directing for the Stage', *The Theatre and Its Double*, trans. Mark Taylor-Batty (London: Bloomsbury, 2024).

[109]IV, 36.

[110]RM, 81–82.

[111]RM, 82.

[112]Jacques Derrida, 'L'Écriture et le théâtre: Mallarmé/Artaud' (unpublished manuscript, 1968–1969), typescript.

If the Mexican Codex is the cultural, religious expression of the emptiness of space, one that Artaud takes to be exemplary of a true and pure culture that lives, then one must conclude that the race-principle of the indigenous people of Mexico, like all principles according to Artaud, has to be grounded, not only on a dynamic origin that is Double (the unity of matter and spirit) but on the Void qua *original ignorance*. This is further evidence of why the race-principle itself cannot be determined and, in turn, cannot determine culture since to do so would negate the effectiveness of the Void. There is, therefore, a *reflective organic* rather than a *determinative mechanical* movement from out of and back into original ignorance. This is precisely how Artaud describes the movement of thought in 'Man against Fate':

> Like life, like nature, thought goes from the inside to the outside before going from the outside to the inside. I start by thinking in the void, and from the void, I move toward the plenum; once I have reached the plenum, I can fall back into the void.[113]

Cosmologically, this metaphysical system positions itself as counter to any gnostic separation between man and the cosmos.[114] Artaud's revolution seeks to overcome the nihilistic tendencies that sprang forth from an Enlightenment understanding of the world where man, and man's reason, find themselves estranged among a thankless and thoughtless universe. Artaud's cosmology does not fix the problem of the loss of value by replacing the lost divine origin with another or turning to existentialist vitalism. The relation between the void and the plenum is synonymous with the movement between death and life: 'Culture is a movement of the spirit that moves from the void toward the forms and from the forms back into the void, into the void as unto death. [. . .] The ancient Mexicans know no other perspective than this coming and going of death and life.'[115] Life, we could say, is nourished

---

[113]RM, 74.
[114]That Artaud is a gnostic has been a popular interpretation since Jane Goodall's 1994 *Artaud and the Gnostic Drama* (Oxford: Clarendon Press). See the 2020 reprint (London: Scarlet Imprint).
[115]RM, 81.

by an original death. Life is always life-death or death-life. In one of the most revealing lines of Artaud's entire 'Messages', countering the exoteric Platonic Good-God-Sun, with the black sun of the Indigenous Mexicans, Artaud writes: 'In a word – and herein lies the real secret – the sun is a principle of death and not a principle of life. The essence of the ancient solar culture is that it demonstrated the supremacy of death.'[116] This metaphysics of life–death, where the dying sun is placed as the condition of life, follows a logic of *entropic displacement* – the displacement of life's internal entropy via the death of life external to it. Such an entropic displacement is the condition of im-possibility of any life's survival, living as such is only possible due to the entropic dying of that which is outside life.[117]

In Artaud's manifestos for a Theatre of Cruelty, that death and life are mutually conditioned, is described as 'cruelty'. As he writes, 'Death is cruelty, life is cruelty, resurrection is cruelty, transfiguration is cruelty, since . . . in a circular and closed world there is no place for true death, ascension is a tearing apart, the closed space is fed by lives.'[118] Death, in other words, is always the condition of life. That which is necessarily cruel is the direction of this entropic logic, 'life always means the death of someone else'.[119] Indeed, it is for this reason that cruelty is necessity. There is no escape from death when life is cruelly conditioned by it.

If we connect the previously discussed metaphysics of space to this metaphysics of life-death qua cruelty, one is left with a strong definition of the Theatre of Cruelty. Since thinking and culture are said to be analogical to this movement between the void and the plenum, death and life, then, to hold onto a thought, to keep thought *present* requires effort and energy. As such, while principles such as the white-male-principle can be fixed and mummified (a comparably Nietzschean idea) by death's persistent, energetic investment, they can also fall to ruin. 'To be cultured is to burn forms, to burn forms

---

[115]RM, 128.
[117]See Joel White, 'Outline to an Architectonics of Thermodynamics: Life's Entropic Indeterminacy', in *Contingency and Plasticity in Everyday Technologies*, ed. by Natasha Lushetich, Iain Campbell and Dominic Smith (London: Rowman and Littlefield, 2023), 183–199.
[118]V, 100.
[119]V, 98.

to win back life. Culture is learning to hold oneself up straight in the incessant movement of those forms we successively destroy.'[120]

For Artaud, this mummification of thinking is tantamount to the creation and perseverance of false idols. True culture destroys these idols or recognizes that they are only alive because of the sacrifice of that which is external to them. For Artaud, the telos of the Theatre of Cruelty is to *stage* the *cruel* destruction of such idols. The Theatre of Cruelty's purpose, as per 'The Conquest of Mexico', is to participate in the logomachic war of principles. It aims to destroy the idol of the white-male-principle's superiority by staging its entropic downfall, a theatrically staged inversion or perversion of the *Triumph of the Will*.

This perversion of racial superiority based on a highly complex negative theology does not, however, absolve Artaud of his Orientalism, primitivism or constant recourse to the 'Nobel savage' trope. To talk like Edward Said, it is clear that the Indigenous are 'Other' and that this 'Otherness' is a fantastical construction of Artaud's European desires for renewal.[121] Apart from experiencing the rituals of the Tarahumaras, most of Artaud's knowledge of the Indigenous people stems from reading the works of white racist European Orientalists like Fabre d'Olivet. While, for Artaud, the Indigenous people are *more* civilized and cultured than Europeans, this argument also hinges on proximity to the metaphysical system described above, which is also described as a certain being-at-one or harmony with the chaosmos. Such a primitivism – one which places the Other as essentially outside of history – is racist in a conventional sense of the term despite Artaud's inversions. What is more, Artaud's primitivism – or in the case of the Mexican Indigenous people *Indianism* – is also counter to the political and epistemological celebration of *métissage* and *créolization* as the production of difference, that thinkers like Eduard Glissant rightfully expound.[122] It must not be forgotten that the first Mexican *mestizos*, whom Artaud criticizes, descend from Mexican Indigenous women enslaved and offered to the Spanish conquistador Hernán

---

[120]RM, 81.
[121]See Edward W. Said, *Orientalism* (New York: Pantheon Books, 1978).
[122]See Eduard Glissant, *Traité du Tout-monde* (Paris: Gallimard, 1997).

Cortés by the Tobsaco people. The brunt of Artaud's prejudice against the Mexican métis certainly reveals itself once this is considered.[123]

Artaud was, nonetheless, fully aware of what it meant for a European to travel to Mexico in search of some form of lost racial idea, calling his only desires 'Baroque', in other words, extravagant and distasteful.[124] For these reasons, Artaud was also highly critical of H. P. Blavatsky's Theosophical Society, charging it with being an organ of the British intelligence service and making a mockery of Eastern monism – being precisely Orientalist in the Saidian sense of the term. Artaud's most vehement critique of Orientalism was, nonetheless, saved for Hermann von Keyserling, one of the more widely read but now mostly forgotten German 'prophets' of European decadence:

> There is no sacred philosophy or great culture which Keyserling has not touched to vulgarize its doctrines in an odious manner, whereas, for their part, the ancient Brahmans of India sometimes sacrificed their lives for the same principles.[125]

Compared to Blavatsky or Keyserling, Artaud does not engage in the same form of intellectual cultural appropriation. He does not level actual culture, whether living or historical, to an object of conspicuous curiosity. There is a sincerity in Artaud's activities that immunizes him – to a certain extent – from such bourgeois pastimes. Putting to one side their political convictions, Artaud saw himself as one of the 'serious men' cited in 'The Universal Bases of Culture', as a 'Spengler, Scheler' or a 'Heidegger'. To his mind, he was rigorous and philosophically singular, Nietzschean in his diagnosis of European decomposition and Promethean in his response.

The need to turn to other civilizations for cultural and political inspiration and renewal consisted of revolting against what Vandana Shiva calls a 'monoculture' of the mind.[126] Indeed, for Artaud, 'And

---

[123]Hugh Thomas, *Conquest: Montezuma, Cortés, and the Fall of Old Mexico* (New York: Simon and Schuster, 1993), 171–172.
[124]RM, 201.
[125]RM, 103.
[126]See Vandana Shiva, *Monocultures of the Mind: Biodiversity, Biotechnology and Agriculture* (New Delhi: Zed Press, 1993).

just as individuals have diseases, there are diseases of the masses. Thus, the generalization of industrial crops has given rise to a collective form of *scurvy* in the European organism.'[127] This scurvy of the mind risks the destruction of differences at the level of culture. Through the universalization and industrialization of mechanical techniques, 'we would risk making them [the Mexican Indians] lose all that they could preserve from their ancient culture because culture and civilization are connected'.[128] In other words, cultural and political colonialism risks what Boaventura de Sousa Santos calls the 'epistimicide' of non-European ways of thinking.[129] There is, therefore, no true revolution that is not simultaneously a revolution against such a universal idea of the mind. For Artaud, European fascism and European Marxism both ultimately fail as revolutionary projects; they mistake mechanical, technological and cultural homogenization for progress.

Ni Droite, Ni Gauche?

In the first section of 'Artaud's Revolution', I questioned whether Artaud's revolution would not be closer to a reactionary or conservative revolution, especially given that in 1926 Artaud expressed his desire for a revolution that would institute a 'regression in time'. Pushing this line of argument furthest, Jannarone's *Artaud and His Doubles* claims that there are darker sides to Artaud, Doubles that align his aesthetic and political projects to that of a 'Reactionary', even fascist.[130]

While it is important to assess the possibility of such a claim given Artaud's sources, his explicit anti-Marxism and use of race as the key driving force of his palingenesis, the main scholarly problem with Jannarone's argument is that her evidence is, for the most part, circumstantial insofar as there are no explicit references to Artaud's mention of fascism; that is, apart from a footnote that details

---

[127]RM, 119.
[128]RM, 108.
[129]Boaventura de Sousa Santos, *Epistemologies of the South: Justice against Epistemicide* (Boulder, CO: Paradigm Publishers, 2014).
[130]Though she does admit that Artaud would not have made a very good fascist citizen; Jannarone, *Artaud and His Doubles*, 195.

Artaud's infamous dedication to Hitler for his 1937 *The New Revelations of Being* and their supposed meeting at a café in Berlin, written by Artaud in 1943 while at Rodez.[131]

While Jannarone does cite *The New Revelations of Being*, she does not mention that, through the medium of tarot reading, Artaud prophecies that the world 'will be balanced by the Right. And that the Left will fall under the Supremacy of the Right'.[132] Whether Artaud, who signs this text under the pseudonym 'The Revealed', supports this prophecy is hard to tell, it is after all a tarot reading. It must be said, however, that certain parts certainly read as though the arrival of balance through the 'Male Right', which must direct the 'Female Revolution' to overthrow the supremacy of the 'Feminine Left', is desired by Artaud.[133] If this is the case, and Artaud does support such an overthrow, not only does it represent an inversion of Heliogabalus's role as the balance bringer, but it would constitute an explicit support for the rise of European fascism. The dedication to Hitler would also, therefore, make perfect sense.

In place of a deeper analysis of Artaud's politics, and texts such as *The New Revelations of Being*, Jannarone's arguments hinge on comparing Artaud's aesthetics from the theatre writings with a set of reactionary artists and theatre makers and definitions of fascism that are exterior to Artaud's work. Synthetic comparison is, however, never the ground for analytic determination. Most significantly, there are no references to the *Messages révolutionnaires*, despite these being available in French.[134] As written earlier, a true assessment of Artaud's intertwined aesthetic and politics projects cannot be made without taking the 'Messages' into account.

---

[131]VII, 423. Artaud also sent a spell to Hitler in 1939, saying that they had met at another bar, Café L'Ida in Berlin. This spell was intended to lift the 'bars' and was sent as a 'warning', not an 'invitation'. It also says that Paris needs 'Gas'. Antonin Artaud, Bibliotèque natiuonale de France (BnF), Collection Serge Malausséna, 'Sort à Hitler'.

[132]For Artaud, the 'Right' is male and the 'Left' is 'Feminine', which constitutes the 'Republic', 'Democracy' and 'Revolution'. See VII, 128–129.

[133]VII, 128–129.

[134]As Sollers asks in "L'État d'Artaud," why is it that no one reads Artaud? This paper opened the famous 1971 Cerisy conference organized around the ideas of Artaud and Bataille and the Cultural Revolution in China. Phillipe Sollers, "L'État d'Artaud," in *Artaud*, ed. Phillipe Sollers (Paris: 10/18, 1973), 19–29.

While there are undoubtedly similarities between Artaud's aesthetics and certain fascist occultist movements and thinkers of the 1930s – as *The New Revelations of Being* demonstrates – in the 'Messages', Artaud, in fact, explicitly rejects many of the very same movements used by Jannarone to align Artaud to their politics. The Futurists, for example, are lambasted for being thoughtless mechanists, for being the artistic movement of the European war machine, and Blavatsky's occultist Theosophy is criticized for being a mockery of Eastern philosophy.[135] Furthermore, if one were to compare a theatrical movement to the Theatre of Cruelty, one might want to start with the movements Artaud praised. In 'French Theatre in Search of a Myth', Artaud applauds the communist theatrical troupe Octobre for their advancements over text-oriented movements such as Jacques Copeau, for their 'invention' of a true theatrical language.[136] Artaud's Theatre of Cruelty was not, as a consequence, a communist endeavour. The ability to align political stance with aesthetic form is, nonetheless, certainly complicated by such a fact.

Jannarone's attempt to align Artaud's philosophy with Nietzsche, and the supposed nefarious political and or philosophical consequences such an alignment might have, also falls flat. In one of his several explicit disavowals of Hitler and Fascism, Artaud writes:

> Hitler's Fascism has its philosophers, whose system is a monstrous mishmash of Nietzsche, Kant, Herder, Fichte and Schelling.[137]

Artaud was astutely aware that what 'Hitler's Fascism' had done to Nietzsche was nothing but a travesty. If anything, fascism is always philosophically poor; it appropriates and adjoins seemingly sympathetic ideas after the fact, rarely arising from actual thought. Fascist Italy, Artaud argues, was not even able to produce one philosopher.[138] In 'What I Came to Mexico to Do', when justifying that all that remains is 'Mexico and its subtle political structure,' Artaud likewise criticizes Japan for becoming simply

---

[135]RM, 155, 175.
[136]RM, 117.
[137]RM, 102.
[138]It is unlikely that Artaud would have written this if he had read Evola, either this or it is a backhanded insult.

'the fascists of the Far East'.[139] Again, regarding the rise of German and Italian fascism in Europe, Artaud writes this rather astute criticism:

> Spain is burning, and the fire in Ethiopia has just been extinguished. On the soil of immense China, war threatens to break out again at every moment; Germany and Italy have fallen prey to a singular order which is nothing but the legalized organization of a disorder. And this order threatens the order and peace of its neighbours, that is to say, the order and peace of Europe.[140]

Regardless of Artaud's use of the metaphors of war and conflict, given that this is written in 1936 and the first German volunteers had already left to fight in the Spanish Civil War on the nationalist side, and Italy was waging war in Ethiopia with the help of Nazi Germany, it is evident that Artaud does not support another total war, especially one that might culminate in a united Europe under fascist rule. As Artaud writes, fascism's pretense to order is nothing but a legalized disorder. While order might well be superficially guaranteed by the juridical status of the sovereign who decides on the state of exception, a deeper cultural and social disorder flourishes.

Artaud was likewise highly critical of political nationalism, arguing for a difference between cultural nationalism, 'in which the specific quality of a nation and its works of art are affirmed', and egotistical 'civic nationalism', which 'resolves itself into chauvinism that results in custom struggles and economic wars, that is, when it does not end in total war'.[141] On Artaud's criticism of nationalism, it is worth highlighting that in the opening lecture given at the University of Mexico 'Surrealism and Revolution', Artaud quotes a pamphlet entitled 'FATHERLAND AND FAMILY' published by *Contre-Attaque* and written by George Bataille.[142] Artaud cites this

---

[139]RM, 120.

[140]RM, 139.

[141]RM, 126.

[142]Bataille was most likely never aware of the fact that Artaud had ever quoted this pamphlet. In 'Le Surréalisme au jour le jour', Bataille recounts, nonetheless, that one

pamphlet to demonstrate that this *new* orientation of Surrealism once again revolts against the same forms of 'material and spiritual oppressions' that provoked the *old* Surrealism to action: 'the Father, Fatherland, Religion, the Family', the central concepts of any fascist nationalism. What is also crucial about this quote, which supports this redirection of Surrealism insofar as it returns to the initial concerns of Surrealism, is that it maintains, 'against the last Stalinist orientations, the essential objectives of Marxism' and in so doing, positions itself against what *Contre-Attaque* called 'fascist drivel'.[143]

Even though Artaud's conferences given at the University of Mexico are, as he writes to Jean Paulhan, 'anti-Marxist' and that ten years before Artaud's 'Messages', Artaud's anti-communism was more than explicit, it is worth reassessing Artaud's relationship to, if not Marxism, then certainly to Marx or Marxian ideas. Indeed, as the above citation indicates, there is certainly ground to argue that what Artaud was critical of was precisely the Leninist and Stalinist nature of communism insofar as they ideologized or idolized Marxian ideas, fixing them into Marxist idols in the shape of the Party. Artaud writes, 'And, rereading Marx's *Communist Manifesto*, they [the French youth] realize that what is called Marxism is a false ideology that caricatures the thinking of Marx.'[144] Indeed, this is the same ideological criticism that Artaud levels against the Surrealists, that 'Surrealism itself had become a party,' which is to say it had become fixed, idolized. For Artaud, as he writes in 'Surrealism and Revolution', this constituted 'the lowering of Surrealism to Marxism', where 'it would have been glorious to have seen Marxism attempt to raise itself to Surrealism'.[145] Much of

---

night around 1935, prior to Artaud leaving for Mexico, Artaud grabbed his arm and declared that what is needed is a 'Mexican fascism'.[141] As an indirect quote, it is hard to determine what Artaud meant by this. One can assume, nonetheless, that in the same way that Artaud inverts the notion of racial superiority, the Mexican fascism Artaud is referring to is not support for the Catholic clerico-fascism that was strengthening at the time. This is not a Mexican European fascism that supports white supremacy. The one consistent fact that one can say about Artaud's politics is that his support lies with the indigenous people of Mexico. George Bataille, 'Le Surréalisme au jour le jour', in *Œuvres complètes Vol. VIII* (Paris: Gallimard, 1976), 180.

[143]RM, 60.
[144]RM, 70.
[145]RM, 64.

the Marxian content of the 'Messages' can be viewed from this perspective, as an attempt at raising Marx to Surrealism via the affirmation of indigenous Mexican culture.

Different to Artaud's more reactive response to Marxism in the 1920s, where the materialism of Marxism and the concrete idealism of Surrealism constituted an insurmountable contradiction, an 'antagonism', by 1936, 'History', Artaud argues, had now 'advanced' to the point where a 'reconciliation between *Culture* and Fate' had now become possible.[146] In other words, Artaud appears to be arguing for a reconciliation between the cultural or spiritual revolution of Surrealism and the material revolution of Marxism, a unification that aims at a 'heightened idea of what man is' and that does not 'separate man's life from the events of life'.[147] Following a Hegelian or Marxian logic, such a unity of mind and body, spirit and matter might well constitute a new political philosophy of *life* understood in its dynamic organic movement as the unification of mind and matter. It might be said that Artaud epistemologically places a reflexive organicism or life-centred logic as counter to a determinative mechanism or machine-centred logic.

It is, therefore, Mexican culture that Artaud looks to for its alleged ability to nourish the body and mind collectively *and* politically. Artaud's justification for the superiority of the indigenous people is, alongside their anti-dualist metaphysics, their cultural emphasis on ways of living rather than the production of material commodities, as well as their capacity to 'heal the psychic life of the world *through the world*',[148] which is to say, an emphasis on the understanding that man and the cosmos are one. Indeed, from a social point of view, Artaud even argues that they 'demonstrate peace in a society that knew how to give food to everyone and where the Revolution, from its origins, was already accomplished'.[149] Artaud appears to support the emergence of a pure collectivism whereby the bourgeois liberal individual whose love for himself is placed before all else is replaced by the love of the community: 'The ancient Mexicans did not know individual love, a European and

---

146RM, 64–65.
147RM, 65.
148RM, 134.
149V, 19.

Christian idea. / It is important to know that the new civilization, if it is born, proposes to make love.'[150] Indeed, it is precisely on this point that Artaud can be seen as different to his insistence on individual freedom from the 1920s. By 1936, Artaud had replaced his support for individualist freedom with an organicist collective cultural revolution.

In many of the 'Messages', Artaud ventriloquizes his organicist political positions via what he calls the French 'youth', and this is especially the case when discussing his political and philosophical agreements and disagreements with Marx:

> The new youth is anti-capitalist-bourgeoisie, and, like Karl Marx himself, it has felt the disequilibrium of the times, which has given rise to the monstrous personality of Fathers based on land and money.[151]

Artaud agrees, therefore, with Marx that one of the driving forces behind the 'disequilibrium of the times' is economic, that wealth is based on 'land and money', and that such an economic system gives rise to and sustains patriarchy – what I called earlier the white-male-principle. Artaud even goes so far as to say that the 'youth' consider that 'Marx departed from a fact.' However, Marx remained with this fact, organizing the 'matter' that the bourgeois left him, but he 'never raised himself to the level of a metaphysics of Nature'.[152]

In 'Man Against Fate', the second conference given at the University of Mexico, Artaud again aligns his thinking concerning the movements of history with that of Marx via the mouthpiece of the French 'youth', arguing that Marx's notion of life was 'provisionally valid,' corresponding 'to a real movement in history'.[153] Artaud praises Marx for being the first that 'lived and felt life' in its historical sense: 'Karl Marx fought against such a simulacrum of facts; he tried to sense historical thought in its particular dynamism.'[154] Thus, if Artaud praises Marx, it is for thinking of history not as something simply past but for having a

---

[150]RM, 198.
[151]RM, 65.
[152]RM, 65.
[153]RM, 70.
[154]RM, 70.

dialectical understanding of history, one which does not just view history as a collection of determined facts but as dynamic and precisely not subject to 'Fate'.

But for Artaud, Marx, perhaps counter to his own philosophical intuition:

> remained fixated on a fact: the capitalist fact, the bourgeois fact, the clogging up of the machine, the asphyxia of the economy of that era that was caused by a monstrous abuse of the utilization of the machine.[155]

Marx's fixation with the machine, regardless of the validity of its criticism, destines Marxism and 'Historical and dialectical materialism' to remain 'an invention of European consciousness', which is to say that they remain mechanist, holding a rationalist conception of the world whereby the relation between cause (economic base) and effect (cultural superstructure) is mechanically determined, even if dialectically. For Artaud, precisely this fixation with both the economic fact and the machine turns 'historical materialism' into an 'idolatry which, like all idolatry, is religious'.[156] That is, 'the materialist explanation of history as an ideology' stops 'history dead in its tracks'.[157] In a rather explicit line from 'I Came to Mexico to Flee European Civilization', Artaud writes that while he is 'in favour of binding human consciousness to matter', which is to say that ideas cannot be thought of as separate from matter, he, nonetheless, does not 'believe that an economic analysis of the world, that the reduction of all world problems to a simple economic factor, is a good way to achieve this goal',[158] which is to say, an effective revolution. If Artaud condemns Marx and Lenin, then it is as 'mechanists', which is to say, as Europeans.

Artaud concludes his critique of Marx's concept of history, and Lenin's materialism, by explicitly favouring 'Hegel's dialectic' over what Artaud claims is Lenin's pretense to have gone beyond it. Using what is most likely an altered, perverted or perhaps invented reference to Hegel's central chapter, 'Force and Understanding',

---

[155]RM, 70.
[156]RM, 70.
[157]RM, 70.
[158]RM, 144.

from the *Phenomenology of Spirit* (insofar as this chapter of Hegel's *Phenomenology* is concerned with the interplay of forces and the appearance of understanding as a relation between an inner and an outer world), Artaud claims that Hegel's dialectic is comprised of three forces, which he aligns with the three forces of 'an old science known to all antiquity':

> the repellent and dilating force,
> the compressive and constricting force,
> the rotational force.[159]

While Hegel's 'forces' are not the same as those mentioned by Artaud, there is certainly a philosophical affinity between both of their forceful idealisms. Artaud continues to describe the interaction of these forces as a set of rotating forces that move from the inside to the outside, from the void to the plenum, in a reflective oscillating manner. For Artaud, the cutting off or arresting of this force on the outside 'to examine what it is capable of' constitutes misunderstanding 'thought in the movement of its internal fate'.[160] In its application to our everyday life, this produces what Artaud calls a *'separated consciousness'*.[161] Hegel might determine this as 'false necessity' insofar as a distinction of parts or kinds is taken to be a distinction in substance.[162] The *true fate* or *necessity* of thought, the unity of the absolute, appears only insofar as it can express the unity *and* distinction of these forces. The Absolute, after all, is not a night in which all cows are black.

Consistent with Artaud's magmatism, as outlined above, Artaud argues that *separated consciousness* – that thought itself can be divided into a soul or subject that views a body or an object – is at the heart of cartesian European mechanist conception of the world and thus also the central problem with Marxism. It is an inadequate theory of consciousness since, for Artaud, such a division of consciousness fundamentally does not align with the real concrete processes of thought.[163] Artaud explicitly cites Bergson to support

---

[159]RM, 74.
[160]RM, 74.
[161]RM, 69.
[162]G. W. F. Hegel, 'Force and Understanding', in *Phenomenology of Spirit*, trans. A. V. Miller (Oxford: Oxford University Press, 1979).
[163]See Julia Kristeva, 'Le sujet en procès', in *Artaud*, ed. Sollers, 43–109.

his integrated notion of consciousness, arguing that 'consciousness is, in reality, a block, what the philosopher Bergson calls *pure duration*'.[164] While the arrestation and division of consciousness is a necessity for reason, insofar as '[t]o think, we have images, words for these images, and representations of objects', the European conception of man exalts these 'deathly simulacrum' beyond measure, thinking them to be *real distinctions*.[165] This not only has the consequences of transforming dynamic things into static objects – commodities – but fixes the subject in its relation to these commodities. That is, even the subject itself is now just an object. Whereas Marxism attacks the social and economic basis for the production of these objects, it believes that an overturning of these relations is revolutionary enough. Marxism speaks of the 'consciousness of the masses', which is to say that Marxism has a notion of *false consciousness* and *class consciousness* whereby the worker can free themselves, theoretically speaking, from the self-estrangement of work through becoming aware of their class, that is, their relation to the production of capital. However, 'it does not destroy the notion of individual consciousness', what Artaud also calls 'capitalism of the conscience', where the 'soul' itself is just a commodity. As Artaud writes in 'First Contact with the Mexican Revolution': 'Marxism, by preserving the sense of individual consciousness, prevents the Revolution from returning to its sources, which means that it halts the Revolution.'[166]

For Artaud, the destruction of false consciousness through the raising of class consciousness will not work to rid society of the power of individualism, which Artaud argues 'in all its aspects, is rotten'.[167] Indeed, '[g]iving everyone the means to eat does not equate to healing the world'.[168] What is 'better' is 'to remove from each person the taste for property in general'.[169] That is, Artaud's call for a 'total revolution' is one where we 'enter iron-fisted into the world of consciousness so that the revolution occurs first within this world'.[170] For Artaud, as per his definition of Surrealism, this

---

[164]RM, 70.
[165]RM, 70.
[166]RM, 108.
[167]RM, 144.
[168]RM, 144.
[169]RM, 144.
[170]RM, 145.

means the *demoralization* or *devalourization of value*, entering 'fully armed into the realm of consciousness' to understand what perverts man's unified notion of life.[171] As an example of such a pervasion, of a value that must be devalourized and thus cannot be solved by class consciousness or even the eventual installation of the dictatorship of the proletariat, Artaud raises the example of a traitor or a counter-revolutionary. He writes:

> when, in a proletarian government, a proletariat betrays and becomes reactionary, is it because they have eaten too much or because they have eaten too little? I demand you to respond, and when doing so, do not believe, I beg you, that I oversimplify the question.[172]

In other words, is the perpetuation of self-interest the fault of the individual counter-revolutionary or has the revolution itself failed? Indeed, Artaud argues that while 'Shooting traitors is always good,' such a 'simplistic approach' to the idea of betrayal will not rid society more generally of self-interest's spiritual causes. Property, value and self-interest, as real abstractions, must first be destroyed as ideas with real concrete bodies.

The groundbreaking nature of Artaud's theory of ideology, what above I have called a 'logomachy', can only really be grasped once his magmatism, that is, his quasi-Bergsonian theory of ideas as self-differentiating principles sustained by energy, is connected to this critique of bourgeois ideals. Artaud writes, 'Alongside the

Thus, one of the most astute arguments levelled against Marxism by Artaud is that being steadfast in its materialism, it refuses to give space to a true analysis of ideas: how ideas are sustained and their role in the maintenance of bourgeois society. Artaud even argues that if 'materialism did not believe in the life of ideas, it would renounce speech'.[173] Marxist materialism is thus 'forced to admit that a life of ideas exists' since it admits the capacity of ideology, that the influence of words, too, in turn, influence the actions of individuals.

---

[171]RM, 145.
[172]RM, 145.
[173]RM, 146.

capitalization of forms, there is the idea of the petrification and conservation of forms, which is also bourgeois.'[174] Artaud's politics and revolution can only be grasped once a Marxist organic-energetics of cultural hegemony replaces Marxist materialism. As Artaud concludes in 'I came to Mexico to Flee European Civilization':

> And yet, I wonder what would happen to the materialist conception when science, in its most recent development, teaches us that there is no matter, that all life is energy, and that matter, in its multiple forms, is nothing other than an expression of this energy.
>
> Atoms are examined so that matter might be understood, but under the scrutiny of science, each atom disappears and transforms into a particular version of the dynamism of energy. Human thought is also an energy which adopts forms. What then prevents us from viewing this energy through its particular form and harnessing this intense source of energy?[175]

While Gille Deleuze and Felix Guattari, to a certain extent at least, developed an organic-energetic philosophy of thought in the latter half of the twentieth century, one that directly stems from Artaud's energetics, the relation between thought, ideas, signification and the science of energy, thermodynamics, has yet to be fully developed. Despite science having replaced the dominance of matter and force with concepts such as energy, information and entropy, as of yet, no adequate *thermodynamics of sense* that accounts for how flows of energy are manipulated and channelled into the maintenance of informatic-metastabilized ideas has been fully formulated. Indeed, as I have been suggesting a theory of sense such as this might come under the title of an Artaudian war of principles, a logomachy.[176]

To conclude, there is no doubt that Artaud's emphasis on a cultural revolution, one that attacks ideology through its very living organic structure, preludes many of the cultural Marxists that follow him: Antonio Gramsci's theory of 'cultural hegemony', Critical Theory's Hegelian-Freudian Marxism and its criticism of

---

[174]RM, 148.
[175]RM, 148.
[176]See Joel White, *Of Logomachy: Thermodynamics of Sense* (forthcoming).

the culture industry, Louis Althusser's 'ideological state apparatus' and especially the French avant-garde of the 1960s: Isidore Isou's Lettrists and Guy Debord's situationists. Artaud, especially Isou, directly influenced both. But having said this, Artaud's particular emphasis on indigenous culture, his all-out attack on dualism, individualism and the white-male-principle distinguish him in many ways from these figures. Of course, even if the accusation is still made that identical cultural criticism can be found just as much from the Right as it can from the Left, that Artaud indeed potentially sees himself as a Spengler or a Heidegger, one must not lose sight of the fact that what Artaud envisioned, dreamed of, when travelling to Mexico was 'an alliance between the French and Mexican Youth with the view of producing a unique cultural effort'.[177] Artaud's disappointment in the Mexico youth was not their desire for socialism. This Artaud was praised for being multifaceted and bubbling with ideas, but that it came at the expense of the Indigenous people and their non-European metaphysics. One could say that in the same way that Artaud argues that it would have been glorious for Marxism to have risen to the level of Surrealism, so, too, should Marxism rise to the level of Indigenous thought. Although impossible to answer, one question that remains is what Artaud would have thought of the Zapatista Army of National Liberation and their blend of Indigenous Mayan culture, Marxist anti-imperialism and Catholic liberation theology? No doubt, Artaud, being Artaud, would have declared it too Marxist, too Catholic, all too European.

---

[177]RM, 108.

I

Three Lectures Delivered at the University of Mexico[ii]

Surrealism and Revolution[iii]

I participated in the Surrealist movement from 1924 to 1926 and went along with it in its violence.

I will speak about it with the same spirit I had during this period. I will attempt to resurrect this spirit for you, one which wanted to be blasphemous and sacrilegious and, on occasion, succeeded.

But do not forget that this spirit is no longer; it belonged to 1926, and if you react to it, react only as if it were 1926.

Surrealism was born from a despair and a disgust; it was delivered on school benches.

More than just a literary movement, it was a moral revolt, an organic cry of man, the bolting of the being inside us against all coercion.

And first of all, the coercion of the Father.

The Surrealist movement in its entirety was a deep and interior insurrection against all forms of the Father, against the all-invading authority of the Father present in our habits and ideas.

Here is, for purely demonstrative purposes, the last Surrealist manifesto, which indicates the new political orientation of this movement:

COUNTER-ATTACK
FATHERLAND AND FAMILY[iv]

Sunday 5 January 1936, at 9 pm, Grenier des Augustins, 7 Rue des Grands-Augustins (métro Saint-Michel).

AGAINST THE ABANDONMENT OF
THE REVOLUTIONARY POSITION

PROTEST MEETING

A man who acknowledges the fatherland and fights for family is a man who betrays. What he betrays is that which gives us a reason to live and to fight.

Patriarchy stands between man and the wealth of the earth. It demands that the products of human toil are transformed into cannons. It makes a human being a traitor to his kind.

Family is the foundation of social obligations. The total absence of all fraternity between father and child has served as the model for all social relations based on authority and the employers' disdain for their equals.

Father, fatherland *and* employer, *such is the trilogy which serves as the basis of the old patriarchal society and, these days, fascist drivel.*

Men will one day rise out of pure exhaustion having been abandoned to a life of suffering and extinction, the causes of which they cannot comprehend. They will accomplish the ruination of the old patriarchal trilogy and will found a fraternal *society of fellow workers based on human potential and solidarity.*

From this manifesto, we can see that Surrealism maintains, against the last Stalinist orientations, the essential objectives of Marxism. That is to say, all the virulent points where Marxism touches man and seeks to enter into his innermost secret thoughts. And we must recognize in this stubborn violence the old Surrealist manner, which can only live exasperated.

But the mystery of Surrealism is that this revolt, since its origins, sank into the unconscious.

It was a hidden mysticism. A new kind of occultism, and like all hidden mysticisms, it expressed itself allegorically and through ghosts that breathed the air of poetry.

Everything that had the form of an apparent demand, Surrealism either dismissed it or could not adhere to it.

When Surrealism began, a terrible seething notion of revolt against all forms of material and spiritual oppression provoked us to action: the Father, Fatherland, Religion, the Family, there was nothing we did not curse... and we cursed with our souls more than with words. We committed our soul to this revolt and committed it *materially*. However, this revolt, which attacked everything, was incapable of destroying anything, at least not visibly. Since the secret of Surrealism is that it attacks things in their secrets.

Surrealism had opened a way to get back to the secret of things. As the Unknown God of the Cabeiri Mysteries, as Ein Sof, as the animated hollow of the abysses in the Kabbalah, Nothing, the Void, the Non-Being devourer of the nothingness of the ancient Brahma Sutras and Vedas, we can say what Surrealism is not, but to say what it is, it is necessary to employ approximations and images, and Surrealism is a movement clothed in images. It resuscitates the spirit of the ancient allegories through an incantation in the void.

There are, of course, elements in Surrealist poetry that can be talked about, recalled and recognized. However, other types of poetry always lead us toward a domain, into a particular country that cannot be confused with others. Contrarily, with Surrealism, the path to loss starts right away, making it impossible to claim that its poetry sprang from the place it was observed.

Surrealism needed to emerge.

'Come forth by light in the first chapter,' as the *Egyptian Book of the Dead* says about the Double of man.

And, as Surrealists, we were constantly in need of emerging everywhere in a deathly movement of dissatisfaction. From whence came a violence that would lead to nothing; but something was revealed in a subterranean manner, a violence which ended up being referred to as *demoralization* by the mania of enlightening things.

Refusal and Violence

Violence and Refusal

These two significative poles of an impossible state of mind, of a mysterious electricity, indicate the abnormal characteristic of the poetry of this era which was not poetry in the sense that these words are usually understood, but the magnetic emission of a breath, a sort of strange magic that established itself between us all.

Refusal. A hopeless refusal to live, but which must accept to live.

In Surrealism, despair was the order of the day, and with despair, suicide. But to the question posed in Issue two of the *Surrealist Revolution*: Is Suicide a Solution? the Surrealists responded unanimously with a singular movement of the heart, 'No,' suicide is still a hypothesis: in Jouffroy's words: 'With suicide, he who kills is not identical with he who is killed.'

All Surrealist expressions participated in this suicidal spirit, where true suicide never intervened.

Destruction on top of destruction. Where poetry attacks words, the unconscious attacks images, but a more secret mind still seeks to stick the statue back together.

The idea is to shatter the real, deceive the senses, and demoralize appearances wherever possible, but always with a notion of the concrete. From its stubborn massacre, Surrealism always aims to pull something up.

For Surrealism, the unconscious is physical, and the Illogical is the secret of an order where the secret of life expresses itself.

When it shattered the model or wrecked the terrain, it would put it back together but, in a manner, so as to incite laughter or to resurrect the depths of terrifying images which swim in the Unconscious.

This means that it flouts reason, extracts images from the senses and gives them back their profound sense.

This means that the writers of this period were aware of the occult depths of Man lost since before Time.

And Surrealism freed inanimate sediments from within life, physically decongesting life; it allowed an invaluable electric cord to come forth and animate these stones.

Disorganized life reformulates itself in response to the chaotic anarchy imposed on the objects seen.

To avoid confusion, the Surrealist world is concrete, *concrete*.

Everything abstract, anything not tragically or farcically perturbing, everything which does not manifest an organic state, which is not a sort of physical exudation stemming from the mind's worries, does not belong to this movement. Surrealism invented automatic writing; it is an intoxication of the mind. The hand freed from the mind goes where the pen guides it, and underneath this, an astonishing spell instructs the plume in such a way that it makes it live, and having lost all contact with logic, the hand, because reconstructed in this way, renews its connection with the unconscious.

Through its miracle, it denies even the idiotic and scholarly contradiction between mind and matter, between matter and mind.

*

Each time life is affected by something, it reacts through dreams and through spectral ghosts.

This means that the general Unconscious was probed by something. It brings forth what it was holding back.

When a woman conceives a child, she will dream about it without knowing she has conceived. A man will dream when he is wounded, sick or enters agony. Alongside the dreams of man, there are also the dreams of groups and countries.

I cannot say how many among us, the Surrealists, felt like we were unblocking a sort of group wound, a wound of life, through our dreams.

Surrealism had a noble fixation, a haunting obsession with purity, a fixation with dreams and a hatred for reality.

We would commonly say about such and such a Surrealist: the purest, the most hopeless among us.

It does not matter whether this pure fire was limited to burn only itself. Since for us, what is sincerely pure is that which is without hope. And Surrealism searched for this purity on all possible levels: love, the spirit, sexuality.

*

'The Father,' writes Saint-Yves d'Alveydre in his *Les Clefs de L'orient*, 'it must be said, is the destroyer.'[v]

A disciplined hopeless soul, who, in order to think, places themselves on a higher plan of nature, regards the Father as an enemy. The Myth of Tantalus, that of Megaera, that of Atreus contains this secret in fabulous terms, this kind of inhumane truth, which the entirety of human endeavour seeks to come to terms with.

The natural movement of the Father against the Son, against the Family, is born of hate, a hate which Chinese philosophy cannot separate from love.

And, concerning this general truth, each father in his own being also seeks to come to terms with it.

I lived for twenty-seven years with the dark hate of the Father, of my father, up until the day when I saw him pass away. Then, this inhumane severity, which I would accuse him of oppressing me, gave way. Another being exited from this body. And for the first time in my life, this father stretched his arms out. And I, ill at ease in my body, understood that all of his life he had been disturbed by his body and that there is a lie regarding being itself which we are born to protest against.

*

The Surrealists assembled on the 10 December 1926 at 9 pm, in the café 'Prophète' in Paris.[vi]

The assembly's topic was what Surrealism should do with its movement in the face of the brewing social revolution.

For me, knowing what we know about Marxist communism, the question concerning whether we should rally behind it should never have even been asked.

Does Artaud not give a damn about the revolution? they asked me.

I don't give a damn about your revolution, which is not mine, I responded, leaving Surrealism since Surrealism itself had become a party.

This revolt for knowledge that the Surrealist revolution wanted to be had nothing to do with the type of revolution that claims to know man already: to make him a prisoner in the frame of his crudest necessities.

The points of view of Surrealism and Marxism were irreconcilable. It did not take long to realize this once some of the more well-known Surrealists decided to join the party, that is, the French branch of the Third International of Moscow.

Are you Surrealist or are you Marxist? we could ask André Breton. And if you are Marxist, what need do you have of being a Surrealist?

In short, it was a matter of lowering Surrealism to Marxism, but it would have been glorious to have seen Marxism attempt to raise itself to Surrealism.

In 1926, this antagonism could not be resolved because History had not moved forward. Today, History has taken these steps, and France faces new facts. These facts are the appearance of a historic idea in the consciousness of the youth of today, and this idea, which I wish to develop, I call the reconciliation between *Culture* and

Fate. In the hopeless consciousness of the youth, a new idea of culture was born. And this culture which wishes to know man is making for itself a heightened idea of what man is. It does not accept that we separate man's life from the events of life. It wants to enter the sensory interior of Man, who likewise plays with these Events.

The new youth is anti-capitalist-bourgeoisie, and, like Karl Marx himself, it has felt the disequilibrium of the times, which has given rise to the monstrous personality of Fathers based on land and money. When Marx is reproached for wanting to eliminate the family, he responds with, 'The family, but it was you that destroyed it, where are your ancient virtues now? Outside all virtues, I only see matter. And I, Marx, will organize matter; I will organize it technically and coercively.' One might say that Marx organizes what has been left by the Bourgeoisie of humanity's ancient values.

Before being the exultation of a superior reality, Surrealism was a critique of facts and the movement of reason in facts.

Between the real and myself [*et moi*], there is my self [*il y a moi*] and the personal deformation of the phantoms of reality.

And the current self [*moi*] of the youth considers that Marx departed from a fact, but that he remained with this fact never leaving it to enter Nature. In short, he derived a metaphysics from one fact. He never raised himself to the level of a metaphysics of Nature – above all, the youth wish to rise to this level of nature before being overcome by economic facts.

But if this youth is in favor of organizing matter, it is also simultaneously in favor of organizing the mind.

The youth consider the materialist organization of Lenin to be transitory and punitive, and it believes that Lenin, in Russia, applies this materialist and punitive organization with just cruelty. But, mind matter, matter mind, the youth affirm the interdependence of these two aspects of its being. Because they eat at the same time as they sense things and think at the same time as they eat. They accuse Modern Europe of having invented an antagonism which does not exist in fact. And if they do condemn Marx, it's as a European, and because the new youth love Man, but the whole of Man, so as to save itself from Man.

In this new idea of culture, there is an idea against progress. Modern science teaches us that matter never existed, and it is returning after 400 years to the old alchemical idea of the three principles of sulphur, mercury, and salt that science terms energy, movement and mass. Here, there is no need to speak of progress.

And all of this reveals a superior idea of culture, but for this culture to be healthy, certain ideas must be shattered, ideas which are idols, and if we agree to shatter ancient idols, new ones should not appear under our noses.

The youth no longer want to be fooled, and when they say that times have changed, and today an intellectual, a poet can no longer ignore the times, the youth retort that there is a misconception involving intellectuals and time.

The youth do not distinguish intellectuals from time, and the intellectuals do not differentiate themselves from their time and, just like their notion of time, they think that the mind is not an empty thing and that art is only as good as its necessity. But for them, this idea is a necessary action and does not mean the prostitution of action.

There is a manner of entering into the times, without selling oneself to the powers of the times, without prostituting one's forces for action to the watchwords of propaganda: 'War against war, common front, unified front, war against fascism, anti-imperialist front, against fascism and war, class struggle, class for class, class against class, etc., etc.'

There are idols of stupidity which serve the jargon of propaganda. Propaganda is the prostitution of action, and for me and the youth, the intellectuals who produce literature that reads like propaganda are cadavers who have lost the force of their own action.

An intellectual acts upon an individual and the mass, and through this unanimous mass action there is a cultural idea of the power of the individual. The youth want to understand the economy of Man's forces, not only their impact on individuals. There is a technique for releasing the forces of man like there is a technique in Chinese medicine to heal the liver, the spleen, the medulla or the intestines by touching physical points across the length of the body, but that are at a distance from the liver, the stomach, the medulla or the intestines.

As the world has its geography, so too does man's, which is of material consistency. But Lenin's dialectical materialism is fearful of this profound way of knowing the internal geography of man.

And yet, a profound culture is not fearful of such geography, even if investigating man's unexplored continents will inevitably lead to this vertigo where the immateriality of life ends.

True culture helps to investigate life, and the youth, who wish to re-establish a universal idea of culture, think that there are places preordained to make the sources of life burst forward, and they look toward both Tibet and Mexico. The culture of Tibet is only of any value for what, in the *Egyptian Book of the Dead*, are called cadavers, the Overturned.[vii] By contrast, the ancient culture of Mexico is worth it for making internal sense burst out through its barriers. It produces the resurrected.

All true culture is based on race and blood. Indian blood from Mexico keeps an ancient secret of race, and before this race is lost forever, I think it necessary to ask about the power of this ancient secret. While present-day Mexico copies Europe, European civilization should ask Mexico about its secret. The rationalist culture of Europe has failed, and I have come to the land of Mexico to look for the basis of a magic culture whose forces may still burst forth from Indian ground.[viii]

Man against Fate[ix]

Last night I spoke about Surrealism and the revolution. I should have said: the revolution against Surrealism, Surrealism against the revolution.

I tried to define the profound disgust and vital anguish that never quite found its bearings and from out of which French Surrealism was born.

In its essence, Surrealism is an affirmation of life against all its caricatures, and the revolution invented by Marx is a caricature of life.

I held the view that this hunger for a pure life, which Surrealism was in the beginning, had nothing to do with the fragmentary life of Marxism. Fragmentary but provisionally valid, corresponding to a real movement in history. I also said that Marx was among the first to have lived and felt history. But in history, there is a whole world of different movements. And if the Surrealist state of mind is a state of mind exceeded by the facts, then the historical movement of Marxism is also exceeded by the facts.

Thus, I present the latest stage of our thought on this matter: the thought of the French youth and those enlightened intellectuals.

Historical and dialectical materialism is an invention of European consciousness. Between the true movement of history and Marxism, there is a kind of human dialectic which does not accord with the facts. European consciousness has been living off an enormous factual error for the last four hundred years.

This fact is the rationalist conception of the world which, in its application to our everyday life in the world, produces what I shall call a *separated consciousness*.

You will understand what I mean in just a moment.

We all know that one cannot grasp thought. To think, we have images, words for these images, and representations of objects. We separate consciousness into states of consciousness. But this is just a way of speaking. In reality, the only value of any of this is that it enables us to think. To view our consciousness, we must divide it; otherwise, the rational faculty enabling us to see our thoughts could never be used. But consciousness is, in reality, a block, what the philosopher Bergson calls *pure duration* [*durée pure*]. There are no stops in thought. That which we place before us so that reason can observe it is, in reality, already past; reason only holds on to a form that is more or less empty of real thought.

What the reason of the mind observes, we could say, always partakes of death. Reason, a European faculty exalted beyond measure by the European mentality, is always a deathly simulacrum. History, which records facts, is a simulacrum of dead reason. Karl Marx fought against such a simulacrum of facts; he tried to sense historical thought in its particular dynamism. But he too remained fixated on a fact: the capitalist fact, the bourgeois fact, the clogging up of the machine, the asphyxia of the economy of that era that was caused by a monstrous abuse of the utilization of the machine. From out of this true fact, there came, *likewise from history*, a deceptive ideology.

The French youth of today, who do not tolerate dead reason, are no longer satisfied with ideologies. They regard the materialist explanation of history as an ideology that stopped history dead in its tracks. And, rereading Marx's *Communist Manifesto*, they realize that what is called Marxism is a false ideology that caricatures the thinking of Marx.

Marx departed from a fact, but he shied away from metaphysics. However, the youth feel that the materialist explanation of the world is false metaphysics. In the face of this false metaphysics, which sprang from Marx's materialism, they seek a comprehensive metaphysics that will reconcile them with actual life.

They blame historical materialism for the birth of idolatry which, like all idolatry, is religious because it introduces mysticism into the mind. The French youth do not want mysticisms; they want us to stop distorting the mind with hallucinations; they are hungry for a human truth: human and without deception.

This youth and I, we sense life as a single thing, a thing which cannot be theorized. Invoking metaphysics today does not mean separating life from a world beyond it; rather, it means reintegrating all that they had intended to remove from this world and reintegrating it without illusions.

For the youth, reason invented the contemporary despair and the material anarchy of the world by distinguishing the elements of a world that a true culture would unite.

If we have a false idea of fate and of how it progresses through nature, this is because we no longer know how to view nature and feel life in its totality.

Chance was unknown in antiquity, and fatality is a Greek concept accused of being excessively obscure by vulgar Latin reasoning, an accusation they often levelled against the Greeks. The pagan world was known for possessing knowledge to cure itself of chance. But, when we invoke knowledge, how many people in the present world can still say what it is?

There is a secret determinism based on the world's higher laws; nevertheless, because we are amid the mechanized sciences, a discipline weighed down with its microscopes, merely mentioning the world's higher laws arouses the mockery of a world where life has become nothing more than a museum.

When one speaks of culture today, governments think about opening schools, grinding out books and spilling printer's ink, whereas, to let culture mature, one should close the schools, burn the museums, destroy the books and smash the printing presses' gears.

To be cultivated is to eat one's fate, to assimilate it through knowledge. It is to know that the books lie when they speak of God, nature, man, death and fate.

God, nature, man, life, death and fate are merely the forms life takes when it is scrutinized by the thoughts of reason. Outside of reason, there is no fate; this high idea of culture, Europe renounced.

Europe has drawn and quartered nature with its separate sciences.

Biology, natural history, chemistry, physics, psychiatry, neurology, physiology, all these monstrous germinations which are the pride of the Universities, just as geomancy, chirology, physiognomy, psychurgy and theurgy are, to enlightened minds – to the pride of a few separate individuals – merely a *loss of consciousness*.

Antiquity had its labyrinths but did not know the labyrinth of divided science.

There is a secret movement in the mind which divides knowledge and presents to a bewildered reason images of science as so many distinct realities.

Satan, so say the ancient books of the Magians, is a self-produced image. By invoking Evil, the black magicians invent it; that is, they create it. Similarly, divided Reason invents the images of science taught in the Universities.

This movement is idolatrous: the mind believes what it has seen.

And to look at life through a microscope is to look at a landscape through the small end of reality.

The French youth are against reason because they accuse it of concealing science. And they are against the science which has petrified reason.

These youth consider that Europe took the wrong path and think that Europe took it deliberately and with criminal intentions. They accuse Cartesian materialism as the origin of this disastrous orientation of Europe.

They reproach the Renaissance, which claimed to glorify man, for debasing the idea of man by a false interpretation of the Ancients.

They know that history is wrong when it talks about paganism and that paganism is not what the books have made of it.

Europe invented the idolatry of the pagans because the form of the European mind is idolatrous; idolatry, as I was saying, is precisely the separation of the idea from its form when the mind believes what it has dreamed. The Ancients, who believed in their dreams, believed in the signification of their dreams. They did not believe in the dreamt forms. Behind their dreams, and at varying levels, the Ancients could sense forces, and they would immerse themselves in these forces. They had a dazzling sense of the presence of such forces, and they sought the means of remaining in contact with the release of these forces throughout their entire organism, if necessary, employing real vertigo. The head of a European today is a cellar in which force-less simulacra move about, images that Europe mistakes for its thoughts.

But this is all going too far to look for the critique of a dead thought. What paganism deified, Europe mechanized.

We are against this rationalization of existence which prevents us from thinking about ourselves, that is, from feeling human, and there exists an idea concerning the force of thought in our idea of man and the dialectical and technical knowledge concerning the force of thought.

Everything that science has taken from us, everything it sections off in its glass retorts, microscopes, scales, complicated mechanisms, and everything it puts into numbers, we aspire to win back from science which stifles our vitality.

Something is trying to come out of us which is not answerable to experiment. And many of us reject the teachings of experiments. We do not believe in the value of experiment or proof by experiment. First, they would have to make us believe in the phantoms of reason and the forms by which experiments seek to reach our thinking.

All forms of experiment conceal reality.

When Pasteur tells us that there is no such thing as spontaneous generation and that life cannot emerge from a void, we believe that Pasteur was mistaken about the real nature of the void and that a new experiment will show that Pasteur's void is not the void: and this experiment has been carried out.

For us, history is a panorama, and it is in time that we judge history, for we are cultured people. Those who eat potatoes are considered to have the morality of adventurers, but in the same place, five hundred years before, those who also ate potatoes supposedly had the morality of degenerates.

Experiments do not allow us to judge reality. Since they do not show us Man. The preoccupation with the external functions of Man diverts us from a profound understanding of Man. And there is a world in thought. The Communist revolution ignores the internal world of thought. When it is concerned with thought, it approaches it via experience, that is, through the external surface of facts.

It takes madmen and grafts strange diseases onto them to see what may result; it injects them with plant viruses just as they were grafting plants onto them to see how the man in them would turn out. At best, caricaturing Totemism, they were experimentally researching the transition between Humanity and the beast, between the beast and the forest.

But let us not forget that Lenin's materialism, also called dialectical, claims to have gone beyond Hegel's dialectic.

Where Hegel's dialectic identifies the internal force of thought as having three terms, Lenin's unites these terms and speaks of the dynamism of thought, saying that it is no longer separate from facts.

There are in life three forces, as an old science known to all antiquity demonstrated:

the repellent and dilating force,
the compressive and constricting force,
the rotational force.

The movement which moves from the outside towards the inside, called centripetal, corresponds to the constricting force, whereas the force which goes from the inside towards the outside, called centrifugal, corresponds to the dilating and repellent force.[x]

Like life, like nature, thought goes from the inside to the outside before going from the outside to the inside. I start by thinking in the void, and from the void, I move toward the plenum; once I have reached the plenum, I can fall back into the void. I go from the abstract to the concrete, not the concrete toward the abstract.

Arresting thought externally to examine what it is capable of means misunderstanding the internal and dynamic nature of thought. It rejects sensing thought in the movement of its internal fate, which no experiment can capture.

I call poetry today the knowledge of this internal and dynamic fate of thought.

To rediscover its profound nature and feel alive in its thought, life pushes away the spirit of analysis in which Europe has lost its way.

Poetic knowledge is internal; poetic quality is internal. There is a movement today that wishes to identify the poetry of the poets with that of an internal magic force that will provide a path for life, making it possible to act upon life.

I would need more time to discuss whether thought is a secretion of matter. Lenin's materialism appears to have ignored this poetics of thought.

Each disease has a corresponding plant, and each disease's colour corresponds to the plant. As he heals individual men, Paracelsus searches for a path for man on the road of disease (and one might say that he aims to cure life). Thus, to cure life, Paracelsus, through the imagination, establishes a relationship between the disease and the plant and cures the disease.

This is the origin of spagyric medicine from which homoeopathy originates.

There are cries for each passion, and within the cries of each passion, there are degrees of vibration; at various times, the world knew about the harmonics of these passions. Similarly, each disease has its own scream, and the form that the gasping for air takes.

There is the cry that the plague victim makes when running through the street, his mind drunk with images, and there is the sound they make when they gasp for air during the agony of death. And earthquakes have their sound. And the air vibrates in a particular way when an epidemic is said to be passing. And between a particular disease and a passion, between a passion and an earthquake, one can establish resemblances and strange harmonies of sound.

However, a living appearance and the determinism of facts are not separate. Every significant historical event has had a colour or a sound entangled with it.

Those genius epochs, to rediscover the movement of history and to postpone the course of fate, have thought through the relation that colour or sound has with the rhythm of gasping air and the trembling of epidemics, with the sound made by plants that resemble different diseases, with the combination of different expressions, and with the modulations of a sob that depicts all the tortures of humanity torn apart by fate.

The ancient games were based on this knowledge that action tames fate. Classical theatre, in its entirety, was a war against fate.

But in order to tame fate, one must understand nature in its whole as well as man's full consciousness synchronized with the rhythm of events.

We have the idea of a unitary culture, and we call this culture unitary to rediscover an idea of unity in all the manifestations of nature, which man rhythmically measures with his thought.

In the same way that Paracelsus' universal cure elevates human consciousness to that of divine thought, the 380 points of Chinese medicine that govern all human functions treat man as a unified extension.

Anyone who asserts that there are numerous cultures in Mexico today, including those of the Maya, Toltecs, Aztecs, Chichimecs, Zapotecs, Totonacs, Tarascans and Otomis, does not understand what culture is and confuses the synthesis of many different forms with that of a single idea.

There is Islamic esoterism and Brahmic esoterism; there is the occult Genesis, the Jewish esoterism of the Zohar and the *Sefer Yetzirah* and here in Mexico, there is the *Chilam Balam* and the *Popol Vuh*.

Who does not see that all of these esoterisms are the same, and mean, in spirit, the same thing? They express a single geometrical, mathematical, organic, harmonious, occult idea reconciling man with nature and life. The signs of these esoterisms are identical. They each possess profound analogies between their words, gestures and cries.

Of all the esoterisms that exist, Mexican esoterism is the last one to be based on blood and the magnificence of a land whose magic only a few fervent imitators of Europe can still ignore.

We must release the occult magic from an earth that has nothing in common with the egoistical world that stubbornly treads all over it and that is blind to the shadow that will soon fall.[xi]

The Theatre and the Gods^{xii}

I did not come here carrying a Surrealist message; I came to say that Surrealism is over, outdated, as are many things in France that continue to be imitated outside of France as if they represented the ideas of this country.

The Surrealist attitude was negative, and I came to say what a whole younger generation in my country, who are hungry for positive solutions and want to regain a taste for life, think. And what they believe in is what they will do.

The new aspirations of the youth in France cannot be spoken about in books or in newspapers in the same way one describes a strange illness, a curious epidemy which has nothing to do with life.

In the body of the French youth, an epidemy of the mind is forming, which is not an illness but a terrifying need. It is a characteristic of the times that ideas are no longer ideas but a Will to be realized.

Behind everything being done in France, a Will is currently ready to be realized.

When the young painter Balthus composes a portrait of a woman, he manifests his will to transform the woman and make her conform to his thoughts. He manifests in his painting a terrible, demanding notion of love and woman, and he knows that he is not speaking in the void, for his painting possesses a secret of action.

He paints like someone who knows the secret of thunder.

For as long as the secret of thunder has not been employed, the world will think that it is science and will leave it to the scientists; but one day, someone will apply the secret of thunder in service of the destruction of the world; it is then that the world will start to consider such a secret.

The youth want us to recouple the secrets of things with their multiple applications.

This is also an idea of culture which is not taught in the Schools; behind this idea of culture, there is an idea of life which can only hinder the Schools because it destroys their teachings.

This idea of life is magic; it supposes the presence of a fire in all the expressions of human thought, an image of a thought that burns; today, it seems to us that this is contained within theatre, and we believe that theatre is created only to make it manifest.

But today, most people think the theatre has nothing to do with reality. When one thinks about something that caricatures reality, everyone thinks about the theatre; however, numerous people in France believe that the theatre alone can show us reality.

Europe is in a state of advanced civilization, which means it is sick. The spirit of the youth in France is reacting against this state of advanced civilization.

They did not need Keyserling or Spengler to sense the universal decomposition of a world that lives on false ideas of life left over from the Renaissance. Life seems to us to be in a violent state of loss. And to sense this violent loss, all that is needed is the invention of a new philosophy.

Things are such that, compared to other ages where the youth ran after love and had dreams of ambition, material success and glory, they now dream of life, they run after life. But this life they pursue, if we may say so, *in its essence*, they want to know why it is sick, what caused the idea of life to rot.

And in order to understand, they look to the whole of the universe. They want to understand nature and on top of nature, Man. Not Man in its singularity, but Man having become great like nature.

When we speak to them about Nature, the youth ask which Nature it is we want to discuss. Because they know that, just as there have been Three Internationals, there are also three natures and three levels to Nature.

This is also science.

'There are three Suns,' said Emperor Julien, 'only the first is visible.' Of all people, Julien the Apostate cannot be accused of paying lip service to Christian spirituality, being one of the last representatives of the SCIENCE of the Ancients.[xiii]

Man is being included in Nature by today's youth; they see the levels of Nature from without as they do from within, also seeing the levels of Man.

And the Youth know that the theatre can give them an enhanced idea of man and nature.

They do not believe that they betray life with such a heightened idea of the theatre; quite the contrary, they think the theatre can help heal life itself.

There are ten thousand ways to look after life and to belong to one's era. In a disorganized world, we do not wish that scholars commit themselves to pure speculation. We no longer know what the ivory tower is. We would like, instead, for scholars to engage with their era, but we do not believe this to be possible without war being declared against it.

War to have peace.

Considering the disastrous spirits of our times, we stand by the accusation of immense ignorance. A strong faction wishes to cauterize this ignorance, and I mean cauterize it scientifically.

Life is neither a lazaretto, a sanatorium, nor even a laboratory; for our part, we do not think culture can develop via words or ideas. A civilization does not disclose what it is through the appearances of its customs. Before pitying the masses, we advocate resurrecting their forgotten qualities so they can become civilized of their own accord.

I am referring to a generation that we should not be worried about yet is itself worried. It is worried that what appears to be the case does not conform to what they believe, and they blame the stupidity of today.

They recognize the ignorance of today and ready themselves for insurrections against it.

When they learn that Chinese medicine, this thousand-year-old discipline, knew how to heal cholera through means that have existed for over a thousand years, and compare this to European medicine, which uses has rather barbarian means against Cholera, such as absconding or incineration, they realize that it is not enough to simply introduce this medicine into Europe, but they consider Europe's vices too and how to heal it of this sickness of the spirit.[xiv]

They recognize that it is not the disease itself but the depth of understanding with which China could comprehend the essence of Cholera.

This comprehension is culture. And there are cultural secrets that texts do not teach.

When confronted with European culture, which maintains itself through written texts and would have us believe that culture itself would be lost if these texts were destroyed, I assert that there is another culture in which different times lived. This lost culture is based on a materialist concept of the mind.[xv]

In contrast to the Europeans, who only know their body and could never imagine organizing nature since they never see beyond their body, the Chinese, for example, know nature through the science of the spirit.

They know the degrees of the void and the plenum, which describe the measurable states of the soul, and out of the soul's three hundred and eighty functioning physiological points, the Chinese know how to detect the nature of different illnesses.

Jacob Boehme, who exclusively believes in spirits, recognizes when these spirits are ill and describes, using a complete notion of nature, those states that reveal the Anger of the Spirit.

These and other enlightened figures provide us with a new idea of Man. And we are in favour of relearning what Man is, since other eras clearly knew it.

We have started to notice the Taboos that a fearful and petty science has erected in front of the remnants of a culture that once knew how to explain life.

The notion of the entirety of man whose cry may climb the course of a storm is nothing but poetry for Europe, but for us, who have a synthetic idea of culture, to be placed in relation with the cry of a storm is to rediscover a secret of life.

All around the world today, there is a current that aims to reclaim culture, a revendication of an organic and profound idea of culture that can explain the life of the mind.

I call organic culture a culture based on the mind's relation with the organs: the mind that bathes in all organs and responds simultaneously.

There is, in this culture, a notion of space, and I affirm that true culture can only be discovered in space and further, that it is an orientated culture, just as the theatre is orientated.

Culture in space is a culture of a mind that does not cease breathing and feels alive in space; it summons to it the bodies of space in the same manner that it calls to the objects of its thought, but which, as a mind, situates itself in the *middle* of space, its blind spot.

This dead centre of space through which the mind must enter is perhaps a metaphysical idea.

But without metaphysics, there is no culture. And what does this notion of space suddenly introduce into culture, if not the affirmation that culture is inseparable from life?

'Though thirty spokes may be joined in one hub,' writes the *Tao Te Ching* of Lao Tzu, 'the utility of the carriage lies in what is not there.'

When there is an agreement in the thoughts of men, where can this agreement be said to be made if not in the dead void of space?

Culture is a movement of the spirit that moves from the void toward the forms and from the forms back into the void, into the void as unto death. To be cultured is to burn forms, to burn forms to win back life. Culture is learning to hold oneself up straight in the incessant movement of those forms we successively destroy.

The ancient Mexicans know no other perspective than this coming and going of death and life.

This terrifying interior station, this movement of respiration, is culture, which moves both in nature and the mind.

'But that is metaphysics, and we cannot live in metaphysics.'

But exactly, I argue that life must live once more in metaphysics, and this difficult perspective, which makes people panic today, is the perspective of all the pure races who have always *felt to be at once* a part of death and life.

Therefore, culture is not written, so Plato argues, 'Thought was lost the day when speech was written.'

To write is to prevent the mind from moving in the middle of the forms like a vast breath. Since writing fixes the mind and crystallizes it into a form, idolatry is born from this form.

True theatre, like culture, was never written down.

The theatre is a spatial art, and it is by bearing down on the four points of such a space that it risks touching life. In the haunted space of the theatre, things find their figure, and under their figure, the sound of life.

There is a movement which wishes to withdraw the theatre from everything that is not space, to send textual language back to the books from where it should never have left. This spatial language, in turn, acts on the nervous faculty; it ripens the land below it.

I will not repeat the spatial theory of theatre, which acts as much through gesture and movement as it does through sound.

Occupying space, it tracks down life and forces it out of its lair.

It is like the six-pointed crosses which spreads an occult geometry across the walls of certain Mexican temples.

The cross of Mexico is always encircled; it is in the centre of the wall, and it comes from a magical idea.

To make the cross, the ancient Mexicans placed themselves in the centre of a space, and the cross would grow around them.

Unlike what scholars argue today, this cross does not serve to quantify, but it is a cross that reveals how life enters into space and how to find the depths of life from the exterior of space.

Always the void, always the point, around which matter thickens.[xvi]

The cross of Mexico specifies the rebirth of life.

For a long time, I have looked at the Gods from Mexico in the Codex, and it appeared to me that these Gods were before anything, Gods that were *in space* and that the Mythology of the Codex was hiding a science of space with its Gods looking like shadowy holes, and its shadows are where life rumbles.

That is, without literature, because these Gods are not born by chance, and they exist in life as they would in a theatre, and they inhabit the four corners of man's conscience here where nests sound, gesture, speech and the breath which spits out life.

Who still thinks about sensing the Gods and searching for the place of the Gods? To search for their place is to search for their force and to endow oneself with the force of a God. The White world calls these Gods idols, but the Indian spirit knows how to make the force of Gods vibrate by locating their musical forces; the theatre, through a distribution of these musical forces, calls to it the power of the Gods. Each has its place in a space that vibrates with images. These Gods come out towards us through a cry or a particular facial expression, and the colour of the God's face has its cry; the cry is worth its weight in images in the Space where Life ripens.

For me, these spinning Gods, who are all tangled in lines that sound out through space, as if they were scared of not having felt the space around them well enough, give us a concrete means of understanding the formation of life. This fear of empty space, which haunts Mexican artists and makes them throw down line after line, is not only an invention formed of lines, of forms that please the eye but specifies a need to let the void be *ripened*. Filling the space to cover over the void is a means of discovering the way of the void. One emerges from a blossoming line only to fall vertiginously into the void.

And the Mexican Gods, which spin around the void, reveal a numerical means of recovering the forces of a void without which there is no reality.

And in the end, I believe that the Mexican Gods are the Gods of a life that is victim to the loss of force and vertigo of thought; and that the lines raised above their heads reveal a means of melodically and rhythmically lifting thought above thought.

They invite the mind not to petrify itself but, on the contrary, if it's possible to speak this way, *to march forward*.

'I am advancing to war,' says the God who is holding a weapon of war in his fist, and who carries it in front of himself. 'And above this advance, I think,' says a line of lightning that zigzags above his head. – And this line once again multiplies at some point in space.

'And if I think, I sound out my forces, says the line behind him. I call out to the force from which I have emerged.'

This is how, in their inhuman form, these Gods, which are not happy with simply being the stature of a man, could emerge from him. – Because moreover, I think that there is harmony in these lines, a type of essential geometry which corresponds with the image of a sound.

For the theatre, a line is a sound, a movement is music, and the gesture which emerges from a sound is like one clear word in a sentence.

The Gods of Mexico have open lines, specify everything that emerges, but reveal at the same time the means of entering something.

The Mythology of Mexico is an open Mythology. And Mexico, that of the past and that of today, holds in its turn open forces. It is not necessary to go very far into the landscape of Mexico to sense all that emerges from it. It is the only place on earth which proposes to us an occult life and *proposes it on the surface of life*.

II

Mexico[xvii]

Post-War Theatre in Paris^{xviii}

Through a description of French post-war theatre, I will distinguish what was theatrical about this movement and what belonged to the French spirit.

To do so, it is not enough to have attended all the shows from 1920 to 1936 that left their mark on Paris, as I did, having been involved in the intimate life of the theatre, in its sorrows, its failures, its hopes, its difficulties, and sometimes also in its triumphs.

I worked either as an actor or dramaturge in no less than ten theatres: l'Œuvre, l'Atelier, the Vieux-Colombier, the Comédie des Champs-Élysées, the Studio des Champs Élysées, the Théâtre de Grenelle, the Théâtre Pigalle, the Théâtre de l'Avenue, the Théâtre des Folies-Wagram.

I knew, intimately, and worked with, all the outstanding individuals of the theatre: Lugné-Poe, Silvain, Charles Dullin, Jacques Copeau, Louis Jouvet, Georges and Ludmilla Pitoëff, Suzanne Desprès, Gaston Baty, Valentine Tessier, Génica Athanasiou, Roger Karl, Falconetti.

I was present during the most established period of the Théâtre de l'Œuvre, before the departure of Lugné-Poe, and lived the first adventures of the nascent l'Atelier on a daily basis, which perilously maintained itself for three years, constantly bordering on disaster until the day when it finally gave in.

This is not a simple list of actors, an inert prize list, that I want to give here, but the life and breath of the French theatre which, only a few months ago, gave birth to a mysterious phenomenon.

In Paris, in 1920, as the Vieux-Colombier reopened its doors, some great actors triumphed on the stage of the Comédie-Française: Silvain, De Max, Paul Mounet, etc.

In the avant-garde theatres, we had fun making people laugh by imitating the tics of these great actors: we imitated Paul Mounet's sonorous voice that came from the throat: that big, heavy voice of Cerberus that was just like an earthquake, and his passive and mechanical style.

We mimicked how De Max used his mouth and other peculiarities, such as turning round and straightening up with learnt mannerisms. We would say: 'There you go, that's precisely what we mustn't do.'

But, in my opinion, despite their mannerisms, these tragedians were the last to uphold the heroic tradition of the theatre. And now that they are no longer with us, it must be said, no tragedy has been performed in Paris since.

Silvain had a funny way of wrapping his arms around himself at the height of the solar plexus; he also used to accentuate certain syllables with a slap on the chest.

De Max, without knowing the meaning of his gesture, would poke at his solar plexus with the tip of his index finger, and he would try to find, again with his index finger, the surviving remains of the third eye, as well as that spot that, in Indian metaphysics, is called the pineal gland.

In all of these actors' outrageous gestures, one must recognize the instinctive survival of magic which, for those who practice it, they no longer know what it means and, for those who laugh at it, they laugh without knowing why. And I would even say that if they could only understand what is laughing in them, they would be afraid of themselves at that very moment.

This is the same reason why at the Colonial Exhibition in Paris in 1931, there was a movement of religious terror that seized the crowds when they saw the Balinese Theatre actor approach them and, after having taken three or four steps and executed a curious upward movement of the hips, touched the third eye on his head.

When De Max touched his head, it should be understood as: 'I think with my obscure head. I search in my tormented head for the lost place of thought.'

But when the actor of the Balinese Theatre touches his head, it should be understood as: 'I am aware of a lost eye; I point to the lost place of an eye belonging to the head of a criminal humanity. I appeal to that science which men lost for the first time in the Dark Ages. That is, sixty centuries ago. For, as is well known, the Dark Ages, for the Hindus, began 3120 years before Christ.'

This is what real theatre suggests to us when we look inside it.

In Germany, they invented the staging of art; in Russia, the staging of the masses; but in France, one of the few countries in the world where from nothing one has managed to draw something, in France, it has been possible, almost without any means at all, to rediscover the secret life of the theatre just as Arthur Rimbaud was able to rediscover the secret life of poetry . . .

But I will return to the alchemy of the theatre in France, to its new beginnings in the post-war period when life in Paris was awakening.

It was Lugné-Poe who introduced Jarry, Strindberg and Ibsen to the French and who brought *Creditors*, *Hedda Gabler*, *Ghosts*, *A Doll's House*, etc., to the stage of Cité Moncey, that small private theatre situated at 55 rue de Clichy, Paris.

L'Œuvre was likewise a 'closed' theatre to which only subscribers had access. One day, I went there to see a performance without having previously paid for a subscription and met Lugné-Poe, who invited me in without paying and offered me a job in his theatre. That same year, I started working there as an administrator, handyman, prompter, actor and extra.

From the wings, I watched Jean Sarment's acting debut in *Ghosts*, *Hedda Gabler*, *A Doll's House*, etc., and, on the stage itself, the following year, acting in Lugné-Poe's astonishing interpretation of Crommelynck's *Le Cocu Magnifique*.

Lugné-Poe created in this role, introducing to the French stage a Brueghel-like composition, an unforgettable type of intellectual buffoon who had a voice that seemed to growl from the darkness and who induced cascades of laughter followed by cascades of expressions that rolled from his head to his feet.

Lugné-Poe was often unequal as an actor, and dramatic performance bored him. He acted with a certain contempt for the audience. But when he got into his role, the audience would burst into laughter. He is, from head to toe, a complete actor. His voice changes in surprising ways; his fingers become points, and his fiery looks are sometimes reminiscent of a now lost tradition of the theatre. It is as if we were in the presence of an actor from the French Medieval Mysteries.

Demonstrating a completely different side of the theatre is Suzanne Desprès who, without gesture and only with her voice, cries in a sobbing silvery voice for her severed hands in d'Annunzio's moving work.[xix]

Around the same year, 1920, Durec, who died shortly afterwards, played the role of a magician in *Desire*, an Icelandic play by Sigurjónsson, who, trapped by his evil spells, believes himself to be the possessor of a secret.[xx] I do not remember ever having heard such a possessed voice in any theatre until the day I heard Marguerite Jarnois screaming for her soul in *The Dybbuk*.

1920 was also the year when Jacques Copeau, at the Vieux Colombier, brought to the stage Unanimism, which is also a school of naturalism and simplicity. Unanimism is a populism before its time, but a populism that deliberately exalts the forces of reality.

Charles Vildrac, Luc Durtain, Georges Chennevière, Georges Duhamel, Jules Romains, and, in a way, Jean Schlumberger belong to this school.

Above all, the décor made Charles Vildrac's *Paquebot Tenacity* such a success. In front of a glass door that opens onto a verdigris light, Copeau evokes all the damp nostalgia of a port in a Nordic country.

The Vieux-Colombier was the first French stage equipped with modern lighting and the first to adopt stylized decor. It was the first attempt in France at what has been called 'constructive decoration'. From the perspective of the set, walls and planes are used as a huge set of cubes to create a palace, an underground, an alley, a cave, a mountain and an immense open space.

I will never forget, in André Gide's *Saul*, performed in 1922, Saül-Jacques Copeau was engulfed in a ghostly green light coming from this vault that was open to the sky.

As a part of his staging, in addition to the stylization of the set, Jacques Copeau would stylize costumes as much as he would attitudes: in the *Twelfth Night*, *Turandot*, *The Brothers Karamazov*, and *Death of Sparta*,[xxi] he created vast frescoes in which he revealed himself to be a connoisseur of museums, a lover of painting with refined taste and a talented writer.

The spirit of Jacques Copeau's theatre consisted in subjugating the staging to the text by making the staging emerge from the text using an intelligent twist. For Jacques Copeau, the text, the word, counts above all else. He has, therefore, a Shakespearean conception of gesture, movement, attitude, and scenery. In short, there is a submission of the theatre to the language of written literature. The main problem with this is that the French theatre continued this approach.

In October, Charles Dullin, who had upped and left the Vieux Colombier, founded the Théâtre de l'Atelier.

Before the war in 1913 at the Théâtre des Arts, Dullin had already shown himself to be a capable actor with what could be called his dark and tenebrous interpretation of Dostoyevsky's Smerdiakov from *The Brothers Karamazov*.[xxii]

Charles Dullin was one of the last actors in France to possess a real, crushing intensity in action, and his acting sometimes evoked the image of a drilling machine breaking through the hardest of walls.

To establish the Théâtre de l'Atelier, Charles Dullin not only left the Vieux-Colombier but also left the Comédie Montaigne directed by Gémier, where, in 1920, Marguerite Janois revealed herself through a performance of Crommelynck's *Les Amants puérils*.

A new interpretation of Paul Claudel's *The Annunciation of Marie* was given on this stage, a triumph for Eve Francis. In the scene of the Mystical Childbirth, the actress showed herself to be particularly moving. At the Comédie Montaigne, Lenormand's *Simoun* was created, a play where the desert wind blows over men.[xxiii]

The beginnings of the Atelier were like that of an epic. Charles Dullin wanted to resurrect the spirit of the old *compagnons* of the Middle Ages, of those travelling companies where the actor was at once a craftsman, poet, author, beggar and adventurer.

In his troupe, everyone worked with their hands and heads. Actors became masons, painters, stagehands, administrators, improvisers and tailors. One was intoxicated with work. Work above all. Food was for afterwards. And this heroic love of the theatre often meant we forgot to eat.

L'Atelier lasted for three years in uncertainty about its future, each day on the edge of a precipice from where its creditors were calling. Such heroism was finally rewarded with the triumph of Ben Jonson's *Volpone*, a work in which a blood-red set vibrated like a flag quivering in the sun.

From 1921 to 1936, the Atelier had its greatest successes with Prosper Mérimée's *L'Occasion*, Molière's *L'Avare*, Calder's *Life is a Dream*, Jean Cocteau's *Antigone*, Ben Jonson's *Volpone* and Aristophanes' *Birds* and *Peace*.[xxiv]

I have some personal memories of Jean Cocteau's *Antigone*. I played the soothsayer Tiresias, Charles Dullin played Creon, and Génica Athanasiou played Antigone.

If there was ever to be a truly human triumph in this play, then it was achieved by the tragedienne Génica Athanasiou for her interpretation of Antigone.

I will never forget the golden, quivering, mysterious voice of Genica Athanasiou-Antigone bidding her farewell to the sun.

Her lament came from beyond time as if carried by the foam of a wave on the Mediterranean Sea on a day flooded with sunshine; it sounded like the music of the flesh, the type that would spread through icy darkness. It was, in effect, the voice of archaic Greece, the moment when, in the depth of the labyrinth, Minos suddenly sees the Minotaur crystallize at the sight of virginal flesh.

In 1925, the Vieux-Colombier ended in style. Jacques Copeau, disappointed by the relative failure of his work, *La Maison Natale*, left the stage.[xxv]

Copeau cultivated the graceful, fantastic, fairy-tale genre; he never bothered with tragedy. But the Vieux Colombier left a legacy to modern France of some of its greatest actors: Louis Jouvet, Charles Dullin, Roger Karl, Valentine Tessier, Bacqué, Bouquet and Auguste Boverio.

The cycle at the Vieux Colombier began with *Les Fourberies de Scapin*, in which, like a runner, an actor is to throw themselves into the text, and it ended with *La Maison natale*. The Compagnie des Quinze, led by Michel Saint-Denis, took Jacques Copeau's artistic [*plastiques*] principles concerning staging to the extreme.

In 1923, Jacques Hébertot launched Rolf de Maré's Ballets Suédois at the Théâtre des Champs-Élysées. Under his direction, the theatre became a large factory where various trends met.

Jean Cocteau recounted in a recent book an anecdote about the mysterious way which Picasso, at the crepuscule of one evening in December 1922, invented the décor for *Antigone*.[xxvi]

Here and there, behind rocks of blue canvas, some lamps were available. A wall, also of blue canvas, rose to the height of a vaulted arch, and in the centre a panoply of masks twirled. Beneath the panoply hung a wide strip of cardboard about two meters wide and one meter high. The material of this strip was grainy and reddish, the colour of colonial stones. It was the red of burnt blood, but a drop of water would have been enough to turn this ruddy blood to a faded pink.

Picasso rolled up his sleeves and strode forward as if he'd been a tamer, a wrestler, a surveyor, a conjurer... and we could see his stocky black back undulate. Lines ran up the pink plate. Picasso would launch himself backwards, reflect, orient himself, and the lines around him would spring forth like a living geometry. More than drawing, he was sensing. The lines sprang up; one might say, fatally. And these lines made up a geometry that would support something or other that, in the middle of the wall, would quickly set fire to another unknowable thing... His hand went back and forth – like a seer's hand – and all at once, in front of us, as if summoned by genuine magic, we could see in front of us a brilliant column – a Doric colonnade. In truth, Picasso was doing the work with all the vigour of a male.

In 1923, Gaston Baty, who had started as a director with Gémier at the Comédie Montaigne, built the Baraque de la Chimère in the Saint-Germain-des-Prés area.

La Chimère succeeded in revealing several minor authors, and it was from their works that the critics deduced the 'theory of the theatre of silence', which the authors themselves rejected.

The star of Gaston Baty's show was Marguerite Jarmois. She acted with her eyes, if I may say so, with her lips. Beneath her eyes, in which tides overflow, her mouth, like a recumbent blade, pulses ready to leap, to live.

For me, it was in *Dybbuk* that Marguerite Jamois performed the greatest work. The premise of this play is well known. A young theology student is forced to separate from the woman he loves and who was *theologically* destined for him. The student dies right when he is about to reveal his great secret, and the way it all unfolds makes him seem already dead when he reveals his secret. At the moment of his death, his spirit begins to prowl around. It becomes incarnate in the woman, and, in an extraordinary scene, Marguerite Jamois speaks with the very same voice of the man who had claimed that she was destined for him, that is to say, the woman, which is to say, herself.

I saw Jamois in almost all her works. I saw her perform these closed beings with closed eyes and a closed mouth. In this work, she embodied a being that was locked up in itself but who spoke from the depths of itself, and the voice with which this being exclaimed its right to restoration is one of the most terrible things I have ever heard.

Gaston Baty also had his theory of theatre. For him, the text, contrary to Copeau's conceptions, is only one of the many elements of the stage, and light plays its part in the whole. But, if one were to attend one of Gaston Baty's stage productions, it would appear that he has not yet managed to realize his ideas fully.

If, in the theatre, the text is not everything, if light is also a language, then the theatre retains the notion of another language that uses text, light, gesture, movement and noise. This is the Word, the secret Word that no language can translate. It is, in a way, the language lost since the fall of Babel. In France, some men thought they would find it again in the theatre, this lost language, this sort of ancient madness, this vertiginous utopia.

In Paris, Gaston Baty achieved some of the greatest public successes of post-war theatre with *Maya*, *The Dybbuk* and, most recently, *Crime and Punishment*.[xxvii]

In 1923, Jacques Hébertot brought together four avant-garde directors to his home of a theatre on Avenue Montaigne in Paris: Louis Jouvet, Gaston Baty, Georges Pitoëff and Komisarjevski. At the same time, it provided a home for the Ballets Russes, the Ballets Suédois and Jean Cocteau's *Les Mariés de la Tour Eiffel*, as well as for the avant-garde music and painting of 1920 to 1926.[xxviii] It was possible to see sets by Picasso, Georges Braque, Othon Friesz, André Derain, Giorgio di Chirico, and even Surrealists such as Max Ernst and Joan Miro.[xxix] The Surrealist group protested what they called a betrayal of Surrealist painting, and there was a memorable scandal in which Max Ernst and Joan Miro were confronted. We saw multicoloured butterflies tumbling down from the galleries while they accused them of betraying the pure poets. Aragon, shouting at the top of his lungs, ran like a madman across the parapets of the dressing rooms on the third floor, almost falling over. And like a shroud, a huge black flag fell onto the naked shoulders of these women who were from all over the world.

During the same period, on the second floor of the theatre, Georges Pitoëff staged François Molnar's *Liliom* and Andreyev's *He Who Gets Slaps*. And Komisarjevski introduced *R. U. R: Rossum's Universal Robots* by Tchapek.

Georges Pitoëff had made a name for himself in Paris in 1919 with Lenormand's *Les Ratés* and an Irish play, *The Playboy of the Western World*.

In the field of staging, Pitoëff's discoveries treated lighting and atmosphere. Thanks to him, for the first time, Russian plays such as

Tolstoy's *The Power of Darkness* and Chekhov's *Uncle Vanya* were shown to French audiences in a truly Russian atmosphere.[xxx] Also, for the first time on a French stage, Georges Pitoëff gave us the feeling that an actor was playing with his own life, ready to give it up at any moment. But the great revelation of Pitoëff's theatre was undoubtedly Ludmilla Pitoëff. Whoever has not seen Ludmilla Pitoëff crying in front of the corpse of *Liliom* does not know what it is to cry, not only on stage but in life too, because Ludmilla is a soul where you can feel life pulsating.

Louis Jouvet, who was first an actor with Copeau, knew how to cultivate authentic violence as an actor, among other things. And at Hébertot's, he produced a theatre based on the technique of pure staging. No one is like Jouvet, for he knows the stage as an actor, director, architect and stagehand.

Later, Jouvet established his theatre, and the Jouvet style of scenery and lighting is now known in Paris and worldwide.

Louis Jouvet's greatest theatrical discovery was Jean Giraudoux, who went from being a sophisticated and stylized writer to a stylized and sophisticated dramaturge. And all those who have a taste for free gymnastics, and the antics of thought will take pleasure in the plays of Jean Giraudoux.

In 1925, a year that seems to have been fateful for the theatre and out of which a whole world would emerge, a mysterious man appeared who would live in rooms without any furniture. He was later called 'the dervish' because he claimed to have spent several years of his life among the dervishes of the Caucasus.

During the revival of Maeterlinck's *Pelléas et Mélisande*, in a stage setup created by Copeau,[xxxi] I was surprised by an extraordinary lighting system; here, the light was alive, for it smelt and gave off a scent; it had become a sort of new character. Lighting his sets and actors seemed to be the last of the 'dervish's' concerns.

A light that does not illuminate and from which a strong odor seems to emanate, in this, I thought, a rare spirit resides.

And one evening, in a café a hundred meters from the theatre, I found myself in front of a short-tempered character with a large moustache, his face twisted like vine shoots, who answered with insults to every question.

And amid these insults, a strange idea of nature and life seemed at times to emerge.

'Salzmann,' I was told, 'is the author of the lighting style that has made such an impression on you.'

So, I told Salzmann.

'Would you believe,' he replied, 'that these fools did not know that light is sense itself, that there is no light without sense?'

And for more than three hours, walking from the Place de l'Alma to the Gare Saint-Lazare, we spent together talking on an awful February night.

For him, everyone was an idiot. And, in the minds of today's humanity, life was nothing more than an obscured notion. And the men of the theatre were the most idiotic of all. 'These dark lights that moved you,' he said to me, 'the reason why the others find them too dark is that they have not yet arrived at a notion of the senses that surpass that of the five senses: smell, taste, touch, sight, and sound as if the theatre was not made to transgress the world of the senses. We experience the life of the senses daily. If the theatre does not help us to go beyond ourselves, what is it for?! . . .'

And I spoke to him about a lost language that could be rediscovered through the theatre. He answered that real poetry, not the poetry of poets, holds the secret of this language and that certain sacred dances come closer to the secret of this poetry than any other language.

Salzmann was an engineer, an architect, and an inventor. He had built on the stage of the Théâtre des Champs-Élysées a kind of luminous arch which carried no less than sixty thousand light bulbs.

Salzmann died last year in Switzerland of a cancerous throat tumor.[xxxii]

On the stage since then, we have seen lighting done in the style of Salzmann, where there is a certain way of handling light as if playing the organ of colours. We find the same lighting now in that of Louis Jouvet, who was directly influenced by these ideas.

In June 1927, the Théâtre Alfred Jarry was founded. At the Théâtre de Grenelle, now demolished, it gave two performances of Roger Vitrac's Surrealist play, *Les Mystères de l'Amour*.

In the role of Lea, Genica Athanasiou achieved the second triumph of her career. Genica had to multiply and transform herself from a butcher into a tamer, a seductress and a passionate aesthete in the style of Burne-Jones. However, the play owes its success to how it was staged. A cupboard, a stove and a coffin were all subject to a Surrealist order, which is a disorder for ordinary reality, and responded to the deep logic of a dream about to suddenly come to life. Multicoloured lights, responding to the same strange logic, to the same concern for balance and musicality, were spread profusely over things, coming from many different angles.

From 1927 to 1930, the Alfred Jarry Theatre staged: *Les Mystères de l'Amour, Partage de midi, Le Songe* and *Victor ou les Enfants au pouvoir.*

The extraordinary July 1931 performances of the *Théâtre Balinais* at the 'Colonial Exhibition', a brilliant success, are part of France's theatrical movement. There is, indeed, a strange similarity of spirit between the performances of the Théâtre Alfred Jarry and those of the *Théâtre Balinais*. One would say they both feed on the same magical sources of a primitive unconscious, this unconscious in which the bitter impulses of its research made the Alfred Jarry Theatre plunge; secret sources which the Balinese Theatre seems to know by tradition.

Since the war, French theatre has been effectively driven by a confused desire to return to a certain tradition.

It is not a question of this or that tradition, which is more akin to a certain form of social conservatism. The general anxiety has also infected French theatre and participates in this immense revision of values that characterize today's world.

If the Freudian 'unconscious' made its appearance with Lenormand and Pirandello, its appearance was, by no means, a great success.

On all sides, people are turning back to the source: that of the fatherland, that of the family, that of love, that of fatherhood. And with it, all the great problems of humanity are once again evoked, weighed up and activated. In 1932, several plays showed a real obsession with it. For instance, in works such as Bruckner's *Criminals [Die Verbrecher]* and *The Pains of Youth*, we are returned to the very sources of morality and the desperation of life.[xxxiii]

This is a necessary sign of a disorder and a search, where the search still prevails over the disorder.

What results from this gathering, this explosion of values, is a depreciation, an abandonment, a loss of the feeling attached to human individuality. Separate feelings are shunned. One no longer sees two beings face to face striving through love to unite their singular individualities, but two beings trying to reach an idea of humanity one over the other.

It is not by chance that the French avant-garde theatre first directed its main research attention toward staging. Due to the development of external staging possibilities, the rediscovery of that physical language became urgent, which, for four centuries, the French theatre had completely forgotten. By developing these possibilities, it is not a question of the French theatre's search for decorative effects; no, what it claims to find under these effects is a universal language that would unite the theatre with the entirety of space.

French theatre seeks space to multiply its expression in space; it wants, like Mexican art, to let space blossom and unfold since it believes that the theatre had, until now, forgotten how to let space speak.

And to let space speak is to give a voice both to surfaces and the masses; and that is why, today, we despise individualities. For too long, the 'ménage à trois', which represented theatre in France for most foreigners, has no longer been part of French theatre. A few Anglo-Saxon tourists now come to the boulevards to see that which survives of this outdated theatre.

In Paris, Jean-Louis Barrault represents this search for a theatre that takes place in space, within a hidden inner life. While it is not just a social theatre, although it is certainly a theatre of the masses, it is also more than a social theatre, the theatre of human anguish in reaction against fate. It is the theatre of a human revolt that does not accept the law of fate. It is a theatre full of screams that do not come from fear but from rage, and even more than rage, from the feeling of the value of life.

It is a theatre that knows how to scream but has an enormous awareness of laughter and knows that in laughter, there is a pure idea, a beneficial and pure idea of the eternal forces of life.

Open Letter to the Governors of the Mexican States^{xxxiv}

Distinguished Governors,

I have come to Mexico on a mission from the Secretary of the French National Education.

The goal of this mission is to study all of the diverse expressions of Mexican theatrical art, but I want to do so by living it rather than just experiencing it from the stage.

And it is, above all, the indigenous art of Mexico that interests me. European culture, in my opinion, has failed, and I believe that Europe abandoned authentic culture through the rampant development of its machines, and I, in turn, wish to betray the European concept of progress.

The rituals and sacred dances of the Indians are the most beautiful form of theatre possible and the only one that can be justified.

Up to now, these rituals have only interested archaeologists and artists.

The archaeologists have spoken about them as scholars do, which is to say very badly, and the artists have spoken about them as artists, which is to say even worse. They have been unable to extract from them their hidden science and profound significance.

There are predestined locations on the planet designed to preserve the world's culture. And in France, the younger conscious generations, who are equally frightened, anxious, and dare I say, desperate, are also turning their souls to these predestined regions.

Present-day Tibet and Mexico are nodes of world culture. The culture of Tibet is made for the dead; there, one can still learn the technical means of dying well so as to separate oneself from life.

The eternal culture of Mexico was always made for the living. In the Mayan hieroglyphs, in the vestiges of the Toltec culture, one can still discover the means of living well: chasing away slumbering organs, maintaining the nerves in a state of perpetual rapture completely open to the immediacy of light, water, earth and wind.

Yes, I believe in a force that is dormant in the earth of Mexico. And for me, it is the only place in the world where sleeping natural forces can still serve the living. I believe in the magical reality of these forces, just as we believe in the healing power of certain waters.

I believe that the Indian rituals are the direct manifestations of these forces. I do not want to study them as an archaeologist or an artist; I will study them as a sage [*savant*], in the true sense of the word, and I will strive to allow their soul-healing powers to infiltrate my entire consciousness. When human magnetism is depleted, it must return to the Earth to replenish its strength.

The primitive rituals of the Indians communicate with the earth, and their dances, animated hieroglyphs, and occult movements unconsciously translate its laws.

Between the earth and man, the spirit of man periodically interposes itself, disturbing the pure forces of the earth by extracting from them the mire of divine superstitions.

But just as periodically, the natural forces of the earth come to light again and put an end to the false spirits of the gods.

I want to thank the Government of Mexico here for allowing me to contact the true culture of Mexico, and I want to thank in advance the State Governors for their help, hoping that they will allow me to visit any place where the red earth of Mexico continues to speak its true language.

The Universal Bases
of Culture^{xxxv}

Today, in Europe, culture, and the same goes for schooling and education, has become a luxury that can be bought. This is the best proof that the meaning of words is being lost, *and* there is nothing like confusion in words to reveal the state of decadence that has now become generalized across Europe. This is why, before discussing culture, I must clarify the meaning of this word. Before saying what it means, I will first say what everyone means or think they mean by it. We speak of cultured men, speak of the earth as cultivated, and express in this way an action, an almost material transformation of man and earth. However, one can be schooled or learn without being cultured. For schooling is a garment. The word schooling or being schooled [*l'instruction*] means that a person has clothed himself with knowledge. It is a veneer, the presence of which does not necessarily imply that one has assimilated this knowledge. On the other hand, the word culture means that the soil, the deep humus of man, has been *readied for production* [*défriché*]. In Europe, where words have lost meaning, schooling and culture are used in everyday language to express the same thing, whereas in reality they are two very different things. And even if we do not confuse schooling and culture, strictly speaking, we place them on the same level; we consider them to go hand in hand when everything we see around us proves that the scattered, contradictory culture of Europe has nothing to do with the absolutely uniform state of its civilization.

When I arrived in Mexico and spoke about its ancient culture, I was more or less told by everyone: 'But there are a hundred cultures in Mexico!' – This proves that the Mexicans of today have forgotten the meaning of the word culture and confuse standardized culture with a multiplicity of forms of civilization. However distinct its civilizations may have been, ancient Mexico had only one culture, that is to say, a single idea of man, of nature, of death, of life; on the contrary, modern Europe, which has succeeded in standardizing its civilization, has multiplied its conception of culture ad infinitum, and, concerning the very idea of culture, it could be said to be in anarchy.

If Europe conceives of culture as a veneer, it is because it has forgotten what culture once was in the times when it truly existed; for words have a rigorous meaning, and it is not possible to completely pull out from the word culture its deepest meaning, its meaning related to the integral modification, one might even say, magical, not just of man but the being in man, for the truly cultured man carries his spirit in his body. It is his body that he works through culture, which is equivalent to saying that he likewise works his spirit.

Europe has long imagined that culture is contained in books, and every European nation has its books, which is to say, its philosophy. In recent years, many systems have arisen, each corresponding to the arrival of a new book, and not only does each nation have its own, but each political party too. And unlike the great ages, when philosophers governed over life and gave birth to politics, each new political system has created philosophers who try to miserably justify its demagogy.

Marxism, a political system based on several fundamental economic truths, has produced a whole materialist conception of the world. Italy is so spiritually impoverished that it could not even produce a single philosopher. Yet Hitler's Fascism has its philosophers, whose system is a monstrous mishmash of Nietzsche, Kant, Herder, Fichte and Schelling. In Europe, next to the prophets of the new West, we find the prophets of the decadence of the West. Next to serious men like Spengler, Scheler and Heidegger, we find little masters of decadence, like Keyserling, who are nothing more than travelling salesmen, amateur lovers of a chintzy Hinduism, and, beyond all measure, dishonest vendors of the theme of the unconscious, stolen in its Freudian form and sold in its American this very same unconscious of which they imagine themselves to be able to fabricate a spectroscopy. For me, nothing is more odious than the philosophical snobbery of a Keyserling, especially when this snobbery, from the beliefs on which the primitive and occult life of humanity has been nourished, knows only how to make a fashionable object out of it.[xxxvi]

There is no sacred philosophy or great culture which Keyserling has not touched to vulgarize its doctrines in an odious manner, whereas, for their part, the ancient Brahmans of India sometimes sacrificed their lives for the same principles. Keyserling's case is aggravated by the fact that he claims to have deduced a system, which is to say, a personal dogma, from traditions which represent the collective and anonymous wisdom of immense countries and periods when the men who were the vehicle of these traditions and doctrines were always careful not to appropriate them for themselves. In this, Keyserling obeys the individualistic, anarchic spirit of a Europe that now has as many philosophies as philosophers and cultures as philosophies.

For two or three years now, there have been grotesque talks of a United States of Europe. It would have been more profitable to talk about the total imbalance of European culture since the lamentable state of this dust of a culture that today represents Europe would have been proof to everyone that the United States of Europe was already an obsolete buffoonery.

First Contact with the Mexican Revolution^{xxxvii}

The current world crisis reached France after other countries, but although it does not appear so, it has reached it more seriously. Unlike elsewhere, France, in its current state, suffers from a crisis in *its consciousness*, much more than in its assets and wealth, and the French youth are particularly feeling the effects of this crisis. Anyone who knew Paris three years ago and who returned now would not recognize it. On the surface, the *city* has changed little, but the *life* of Paris, what used to be its vibrancy, youthfulness, bustle, glitter and fun, has changed to a terrible extent. It is, above all, the youth that suffers, and nothing affects a country's deep life as much as the pain of its youth.

I would not say that the French youth has lost hope; I would say that it has been affected in the very mechanisms of its mind since it is about to lose confidence in the resources of life. The government is concerned with keeping the prices of essential articles up so that they are not sold at a loss, thus enabling the French peasants to maintain their former standard of living, but it is not concerned at all, as it is here in Mexico, with the life of the young. And the French youth left to itself – I am speaking especially of young painters, sculptors, actors, filmmakers, etc. – is close to despair.

I need hardly say how moved I was when, on my arrival here, I saw the extent of the care the revolutionary Government of Mexico takes of the artworks of the youth; I spoke with artists, painters, revolutionary intellectuals and also with musicians; The Department of Fine Arts, headed by Professor Muñoz Cota, did me the honour of inviting me to its Children's Theatre Congress as a delegate of the French Republic. I could see that the Mexican revolution has a soul, a living soul, a demanding soul, which the Mexicans themselves are ignorant of how far it could take them. This is the highly emotional thing about the revolutionary movement in Mexico. Young Mexico is pioneering; it is determined to remake a world and does not shy away from any transformation that will rebuild that world. Ask the young revolutionaries of Mexico, and no one will give you the same answer; this chaos of opinions is the best proof of the dynamism of the revolution. The youth all agree that Mexico's life must be socialist, it must be acknowledged, but perspectives range on the tactics to be employed to realize this socialism completely and swiftly in Mexico.

These very divergences possess their own forces of exaltation. The consciousness of today's Mexico is chaos, where the new forces of a world are bubbling up. If the French youth are in despair, then the youth of Mexico is nowhere near it, as I discovered on the occasion of this Children's Theatre Congress, where I was kindly asked to give a talk on the dynamism of the Guignol.

It must be said that the French youth, currently in full effervescence, is stirring up the most audacious ideas, and they do so most of the time without hardly realizing it. In fact, concerning the theatre, a new concept has been underway in recent years. Leaving behind the purely artistic [*plastiques*] research of Jacques Copeau, where the staging merely offers itself as a way of dressing up the text and being strictly conditioned by it, we are trying to rediscover and invent a pure language that is the very language of the theatre. That is to say, literature, the written word, and dialogue cease to hold the cardinal place in a theatre conceived as such. The text no longer conditions staging, but there is a tendency to reshape the text, as in the Mysteries of the Middle Ages, when language, the basic idiom pronounced by man, combined with the organic power of breathing, was considered a servant, a slave of a particular *order* that came from far away, from the very beginnings of language in mythical ages. Little by little, modern French theatre is on its way to rediscovering the very necessity, the *central* and moving necessity, of expression. In other words, the theatre is abandoning literature; it is leaving books behind to rediscover the *air* of the stage, to let itself unfold in the entire perspective of space, because the theatre is an art in space, and the necessity to recover the awareness of the spatial value of expression comes at all costs. Sound, movement, light, gesture, voice and even the form of the voice are part of this new language of the theatre. A word lives above all in the way and from whence it is said, and what lives above all is the rhythmic pulse of the breath, which is solar and lunar, male and female, active and passive. There is a whole technique of breath here that a young actor, Jean-Louis Barrault, fresh out of Charles Dullin's Théâtre de l'Atelier, has begun to study in detail.

I explained this technique in the paper I gave on the dynamism of puppets. I had also already described it in the 'Manifesto for the Theatre of Cruelty', which appeared in the October 1932 issue of the *La Nouvelle Revue Française*, and in an article on the ternary numbers of the Kabbalah and their application to the art of theatre, in an article which will appear in the next issue of the *Revista de la Universidad* under the title 'An Affective Athleticism'.[xxxviii]

These techniques, which seem rather arid and dry, express something elementary and simple. But which is *essential*. Whether we admit it or not, there is a profound idea of culture here, and it is on this essential idea of culture that all the hopes of the French intellectual youth are based today.

The French youth is currently suffering, it could be said, from the throes of real childbirth, but they do have a revolutionary idea of culture. What I came to look for in Mexico was precisely an echo, or rather a source, the real physical source of this revolutionary force. And I am counting on the support of the Mexican youth with the youth of France to help us release this force and this idea.

The effort that I ask of the youth of Mexico, that I also ask of the Mexican revolution, will be great, and it needs to be terribly effective.

We look to Mexico, in short, for a new concept of Revolution, as well as a new concept of Man, which will serve to nourish and to feed, with its magical life, an ultimate form of Humanism, which is currently being born in France with a spirit diametrically opposed to the spirit of the sixteenth century.

You should know this; Europe is currently the victim of a collective hallucination about the Mexican Revolution. It is only a matter of time before it thinks it sees the Mexicans of today, dressed in the garments of their ancestors, *really* sacrificing to the sun on the steps of the pyramid of Teotihuacan. I assure you that I am not joking in the slightest. In any case, they have heard of the vast theatrical re-enactments that took place on that same pyramid and believed in good faith that there was a well-defined anti-European movement in Mexico, just as they believed that today's Mexico wanted to establish its revolution based on a return to the pre-Cortesian tradition. A similar fantasy circulates in Paris in the most advanced intellectual circles. In short, the Mexican Revolution is believed to be a revolution of the indigenous soul, a revolution to reconquer the *indigenous soul* as it was before Cortes.

This was to be the subject of the investigation I was charged with undertaking here.

Yet, the revolutionary youth of Mexico are not particularly concerned with the indigenous soul. And here is where the drama lies. When I came to Mexico, I dreamed of an alliance between the French and Mexican Youth with the view of producing a unique cultural effort. However, this alliance is impossible if the Mexican youth remains solely Marxist. Marxism claims to be scientific, it speaks of the consciousness of the masses, but it does not destroy the notion of individual consciousness. So, leaving this notion intact, it speaks gratuitously and romantically of mass consciousness. However, the destruction of individual consciousness represents a high idea of culture, a profound idea of culture from which a completely new form of civilization is derived. Not to feel alive as an individual is to escape this dreaded form of capitalism, which I call capitalism of the conscience since the soul has become a commodity for everyone.

In France, the youth believe in a renaissance of pre-Cortesian civilization in this sense. They do not wish to commit the same North American error of a civilization that develops on the margins of culture; they want first to achieve a profound and central idea of culture on which all revolution must depend.

By imposing the forms of white civilization on the Indians, we would risk making them lose all that they could preserve from their ancient culture because culture and civilization are connected.

In the end, the problem comes down to this:

In Europe, there is an anti-European movement; I am afraid that in Mexico, there is an anti-Indian movement.

To be concerned with the body and not with consciousness is to risk losing the body. I know perfectly well that the problem of consciousness does not exist for the Marxist youth of Mexico or, if you prefer, that external elements condition it.

But for the revolutionary youth of France, Marxism, by preserving the sense of individual consciousness, prevents the Revolution from returning to its sources, which means that it halts the Revolution.

Medea without Fire^{xxxix}

Seneca's *Medea* is a mythical world; however, Margarita Xirgu's lacks fire and misses this world entirely. One must not lessen myths. Otherwise, one resigns to being only a man, and that's nothing but a miserable anthropomorphism. This is how one discovers oneself a man, how one discovers man, small in stature, feeble in sound, and, in the end, naked.

This tragedy needs monsters leaping out; we need to be shown as being among these monsters, the monsters of the primitive imagination as seen through the primitive mind. Monsters do not show themselves so easily. Jason and Medea cannot approach each other: each has their circle and stands within it. To arrive, Jason has to make his way among the gods, as does Medea. One god faces another god. At every moment, the atmosphere of the drama is raised to its highest point.

The ancients had a range of tragic materials at their disposal: cothurns, models, masks; the symbolism of these masks, lines and costumes. Not to be seen from afar, but to surpass, to leer at man's stature.

'I invoke you,' says Medea with a sinister voice, 'a voice that calls forth crime, which is the invention and imagination of crime.' The peculiarity of modern theatre is that it systematically loses the prospect of representing a tragedy, that is, really tearing away someone's attention through crime. It is a theatre that cheats because it is afraid to deal with the powers that be, powers one cannot pretend to evade.

Tragedy has its technique.

A material and decorative technique.

A physiological technique.

And finally, a psychological technique.

It aims to deceive the senses; that's why it's necessary in the first place not to awaken them. The theatre is the world of true illusion. The spectator's imagination wants him to believe in what he sees and to present him with scenery that shakes and is painted in the style of *trompe-l'œil*, whose purpose is not only to deceive the eye but to disgust and make the eye despair, which would laugh if it could.

In Xirgu's Medea, three moth-eaten dust cloths have been hung up, which pretend to evoke the Cyclopean mountains. And, to finish it all off, these mountains are stylized. I can't swallow this type of stylization based on filthy dust rags. Gordon Craig invented the system, but we have had our fill of Gordon Craig's stylization in Europe. Even more filthy are the bags worn by those servants who almost fall face-first into the room.

I particularly urge you to check out the chorus, the chorus of warriors with rose-coloured arms who look like they've just come out of a hospital for sick children. They are all dressed in green cloth as if a hundred billiard tables had been ransacked to dress them.

Creon's costume is the most implausible of all. He wears a banner and a string of acanthus leaves, each as wide as an elephant's thigh. If this garland of barbaric leaves pretends to signify his royalty, it succeeds much more in showing that kings are taken for vagrant common pochards. And if many kings have drunken habits and degenerate vagabond souls, the mythical kings must always offer us a superior image of royalty. The directors of modern theatre no longer have a sense of what true royal power is, no more than they have a sense of tragedy.

The supernatural atmosphere of horror that emanates from the truly magical text of Seneca, who was an authentic initiate, while modern tragedians are nothing but puppets and jugglers, cannot be conveyed to us by using the lighting of a modern music hall on the dust rags that I described earlier.

On stage, objects must be taken for what they are; this is, in my opinion, the only way to create the stage illusion. One should not take a dust cloth and try to make us believe that it is a mountain but take a mountain and use it as a cloth. You can't carry a mountain on stage, but you can take a mirror and have a mountain reflected in it. The technique is not to try to represent what cannot be represented.

All genuine theatrical traditions have always despised reality, but they have never substituted it with a stunted artifice. Wherever he is, the actor plays with objects from life: tables, chairs, cupboards, and ladders, to which he is limited; the rest he passes on through his gestures. The set is in his arms, in his body, in his feet, in his hands, in his eyes, and above all, in his face, which is as changeable as a landscape where clouds have fun hiding the sun. But this does not prevent natural objects from undergoing a real psychological demonetization: changing plane, they change value; and they change plane because their psychological situation is new, strange, surprising and unexpected. By embroidering everything as if by magic, light adds to the illusion or the disillusionment. Light has a moral value; it does not only illuminate objects. On the stage, objects become monsters to which the actors' words, gestures and movements lend a supernatural soul.

Tragedy is born of myth. Every tragedy is the representation of a great myth. The language of myth is symbol and allegory. Allegory manifests itself in signs. There is a language of signs that is part of the plastic technique and the setting of tragedy.

Xirgu's style of representation lacks allegorical signs: it has only two or three invariable gestures, such as the hand on the head and the arms crossed.

From the point of view of theatrical scenery, tragedy also has its symbolic signs from which came, for example, the lictors' fasces, the cross and the caduceus of Mercury. The Roman armies marched behind a forest of signs. Where were the symbolic emblems of the *Medea* staged at the Palacio de Bellas Artes?

The physiological technique, which aims to transform the human voice through the knowledge of breath and certain muscular points, was absent from this *Medea*. Xirgu's Medea screams uniformly, without nuance, without an inflexion of the voice that would make our insides tingle and our souls leap inside the body. It does not seem to occur to her that the pitch of the human voice can be adjusted to make it sing like a real organ. There are ways to make the voice jump and quiver like a landscape. There is a whole scale of the voice.

Finally, it is in the psychological technique that the poetic gift must intervene. Poetry allows Jason to finally arrive by letting in monsters as he enters with the grace of a god. One can make gods appear on stage and draw magic circles around the inapproachable characters of a truly figurative myth, but I repeat, you need this gift. The principle is to introduce on stage the irrational and monstrous logic of dreams, that logic which, on the one hand, reveals a face and which, from a sigh exhaled close to the ear, suggests the passage of a hurricane. In the language of writing, this technique of images is at the origin of metaphor. The tragic actor walks with secretive gestures, surrounded by metaphors that he constantly creates with his voice, gestures and movements.

Young French Painting and Tradition[xl]

In current French painting, there is a marked reaction against Surrealism, represented above all by the young painter Balthus who, weary of ghost-like paintings, is trying to organize his world, a world of his own in which he nevertheless takes advantage of the in-depth examinations that authentic Surrealist thought made in the field of the unconscious.

Surrealist painting negated the real, a fundamental discrediting launched at appearances. When not denying objects, the Surrealist world disorganizes them. Its conception of things first establishes a divorce between the unlimited and reason. No difference can be found in it between the world of dreams and the world of applied reason.

The forms of Surrealist culture live in a light of hallucination. In the struggle against this divorce and destruction, Balthus once again takes up the world *from appearances*: he accepts sense data, as he accepts that of reason – he accepts them but reforms them; one might even say that he recasts and reformulates them. In short, Balthus starts from what is *known*; there are universally recognizable elements and aspects in his painting, but the *recognizable*, in turn, has a meaning that not everyone can reach or even recognize. Balthus's painting is a revolution that is unquestionably directed against Surrealism but also against academism in all its forms. Beyond the Surrealist revolution, beyond the forms of classical academism, Balthus's revolutionary painting joins a kind of mysterious tradition.

Contrary to what is taught in textbooks and schools, a tradition of painting was lost during the Renaissance. Painters like Vinci, Titian, Michelangelo, Veronese, Giorgione, Correggio, etc., broke with a universal sacred tradition of painting; they betrayed this tradition. Between the plastic secrets of a life whose appearances painting translates and manifests, and the appearances that could be said to be *epidermal*, the whole of European painting has, since the Renaissance, decided in favour of the appearances of life in favour of the *natural*. Since then, we have seen the faces of women and men with a chuckling or tearful attitude, the sun, the wind, the passions, and bad weather. Painting has fallen under the anecdotal authority of nature and psychology. It has ceased as a means of revelation and has become an art of simple descriptive representation. It has lost that universal and secret reason for being, which made it *magic* in the true sense of the word.

In pre-Renaissance painting, faces may seem a little dead psychologically speaking, but this is because so-called primitive art has forever been the *supernatural* manifestation of a science beyond human psychology, which it disdains; the faces in primitive painting transmit to us the vibration of the soul, the profound efforts of the Universe.

Compare the hieratic and sacred primitivism of a Cimabue, a Giotto, a Fra Angelico, with the type of painting that worships matter for matter's sake, such as a Michelangelo, a Titian, a Veronese, and even a Tintoretto and a Rubens, and painters like Piero della Francesca, Simone Martini, Piero di Cosimo, Tura, Antonello di Messina and Mantegna who reconcile the demands of the sun, of time, of darkness, of human psychology, in a word, of *reality* [*actualité*], with those of that old sacred art which was based on the knowledge of what I will call the Energetics of the Universe.

Where Cimabue seeks to manifest essences hieratically, Paolo Uccello paints form with science, and the form is still ardent because it is close to the essence that gave birth to it. It is to this esoteric and magical tradition that a painter like Balthus returns. Surrealism helped him to clarify forms, and, under the fixed convention of these forms, it allowed him to discover in the unconscious of man the rustling life of the naked forces of the Universe.

The pre-Renaissance painting had a form and a figure. In their lines and sketches, the so-called primitives revealed the Pythagorean tradition of numbers. There is a kind of esotericism in their representations, a kind of enchantment, and through its lines, the figure of man becomes the fixed sign and the transparent sieve of magic.

This is how Balthus proceeds, rejecting the anarchic carelessness and the more or less inspired disorder of the painting that calls itself modern, and he gives us landscapes, portraits, and groups that have their number and whose symbol does not appear to us at first sight. Balthus has painted mysterious groups, a street where dreamy automatons march single file; he has produced concentrated portraits where, as on an astrological chart of the sky, a colour, a flower, a metal, fire, earth, wood or water allows the represented character to regain their identity.

Palmistry knows the hand of metal, wood, water, earth or fire.

Similarly, in a portrait by Balthus, the character evokes the element to which his life, character, or spirit most resembles.

Balthus has the soul of an ascetic, and in the way he uses colour, there is a true 'asceticism'. He practices this 'asceticism' when he paints. He suppresses his secret sensuality and repels the temptation to indulge in the artificial and easy intoxication of colour. This way, he achieves a darker intoxication that makes objects sing in their light. He brings objects to life in a light he has made his own. We can say there is a colour, light, and luminosity specific to Balthus. And the characteristic of this luminosity is, above all, to be *invisible*. Objects, bodies, and faces are phosphorescent without us being able to tell where their light comes from. In this regard, Balthus is infinitely more skillful than Goya, Rembrandt, or Zurbàran than all the great masters of painting who, from darkness, ascend, plane by plane, to clarity.

Allied with his science of colour, Balthus possesses a science of space. He knows immediately where on a canvas to place the precise point that vibrates, following the great tradition of painting for which the painted canvas is a geometric space to be filled. But in this painted and vibrating space, in this invisible illuminated space, Balthus's personality calls to him the colours and shapes and imposes his dark claw on them. He curdles them, so to speak, the way a fermenting acid curdles milk.

Balthus does not simply play with ochres, brown reds, earth greens, asphalt, or the blackness of lacquers, for it is a fact that the world he sees maintains itself in this minor key.

Balthus's use of bitter colour means, above all, that life, currently, is bitter. In his agile and concentrated forms, Balthus proclaims the bitterness and despair of living.

One of Balthus's drawings sweats the science of living when life takes us by the throat. This mixture of geometry and tenderness is the work of a man in agony who, by a miracle, has managed to triumph over his own agony.

All of his painting, with the rhythm of a human breath, is impregnated with a vast respiratory harmony that goes from the precipitous breath of anger to the slow and wide breath of agony.

In a portrait by Balthus, there is this principle of synthesis related to ancient Chinese calligraphy and certain primitive paintings.

Through this portrait painted by Balthus, the character joins its historical model. And all this is achieved by something other than *overloading* but by what one might call a stripping down. The head stands apart from time, in a luminous atmosphere, in an exposure to light that immediately gives its reason for being as such and the key to its fate.

With his angular and strangled drawing, his earthquake colours, Balthus, who has always painted hydrocephalic people with emaciated legs and long feet – proof that he himself does not carry his head well – Balthus, when he has finished digesting his sciences, will assert himself as the Paolo Uccello or the Piero della Francesca of this period or, better still, as a Greco who has lost his way.

French Theatre in Search of a Myth[xli]

Weary of Copeau's, Dullin's, and Baty's artistic inquiries, young French theatre is looking for a myth it is about to uncover. For them, the famous 'respect for the text', that invention of Jacques Copeau, only leads to the revival of old texts, but the theatre of today is not looking for texts but for a 'language', and this language is not located in the choruses, but in space, for this is where the theatre's language is situated.

For the myth of modern theatre to be born, it must first make for itself a 'language'. The communist group *Octobre*, under the direction of Jacques Prévert, and the group led by Jean-Louis Barrault, are in the process of inventing this language, each in their own way.[xlii] The *Octobre* group have performed farces that were bloody critiques of bourgeois aspirations and the bourgeois mind. Jacques Prévert had participated in the Surrealist movement. This can be seen in the technique of his jokes, where suddenly, the life of dreams bursts in amid the dreaded caricatures of a world that, before it dies, spurts out its venom. In Jacques Prévert's farces, the lewd homebody spirit of the modern French bourgeoisie is cruelly castigated. Because of this absurd spirit, Edgar Poe and Baudelaire's "The Imp of the Perverse" is given free rein. The lust that seeks refuge in the double-bottomed bed of the old French adulterer is driven away by its phantasms. It scares itself through contemplation. The *ménage à trois* becomes *ménage à six*, *ménage à douze*, *ménage à dix-huit*, *ménage à vingt-quatre*, *ménage à trente-six*, and there are frightening running races of multiples of three that end up blushing on their own accord; then comes a proletarian machinist who throws all this pretty theatre into the bin.

Jacques Prévert's buffoonery is both psychological and objective. What I mean is that lust, the demon of the perverse, the multiples of three, take shape and, as the play unfolds, it acquires the proportions of a nightmare. For young French modern theatre, there is no difference between myth and nightmare: their shared characteristic is that they avenge us. They avenge us for the dreams we have of our wicked life. What is more, if we seek to create a myth for the theatre, that myth will be burdened with all the horrors of a century that have made us believe in our failures in life.

The highest form of theatre is tragedy. And the last living creations of modern French theatre partake of this form, which does not mean that they are in five acts and in verse. This division into acts is an invention of the French psychological tragedy, which has forgotten the penetrating and morbid soul that finds, in the manner of the ancient myths, tragic inspiration in the darkness of an encompassing nightmare.

With its ferocious humor, Jacques Prévert's theatre is a theatre of darkness; so is Jean-Louis Barrault's.

Theatre is born out of darkness like light out of chaos; like light, it emerges to overcome the darkness of chaos.

The theatrical representations of the *Orphic Mysteries* showed forms that were swelling to conquer the darkness; these forms had the face of night and took on the aspect of invading Evil.

Every great myth has one foot firmly planted in Evil; that is to say, in the disaster that threatens all of us, we, as men, and periodically, if an awakening is necessary to annihilate the disaster, it is above all up to the theatre to realize, through its images and its forms, the poetic and magical sign of this awakening.

Jacques Prévert's humor indicates that the life of our times is sick; Jean-Louis Barrault's theatre seeks to find the secret hieroglyphs and signs of a magical life that the stage must resurrect.[xliii]

Through the revelation of these signs and hieroglyphs, the true language of the theatre will finally reveal itself.

The mistake of someone like Jacques Copeau is to rely on the author to renew the theatre. In contrast, the resurrection of the theatre must be the work of a kind of 'Proteus human', who is as much responsible for the animated hieroglyphs of the staging as for the work of the actor, the spoken parts of the discourse being henceforth linked to the rest to compose a single voice, a single being, a single movement.

What I Came to Mexico to Do^{xliv}

I arrived in Mexico looking for politicians rather than artists.

And these are the reasons why:

Until now, I was an artist, a *driven* man. There is no doubt that from the social point of view, artists are *slaves*.

Well, this must change.

There was a time when the artist was a sage, which is to say, a cultured man who doubled as a thaumaturgist, a magician, a therapist, and even a gymnasiarch; all of these are called, in fairground language, 'the man-orchestra' or 'the Proteus man'. The artist used to combine all of the faculties and sciences in him. Then came the era of specialization and also an era of decadence. This cannot be denied. A society that reduces science to debris is a degenerating society.

There is a disease in the polar regions which consists of an essential alteration of the tissues: this disease is *scurvy*. The organism's cells dry up, lacking an essential and vital principle. And just as individuals have diseases, there are diseases of the masses. Thus, the generalization of industrial crops has given rise to a collective form of *scurvy* in the European organism.

This is the ransom that progress has had to pay.

Today's Mexico, which has come to realize the defects of European civilization, must react against the *superstition of progress*.

And since politicians have replaced artists in public affairs, this task falls to them rather than the artists.

Today, Mexico faces a major problem, and I came to Mexico to study the solutions that could be offered here.

And it amounts to nothing less than destroying the spirit of the entire world and replacing one civilization with another.

Dr Alexis Carrel, who also recognizes the defects of the mechanized civilization of Europe, does not fail, in his book *Man, the Unknown*, to advocate the need for a revolution and even suggests ways of carrying it out.

Mexico, which has undergone two or three revolutions in a century, should not fear another one; and when the next one takes place, it will certainly be of exceptional gravity because, this time, fundamental problems will have to be solved.

Only, this future revolution of Mexico's – and this constitutes its originality – will not be a fratricidal revolution because, when it comes to the fate of civilization, a unanimous thought animates present Mexico. This heart-warming unanimity is what I wanted to witness.

The question is this: Europe's present civilization is bankrupt. Dualist Europe has nothing left to offer the world but a set of unbelievably ruinous cultures. It is necessary to draw out from this cultural dust a new unity.

The East, on the other hand, is in full decadence. India is falling asleep to the dream of liberation that will only be worth it after death.

China is at war. The Japanese of today seem to be the fascists of the Far East. China for Japan is a vast Ethiopia.

The United States has done nothing but multiply the decadence and vices of Europe ad infinitum.

What remains is Mexico and its subtle political structure, which has stayed the same since the time of Moctezuma.

Mexico, this sediment of innumerable races, appears as the crucible of History. A unique deposit must be drawn from this sedimentation and mixture of races. From this, the Mexican soul will emerge.

But a unique culture is needed to form a unique soul, and this is where the problem becomes interesting.

There is culture on one hand and civilization on the other, and both civilization and culture are in danger of going in diametrically opposite directions. If there are a hundred European cultures, there is now only one civilization. A civilization that has its laws. Whoever is without machines, guns, planes, bombs and poisonous gas necessarily falls prey to the better-armed neighbour or enemy: look at the case of Ethiopia.

Modern Mexico could not escape from this necessity or law. But, in addition to this, Mexico possesses a secret culture which the ancient Mexicans have bequeathed to it. In contrast to the modern culture of Europe, which has reached a senseless pulverization of forms and aspects, the eternal culture of Mexico has a unique aspect. This is what I was getting at: every culture of synthesis has a secret. Over time and under the external influence of the civilization of Europe, Mexico has abandoned the knowledge and use of this secret, but – and this is the astonishing event of our own time – a movement has arisen in Mexico to recover this secret.

Once Mexico has truly reconquered and resurrected its true culture, neither guns nor planes can do anything against it.

Please pay attention to what I am about to say; these are not catch phrases from some serial drama. Underneath the childish appearance of this statement lies a fundamental truth.

Every important cultural transformation has as its starting point a renewed idea of man; it coincides with a new surge of humanism. One suddenly begins to cultivate man like one would a fertile garden.

I came to Mexico in search of a new idea of man.

Man in relation to invention, science, and discovery, but as only Mexico can provide us. By this, I mean with the framework still to be discovered, but carrying within it the ancient *animistic* relationships that man has with nature, that which established the old Toltecs, the old Mayas, and, in short, all the races that from century to century have made the Mexican soil great.

Mexico cannot, at the risk of dying, renounce the present conquests of science. Still, it holds in reserve an ancient science infinitely superior to that of labs and scientists.

Mexico has its science and its own culture. To develop this science and culture is a duty for modern Mexico, and such a duty is precisely the exciting originality of this country.

Between the now degenerate vestiges of the ancient Red Culture, such as can be found in the last pure indigenous races, and the no less degenerate and fragmentary culture of modern Europe, Mexico can find an original form of culture which will constitute its contribution to the civilization of this age.

The task to be accomplished in this sense is enormous. If I am in Mexico today, it is because I have felt that modern Mexico is accomplishing this enormous task of epic proportions – let us not be afraid of big words.

There are other undiscovered forces, other subtle forces that are not yet within the purview of science, but which someday may become a part of it, hidden beneath the achievements of current science, which routinely uncovers additional forces. These forces are part of the animistic domain of nature as it was known in pagan times. The superstitious mind of man has given religious form to those profound insights which made man, if one may venture the expression, 'the catalyst of the Universe'.

But the conquest of modern Mexico and the vital contribution it can make today consists precisely in the discovery of *analogous forces* – how the human organism works in harmony with and governs the organism of nature – represents the victory of modern Mexico and the extremely vital contribution it can make today. As we witnessed in the era of the *Popol-Vuh*, insofar as science and poetry are the same thing, poets, artists and scholars all have a stake in this matter.

But this time, this rediscovery will be free of all superstition, of all religious significance, no matter how slight.

In short, it is a question of resurrecting the old sacred idea, the great idea of pagan pantheism, in a form that is no longer religious but scientific. True pantheism is not a philosophical system; it is merely a means of *dynamically investigating* the universe.

And this is precisely the lesson that modern Mexico teaches us. It appropriates the forms of the mechanistic civilization of Europe and adapts them to its spirit. What does it matter if this spirit is the destroyer of these forms!

If it destroys them, it will do so in time, when it is itself already armed with its strength, that is, when the spirit of the ancient synthetic culture of the Toltecs and Mayas has regained enough strength to allow Mexico to abandon European civilization without danger. Again, this is not a utopia but a scientific reality that cannot be denied. If we are willing to accept the idea that Man is the catalyst of the Universe, we must deduce that the moral forces of Man vibrate in unison with the forces of the Universe, those forces which, according to the teachings of the high Monist philosophy, are neither physical nor moral, but take on a moral or physical aspect depending on the direction in which we wish to use them.

The Palenque cross contains the synthetical image of this double action.

Inscribed in the stone is the hieroglyphic representation of a single energy which, through the cross of the space, which is to say, by passing through the four cardinal points, goes from man to the animal and the plants.

The Eternal Culture of Mexico^{xlv}

I came to Mexico to make contact with the Red Earth. It is the separate soul, the original soul of Mexico, which interests me most of all, but before I confront it, I want to study the real life of Mexico in all its aspects to be sure of deeply understanding it.

I came here with a blank slate, which does not mean without preconceived ideas, but preconceived ideas partake of the realm of the imaginary, so I distrust them.

Not that I lack an idea about what the true culture of Mexico was once like, but I acknowledge that there is a fundamental difference between civilization and culture. Art's outward form may distinguish a multitude of civilizations, but their variety leaves intact the deep spirit of a culture, and in Mexico, under the multitude of outward appearances that only art discerns, there is hidden a single cultural aspiration: the burnished copper culture of the sun.

I know almost everything that history teaches us about the different races of Mexico, and I must confess that I have also allowed myself to dream, as a poet does, about those things history does not teach.

Between the known historical facts and the real life of the Mexican soul, there is an immense margin where the imagination – and I dare say personal intuition – is given free rein.

I have my ideas about the Mayan, Toltec and Zapotec cultures, but what intrigues me is whether it is possible to find the lost soul of these cultures and their survival in people's contemporary way of life and those who govern them in today's Mexico.

Mexico lies on the road toward the sun, and on this road, we must track down the source of the light's force that caused the pyramids to rotate until they were positioned along the sun's magnetic attraction line. This is not a charlatan's secret.

The regret of a lost science, defined as a fundamental attitude of the human spirit and which I consider of essential importance to recover, is what most closely approaches the lyrical and sterile nostalgia of a dead past.

As certain as it is that I have an idea of Mexico's eternal culture, I also have no judgment or opinion on Mexico's current politics.

Such a subject is not my responsibility, nor is it any of my business. I am here as a spectator; I would even say as a *disciple*. I have come to Mexico to *learn* something and want to bring these lessons back to Europe. That is why my research can only relate to that part of the Mexican soul which has remained pure of any influence from the European spirit. I did not come here to seek out the spirit of European culture but the original Mexican culture and its civilization; I wish to draw lessons from this originality, of which I consider myself a disciple.

We talk about the Latin spirit of Mexico. And the first question I ask myself is to what extent does the European spirit, in its Latin form, still permeate the Mexican soul of today?

The Latin spirit is a rational culture, the supremacy of reason. We must react against this frenzy of inventions, against this frenzy that has produced the agrochemical industry, lab-produced medicine, machinism in all its forms, etc. Machinism renders all human endeavor sterile and leads, in short, to the belittling of man's effort, the discouragement of competition between men, and the uselessness and inconvenience of all research aimed at *quality*. As for lab-produced medicine, it is incapable of perceiving the subtle and fleeting soul of diseases; it treats living man as if he were a corpse.

The Latin spirit is also responsible for the democratic ideas of Europe, for nationalism, not natural nationalism, but a certain form of egoistic nationalism that today's Mexico does not suffer from.

For there is cultural nationalism, in which the specific quality of a nation and its works of art are affirmed to distinguish themselves; this nationalism is irreproachable; and then there is what could be called civic nationalism, which, in its egoistic form, resolves itself into chauvinism that results in custom struggles and economic wars, that is, when it does not end in total war.

As for what concerns lab-made medicine, it should be known that there is currently a reaction in France against this type of medicine which relies almost exclusively on experience and experiments and draws its conclusions from the information provided by the microscope, the dissection of dead matter, etc.

I must point out a return to empiricism which, in its primary form, gives rise to healers and bonesetters and, in its transcendental form, is the basis of great methods such as homoeopathy.

Homoeopathy, with its principle of similitude, is intimately connected with herbal medicine. As such, I will search Mexico for the existence of an old herbal medicine akin to what is known as spagyric medicine in Europe, whose most notable theorist toward the end of the Middle Ages was Paracelsus.

Now, I cannot draw any conclusion regarding these matters. Still, it seems that there are two currents in Mexico: one which aspires to assimilate European culture and civilization, giving them a Mexican form, and the other which, continuing the age-old secular tradition, remains obstinately rebellious to all progress. No matter how small the latter current may be, it is here that all the strength of Mexico lies; it is here that I will come face to face with that which survives of the empirical medicine of the Mayas and Toltecs, the true Mexican poetics, which cannot only be reduced to writing poems, but affirms the relations of the poetic rhythm with the breath of man and, through breath, with the pure movements of space, water, air, light and wind.

The deep culture of Mexico comes from far away. It carries the culture of the racial groups that formerly controlled civilization.

In the face of the evident collapse of the present civilization of Europe, I have come to see for myself how Mexico might strengthen its traditional culture and whether, without trying to resurrect wasteful remnants of its life, it aspires to prove the permanence in it of a spirit which, from my point of view as a poet, I would call *magical*; a spirit which, considered from a strictly scientific point of view, could become the expression of a truly psychological energy.

Thanks to this energy, which is infinitely spread throughout Nature, Ancient man entered into possession, so to speak, of its events. For example, we know that for the Maya, fate did not exist: Nature only has power over us because of our ignorance and age-old blindness.

But when humanism is spoken of almost everywhere again, the opportunity arises to affirm man's great power of control, the true powers of man that make him master of these events.

A culture that views the universe as a whole knows how each component automatically affects the totality. Knowing these laws is all that is necessary.

To know fate is, in short, to master fate, since in the present as it will be in the future, the external world falls under the mastery of the intellect.

One can foresee events and act upon them by employing very precise astrological data drawn from a transcendental algebra. The ancient Maya perfected the collection of such data and the mastery of this science.

Having established this, I conclude that at the bottom of the true solar culture is a secret meaning that I will now attempt to define.

The sun, to use the ancient language of symbols, appears as the *maintainer* of life. The sun is not only the element which fertilizes – the sovereign instigator of germination. It is all of these things making everything that exists ripen, but this is, if one may say, the least of its faculties. It burns, calcinates and eliminates but does not destroy all it removes. Under the heap of destruction, due to destruction, it maintains the eternity of the forces by which life is preserved.

In a word – and herein lies the real secret – the sun is a principle of death and not a principle of life. The essence of the ancient solar culture is that it demonstrated the supremacy of death.

There are in India worshippers of Shiva the Destroyer and worshippers of Vishnu the Preserver. But destruction is transformative. Life maintains its continuity through the transformation of the appearances of being.

Now, the worshippers of Shiva have as their emblem the spirit of fire, the great form-devouring current, that kind of impelling force which changed the burnished men of ancient Mexico into ascertained maintainers of death. And this is not a verbal paradox.

Realizing the supremacy of death is not the same as choosing to forego present life. It involves putting present life in its place, allowing it to exist on multiple planes at once, experiencing the stability of the planes that give the living world its great force of equilibrium, and, ultimately, re-establishing great harmony.

I have come to modern Mexico to seek the survival of these notions or to await their resurrection.

The False Superiority
of the Elite^{xlvi}

Rather than crushing the intellectual elite, we must first understand them, and to understand them, we must define them.

The modern world, which is experiencing a spiritual breakdown and even more so because it despises everything spiritual, must restore the balance between the two fundamental movements through which they manifest themselves; that is, if it is to find peace, whether via the use of the head or the hand, an activity and an identical dynamism whose integration constitutes man whole.

And just as there is a tremendous misunderstanding between the opposing faculties of the mind and matter in the present world, there is competition, or rather rivalry, between the work of the hand and that of the head. Intellectuals [*élites*], it cannot be denied, enjoy no recognition in today's society. Most of humankind is interested in something other than the work of the mind. And it would not be an overstatement to say that those who proclaim to devote themselves to the sole work of thought are about to go hungry because of their selflessness, which was once more widely acknowledged.

But before reducing intellectuals to starvation, dismantling those who make a society great and, most importantly, guaranteeing its *endurance*, society should at least attempt to comprehend them. An eminent man to whom I complained about the sad situation in which artists have fallen in France replied: 'What do you want? In our world, when it's not on the straw floor of the prison cell, artists are forced to perish on a pile of hay.'

I replied that there were times when artists were given their rightful place, which is to say, the first among others, and when society was concerned with providing them with the means of subsistence, even beyond what was necessary.

That money has evolved into what it is today – a major force and, one could argue, a touchstone of life – fine, but this is a fact, not a rule of proof. And just because something is the way it is, does not mean one has to accept it. There are many reasons, and very good ones, for initiating change.

What is the purpose of revolution if not to re-establish the social equilibrium and to inject a modicum of justice into the injustice of life? At the bottom of this rivalry, this struggle between the antagonistic forces of the spirit and matter, we find an error of conception that belongs to the modern world: what I mean is how it was not known by other epochs.

If in the modern capitalist world, which puts money above all else, there is, it cannot be denied, a characteristic contempt for the intellectuals [*élites*], which in turn masks the hatred that all true superiority inspires, it is because the modern world offers the elite another reality, an existence that they would not have otherwise.

Those who work with their hands have forgotten their head, and those who work with their heads generally feel saddened when they have to work with their hands, believing themselves to be diminished.

This explains the contempt felt by the communist masses for the free activities of the mind. It is because the modern world despises the work of the mind that it is in disarray; one might say with some confidence that it has lost its mind; the mind, having been split from life, has, in its turn, become useless. The elite must cease to believe in their superiority; they must acquire a salutary humility to restore the mind to its ancient function as an *organ* and demonstrate the works of the intellect from a valuable material perspective, and as if by magic, this idiotic war between the *sumptuary* refinements of the mind and the work of the hands, which is worthless if the logic of the head does not govern it, will cease.

Whether we like it or not, the elite are the ballast, the sovereign counterweight that keeps life upright.

Intellectuals will occupy their rightful place in society when society is discerning enough to understand that there is an absolute identity between the forces of the body and those of the intellect and that the mind is the filter of life. I am not claiming that the mind is as useful as the body; I am claiming that there is neither body nor mind, but modalities of a unique force and action. And the question of rivalry between these two modalities should not even have to arise.

It is the responsibility of intellectuals to channel their spiritual strength into worthwhile endeavors that might serve as the salt of life rather than speculative ideas that appear to be uninterested and gratuitous but are in reality meaningless and unhelpful. This does not mean that intellectuals should engage in manual labor, but that they should finally understand the *functional utility* of the mind.

If the body and mind are but one movement, then the intellectuals should focus their efforts on the side where the mind connects with the rhythms of the diseased life; and, as in the times when the great unitary culture reigned and from which all civilizations emerged, they must once again become the healers, the therapists of the high functions of life in man, since it is in the disordered organism of man today that the disordered organism of the universe is reflected.

Masculine, feminine. With this, ancient societies famously consecrated the eternal antagonism between the masculine forces of the spirit and the forces of the body or matter, whose passive weight is precisely feminine.

Resurrecting these old notions, without which life is unintelligible, would be a magic trick today.

To do this, we have a magic organ at our fingertips, a weapon that allows us to be a symbol of life.

This weapon of exceptional power and inexhaustible fertility is the theatre. But modern society has forgotten the therapeutic benefits of the theatre, and it would laugh if we told it that in ancient times, the theatre was considered an exceptional means of re-establishing the lost balance of forces and that the ancient theatre's function included healing music and dances.

It has been forgotten that theatre is a sacred act that engages both the beholder and the performer and that the fundamental psychological idea of the theatre is this: a gesture seen and reconstructed by the mind in images is as valuable as a gesture one makes.

That is why there is no better instrument of revolution than the theatre, and it is through the theatre, through this solvent and formidable weapon, that every perceptive revolutionary government directs and ensures its revolution.

There can only be a revolution with the integration of the elites with the masses, who thereby reach a higher spiritual level.

Mexico, with its primitive indigenous races in which healing music and dances are abundant, can undertake such a revolution; and the best of this indigenous healing music awaits the moment of resuming its place among the mass of workers.

P.S. – There is indeed no reason why the popular art of the Indians should not be incorporated into the elite. To put the life of folklore and the research of the great Mexican writers on the same cultural level seems to be a refined way of putting an end to the antagonisms that exist between the elite and the masses, popular art and bourgeois art, intellectual life and instinctive life, the effusions of pure thought and the harmonies, also intellectual, of the organic life of the Indians.

P.S. – I am looking for Dr José Miguel Cornez Mendoza, who is well-versed in the ancient occult medicine of the Toltecs. If he is reading these lines, I ask him to write to me, giving me his address and telling me where and when I can meet him.

Eternal Secrets of Culture^{xlvii}

Every authentic culture has its secrets. Before talking about the universal bases of culture, we should talk about the eternal secrets of culture, secrets that nobody has ever penetrated.

Culture is a refined outpouring of life in the awakening organism of man. And no one has ever been able to say what life is. Thus, to affirm the flowering in man of an eternal spirit of culture is to affirm man's ignorance regarding the sources of true life.

This humility is the very basis of science. Even more than science, ignorance stimulates because it incites above all else one to be careful, not to make mistakes.

Ignorance, an enlightened and conscious ignorance, is the cement of truth.

With his conscience as a barrier, the man who wishes to build on firm ground knows at *once where he must not set foot.*

Undoubtedly, the origin of all that exists is obscure, and the far-sighted man – in the beginnings of his science – creates a path, a margin, a place where the universal obscurity can reveal itself.

For the strange thing is that, not knowing where he comes from, man can use his ignorance, this kind of *original* ignorance, to know exactly where he must go.

And this is where empiricism serves him; empiricism, that is to say, the spirit of hypothesis; that is, the beneficial and fruitful use of his indefatigable imagination.

To help himself, he looks to the past and makes use of the fruits of men's long-ago stumbling in the dark as they attempted to extract the secrets of Nature using imagination and hypotheses.

However, the true secret will not be revealed since it is part of the ineffable. At the bottom of any true culture there are necessarily ineffable secrets because they proceed from this margin of emptiness where our eternal ignorance compels us to locate the origins of truth.

There is no civilization or culture more *rational* than the civilization and culture of China, which has pushed to the extreme the domination of Nature, but with the sole purpose of extinguishing its darkness. There is no trace of occultism or even mysticism in the rational conceptions of China; everything is real and the real is concrete. But, according to the *Tao Te Ching* of Lao Tzu, at the centre of everything, of the universal *whole*, is the void. This means that there is an emptiness that science will never fill; however, if we think of poetry as a useful and rational form of divination, it might help us lay the groundwork for moving forward.

Ancient Mexico contributed to a great extent to the constitution of this secret treasure where eternal Humanity is nourished.

We owe it psychological discoveries of the first order, the same discoveries that the European Middle Ages represented in the allegory of the Macrocosm and the Microcosm, which placed Man, like a Universe in miniature, at the point of convergence of all cosmic forces.

Thus Man, considered as a small-scale Universe, *could not despair*. As a result, this despair – which, as an aside, was termed the 'evil of the century' and that, in France, made a new and frightening appearance at the time of Surrealism, signaled by several, resounding suicides – this despair diminished by itself since all the forces of the world contributed to its demise.

Man and the universe were, therefore, in equilibrium; he breathed with it, and he knew how to heal the psychic life of the world *through the world*.

To awaken the obscure life of the world and to search for complicities in it was a way to fight against certain crimes, against a certain category of unexplainable crimes.

Education was not, as it is today, a mere *mnemonic technique*, it was a material summoning of forces, and if I dare to express myself in this way, I would say that through education the human organism was *kneaded* so that the forces would unfold within it.

This is the function that the theatre once had, this is what the great sacred festivals were used for, with their dazzling calls of sounds, their rhythmic repetitions of images that plunged into the human Unconscious.

Totemism was not some crude magic, a superstition coming from the first ages of Humanity, but the patent application of a science. For what are we made of? Does Man really believe that he is alone, without any correspondence with the life of other species – flowers, plants, fruits – or that of a city, a river, a landscape, a forest?

The spirit of matter is the same everywhere. The religious rites of today appear, thanks to the theatre, as stripped of their superstitious apparatus. The theatre was a social force which knew, by using scientific ritual means, how to act *outside* the consciousness of the peoples that Religion has now fanaticized.

We participate in all possible forms of life. On our human Unconsciousness weighs a thousand-year-old atavism. And it is absurd to limit life. A bit of what we have been and especially of what *we must be* lies stubbornly in stones, plants, animals, landscapes, and woods.

Particles of our past or future *self [moi]* wander in nature where very precise universal laws work to gather them. And it is right that we look for replicas, active, nervous, fluid even, replicas, in all these disintegrated elements.

To be aware of all that which materially unites us to the general life is a scientific attitude that today's science cannot deny since, by its recent discoveries in physics, it reduces the world to being only an energy; and by its latest psychological discoveries it shows us that Man is not an immobilized entity, but that, through the subterranean regions of his consciousness, he participates in the future as well as in the past.

To a greater or lesser degree and according to the strength of his own genius, the Unconscious of each human being possesses archaic images that the ancient races of Mexico clothed with an impenetrable mantle of allegories. At the same time as the *indispensable* social and economic revolution, we are all waiting for a revolution of the conscience that will allow us to heal life.

It is up to modern Mexico to undertake this revolution.

The Occult Forces of Mexico[xlviii]

I have already spoken about the collective hallucination that now reigns throughout France in intellectual circles regarding the Indianist policies of contemporary Mexico.[xlix]

However, it is worth clarifying.

For France, the Revolution of modern Mexico is a Revolution of Man. I mean that it aims at the internal constitution of Man and not merely the constitution of Society.

It is a Revolution against Progress, against the ideas of the modern world, against the scientific civilization of today.

There has been talk of Mexican Indianism, of the present Mexican government's Indianist policy, that is, of a revival of the Indian spirit. And the French youth, animated by an immense desire for universality, was thrilled by the idea that a people was returning to its cultural origins and the sources of the primitive spirit.

But these are false rumors. There is no such true reawakening of the Mexican Indian spirit, and the Revolution on Mexican soil is not as we had imagined in France.

Even if these rumors were false and did not come from Mexico, it would still be very important to know where they came from.

Because the thought of the French youth – and in this case, it could very well be universal thought – wants to return to the sources, to the dreams of the primitive unconscious that enchant it. It wants to turn these dreams into reality, even if the Revolution of Mexico is not Indianist in the exclusive sense that the young intellectuals of France understand as. Because of this, it finds a chance to save life in the buried traditions of Mexico.

A German book is currently enjoying great success in France among the intellectual circles of the youth. This book is entitled: *Sources of Magical Inspiration from the Spirit of Primitive Peoples*.[1]

The French youth wants to understand life and the original powers of life; it wants to penetrate in its totality the fundamental trembling of life.

They imagine that the Mexican intellectuals are heading a similar movement to revive the inspired soul, the magical soul of the ancient Mexican peoples.

And I will say it again: this is not some moral chimaera. If the modern era is experiencing a catastrophe, it is because it has forgotten that there are powers of life hidden beneath the earth. There are other material ways of appreciating the synthetic forces that sustain life.

Although it may seem paradoxical, young intellectuals in France believed that Mexico, which has not renounced the conquests of the modern world, craves new blood and that this blood is none other than the vehement blood of the old peoples, whose eternal strength can be revived under a new appearance.

The French youth has noticed a kind of essential exhaustion in the spirit of the modern world; this world which lost its vigour the day Man turned in on himself and gave up looking for his strength in the diffuse life of the Universe.

In reality, it is nothing other than the magical springs of the Primitive Spirit; that Primitive Spirit in which an uninterrupted exchange of forces takes place between Man and the Universal.

When awake and in contact with everything around him, man draws forces from everything around him, from universal life which completely submerges him.

European culture has never understood how Man can be taken possession of by natural forces, but Ancient Mexican culture has. The French youth is turning to Mexico as a land of resurrection. And, in search of a vigorous idea of Man, they believe that the Mexican Revolution seeks to bring back the old cultural principles.

It is the unilateral development of Progress that has made men lose an essential idea. In Europe, man is bored and gives no explanation for this decline in the desire to live. He needs to understand that by considering life only under its material aspect, he has come to confuse life with merely dead appearances.

Now, a simple glance is likely enough for the world of dead appearances to unravel.

Spain is burning, and the fire in Ethiopia has just been extinguished. On the soil of immense China, war threatens to break out again at every moment; Germany and Italy have fallen prey to a singular order which is nothing but the legalized organization of a disorder. And this order threatens the order and peace of its neighbors, that is to say, the order and peace of Europe. Regarding France, the country is virtually in a state of revolution.

We are as if on the eve of a new Babelian *Confusion of Languages*. Modern man no longer understands himself. Humankind needs a rejuvenating bath. It needs to locate untapped virgin sources of life. And these immutable elements of life are provided by Mexico's timeless culture.

The Mexican soul never lost contact with the earth, with the telluric forces of the soil.

However small my contribution may be, I only ask that I be allowed to contribute to this search for living sources, a search that one day will be transformed into resurrection.

In all points of the Mexican soil where these springs of culture emerge, I ask that I be allowed to discover them, to make them spring forth. I did not come to Mexico as someone curious but as a worker. I understand the wonderous meaning of the current Mexican Revolution. This Revolution, made for the Mexicans, ignites the need for ideals of the whole French youth. However, the French government cannot take an official interest in it. This is precisely why I am asking the Mexican government for the means of action my government cannot provide me.

No one has yet thought of making the Mexican soul's hidden forces manifest, *enumerating* them, and gathering them methodically. I know the names of these psychological forces and want to write a book about them, but I lack certain elements that can only be obtained from the land: the rites, the beliefs, the festivals, and the customs of the indigenous tribes. I will write a book from this research, and this book will serve as propaganda for Mexico.

I ask the Mexican government to let me undertake this work because for me and for the young French intellectuals it would be very sad, very sad indeed if the Mexican Revolution did not answer our hopes. I have no other ambition than to contribute to the glory of the land whose guest I am today.

The Social Anarchy of Artli

It is the social duty of art to provide an opening for the anxieties of its age. The artist who has not tapped into the soul of their age, the artist who is ignorant that they are a *scapegoat* that they must magnetize, attract, let the restive anger of the times fall on their shoulders so that the age may be discharged of its psychological discontent is no artist.

Epochs, like men, have an Unconscious. And *those obscure parts of darkness* which Shakespeare discusses also have their own life, a life that *must be extinguished.*

Works of art serve this end.

The materialism of today is, in reality, a spiritual attitude since it prohibits us from getting at the substance of values which escape the senses, thinking that in doing so, it better destroys them. Materialism calls these values 'spiritual' and disdains them, thus letting them poison the Unconscious of the age. Yet, nothing that reason or the intellect can attain is spiritual.

We possess the means to fight, but forgetting how to employ them, our age begins to perish.

In its beginnings, the Russian Revolution slaughtered many artists, and everywhere, people rose against this contempt of spiritual values that the executions of the Russian Revolution appeared to signify.

But, looking more closely, what was the spiritual value of the artists whom the Russian Revolution gunned down? In what manner did their work, written or painted, bear witness to the catastrophic spirit of the times?

Today more than ever, artists are responsible for the social disorder of the age, and the Russian Revolution would not have gunned them down had the latter grasped the actual meaning of this.

This is because, in every authentic human feeling there is a rare strength which demands respect from all.

During the first French Revolution, they committed the crime of guillotining André Chénier. However, in an age of gunfire, hunger, death, despair, and blood, and at a time when nothing less than the balance of the world was at stake, André Chénier, who was lost in his own meaningless and reactionary dream, could easily vanish without causing any actual harm to poetry or to his times.

And the universal, eternal feelings of André Chénier, if he felt them, were neither so universal nor so eternal that they could justify his existence in an age when the eternal was disappearing behind innumerable private preoccupations. And yet it is precisely art which must seize these private preoccupations and raise them to the level of emotion capable of governing the age.

Nevertheless, not all artists can achieve this sort of magical identification between their feelings and the collective fury of man.

And in the same manner, not all ages can appreciate the social importance of artists and the safeguarding function which they perform for the benefit of the collective good.

The contempt for intellectual values is at the root of the modern world. This contempt hides, in reality, a deep ignorance of the nature of these values. But we should not wear ourselves out seeking to convey to an age which, among its intellectuals and artists, has produced almost nothing but traitors, and among the people has resulted in a community or mass that does not want to know that the spirit, that the intellect, must direct the march of time.

The capitalist liberalism of modern times has consigned to the bottom of its priorities the values of the intellect, and modern man, faced with these few elementary truths, which I have just stated, acts like a beast or a panic-stricken man of a primitive age. And the only way of coping he finds is to wait for these truths to become acts, to actualize themselves as earthquakes, epidemics, famines, wars; that is, he waits for the thunder of cannons.

I Came to Mexico to Flee European Civilization, . . .^{lii}

I came to Mexico to flee European civilization, wrought by seven or eight centuries of bourgeois culture. I came because of a loathing for this culture and this civilization.

Here, I was hoping to find culture in its vital form, but I've found nothing more than the cadaver of European culture, a cadaver which Europe is already beginning to rid itself of. There are those in Europe who have become conscience of it, even some in France. These are revolutionaries, and like them, I am a revolutionary. But we want to present the problem of revolution in its totality and to develop the idea of total revolution fully; hence we believe that Marxism is insufficient.

As Marx conceived it, revolution presents the problem of social revolution mechanically. We believe, however, that a social revolution is only one separate aspect of total revolution, and to consider revolution exclusively through its social aspect prevents us from following it through to its just end.

For us, the problem of the abolition of class cannot be solved by simply substituting one class for another; rather, we must inquire into how man lives to find the reasons for an eternal perversion.

When I am presented with the idea of immediate access to food, I reply that we must, without delay, find the means to make food available to all. But when I hear: 'We must with the utmost urgency find food for all! Then the arts, science, and thought will be able to develop!' I respond, 'No.' Here the problem has been inadequately and clumsily formulated.

There is no revolution without a revolution in culture, that is, in a universal manner, the manner which belongs to us all, to man in general, of understanding life and of posing the problem of life.

It is good to dispossess those that possess, but to me, it is better to remove from each person the taste for property in general.

Culture is eating, but it is also knowing how we eat, and for me, when I think, I eat, I devour and assimilate thoughts. From the outside, I receive the impressions of nature and only then expel them outside as thoughts. It is the same vital act, the same life function that allows me to think and eat. To separate the activity of the body from that of the intellect poorly poses the question of life. The materialist conception of the world separates reality into two functions. The Marxists think we must nourish the body to allow the mind to function freely. This is a lazy attitude, a false notion of human happiness.

All creation is an act of war, a war against hunger, against nature, against sickness, against death, against life, against fate.

I am not for the sybaritism of individual peace. I am not for peaceful arts. To create in peace is a bourgeois attitude, and if I am against all bourgeois attitudes, it is because I have a tangible notion of the spirit of property. Hunger, coldness, love, sickness, and insomnia are not states from which artistic enjoyment can be drawn. Artists should not pay with coldness, hunger and sleeplessness to obtain artistic enjoyment. But I also do not accept that artists possess their own individual satisfactions since I am against the spirit of possession in all possible cases.

There is a war between Marxism and me which rests on a distinct notion of individual consciousness. Marxism claims that it is impossible to directly apprehend consciousness since consciousness is something we have no knowledge of. It wants to force individuals to behave socially in an equitable manner by making them comply with the determinism of facts. In this position, there is a contempt for human consciousness which I share, and with Marxism, I believe that the individual, in all its aspects, is rotten.

I am in favour of binding human consciousness to matter. Yet, I do not believe that an economic analysis of the world, that the reduction of all world problems to a simple economic factor, is a good way to achieve this goal.

Giving everyone the means to eat does not equate to healing the world. Beside the satisfied stomach are the vices of the conscience, the passions, the particularism of individuals, the spirit of madness and crime, and the betrayal of individuals. All revolutions have their traitors, and when, in a proletarian government, a proletariat betrays and becomes reactionary, is it because they have eaten too much or because they have eaten too little? I demand you to respond, and when doing so, do not believe, I beg you, that I oversimplify the question.

Like you, I have a material conception of life and of being. But for me, it does not suffice to feed man; I want to understand how man's life perverts itself. Just as human organs have their diseases, the human consciousness has its alterations, which for me, are diseases. To steal, betray, and deceive are diseases that must be mastered. Hoarding is also a disease. I try to have a clear idea of human biology and want to tackle the question of human biology to prevent my ignorance from one day being able to take revenge.

Marxism has badly presented the problem of human biology. It denies the world of consciousness, whereas I want us to enter iron-fisted into the world of consciousness so that the revolution occurs first within this world. We know that the Marxist position will one day achieve a mechanical explication of consciousness, but before this can come to completion, what new lunacy will have the time to put an end to the revolution? I do not know.

Marxism cannot explain consciousness and refuses to recognize the world of consciousness because it believes that to do so would be to recognize the absolute reality of the spirit. And I say that in doing so, it adopts a spiritualist attitude. Its fear of studying consciousness understood as a world in and of itself ensures that, to speak about the phenomena of consciousness, it has to continue applying an old spiritualist language that insists on a distinction between matter and spirit. Before spirit, the materialist finds himself disarmed. We must enter fully armed into the realm of consciousness; for, although my philosophy of life is anti-materialist, I have a material idea of the spirit. I believe that life exists. I do not believe that life is born of matter, but I believe that matter is born from life.

There is mysticism in Russia. Materialism is a mysticism; anti-imperialism is a mysticism; the struggle against fascism is a mysticism; the destruction of the family is a mysticism. I mean that in these, there is a collection of ideas which, simply by being formulated, provoke a direct action in the mind. The human mind, which moves quickly, adjusts its external actions and behavior in life concerning its ideas. Taking place here is an immediate alchemy of consciousness. Those who betray their ideas are gunned down in the name of the value of these ideas and the human and material activity they entail. This presupposes the admission of a certain kind of life pertaining to consciousness, of a consciousness which forms and deforms reality.

And if materialism did not believe in the life of ideas, it would renounce speech. It is thus first forced to admit that a life of ideas exists and to judge these ideas according to unverifiable laws. It takes this stance since it can have no other and the materialist explanation of the world has left an entire collection of unexplained facts, ceaselessly transforming the world's life.

Shooting traitors is always good, but it is a somewhat simplistic approach. Who would dare say that the spirit of betrayal is eradicated in such a manner? I claim that the spirit of betrayal is curable and material and can be materially affected.

Revolutionary biology has given up on an entire collection of notions within consciousness which also belong to the counter-revolutionary consciousness: the bourgeois idea of man, nature and life.

And that is why I say: there is no revolution without a revolution in culture, that is, without a revolution of modern consciousness concerning man, nature and life.

For me it is a bourgeois idea which separates the problem of life from the problem of culture, the problem of life in man from the problem of life in nature, the problem of the body from the problem of the spirit, and the problems of physiological illness from the problems of mental illness.

The analytical concept of the world is a lie of European culture, a lie of the white mind. Thus, there is no revolution without a revolution against the culture of Europe, against all forms of the white mind, and I do not distinguish the white mind from the forms of white civilization.

The white mind is materialist, but if life is born from matter, fifty thousand years of experience would be needed to draw out life's laws from the experience of matter. If one believes that life governs matter, one can immediately organize matter through knowledge of life.

The bourgeois world has never known life but only ever matter. It is upon a restricted idea of matter that the European world has lived. To know life uniquely through experience is to think that each experience in itself has the value of a particular life, and from this, it follows that each form of art has the value of a particular life: that works of art are worth something in their form and through their form and books through their written content.

There is an idea of capitalizing forms just as there is a capitalist form of life. Like me, you think that culture cannot be found in books, but rather it is a manner of being in life, eating, drinking, sleeping, loving, thinking, dreaming, this is culture, but you have an experiential idea of life, and I would like to know how you reconcile this contradiction.

If you admit that culture is a living thing, you cannot recognize an existence in itself of written forms of life, of painted or sculpted forms, since you think that what lives is not the forms but the life that lies beneath. Hence, as I am, you must be ready to burn all forms which do nothing more than imitate life. Alongside the capitalization of forms, there is the idea of the petrification and conservation of forms, which is also bourgeois.

Because I have a unitary idea of culture, I say that thinking, sleeping, dreaming, eating are all but one and the same thing. All of this is life. But this same taste for collecting, which accumulates pictures and books and amasses stones in museums, is nothing but the impulsion to hoard the bare necessities of life. It asphyxiates the world's production and appropriates for the benefit of a few individuals an entire collection of material riches, the enjoyment of which belongs to all.

If I say that culture, in its reality, is not that which is written, it is because I feel that life moves, and culture is bound to the concept of life as movement. Capitalist Europe believes in the culture of books since, in its conservative soul, it has an idea of life as that which does not move.

I do not believe in a culture of books; I do not believe in a culture of written things, for I consider life in man, free; free, by which I mean never having been bound.

And yet, I wonder what would happen to the materialist conception when science, in its most recent development, teaches us that there is no matter, that all life is energy, and that matter, in its multiple forms, is nothing other than an expression of this energy.

Atoms are examined so that matter might be understood, but under the scrutiny of science, each atom disappears and transforms into a particular version of the dynamism of energy. Human thought is also an energy which adopts forms. What then prevents us from viewing this energy through its particular form and harnessing this intense source of energy?

At the same time as matter, science also destroys space. It is said that space is nothing other than a form that allows the human mind to distribute the diverse forces of energy, allocating to each its place. All major cultures deny this notion of space. For seven or eight million years, China has dealt with the void and asserts that the void can be found at the origin of life. The Mexican cross emerges from the void; it represents an idea of space that emanates from the void. The central point where the completed cross's six branches meet represents the void.

The cross of the Christian religion is the symbol of a human idea; it represents the death of Christ. It is an anthropomorphic idea. The Mexican cross, emerging from the void, shows us how life enters space. It shows how the void of space might provide an opening for life.

III

Franz Hals. Oritz Monasterio. Maria Izquiero[liii]

Franz Hals

Franz Hals was born in 1580, either in Mechelen or Antwerp. Historians do not agree on this point. He spent his entire life in Harlem – the city of images – and died in poverty in 1666.

In any case, he is one of the most authentic representatives of specifically Flemish painting, which, like all the great schools of painting, is both myth and reality. The reality of Flemish painting is represented by the Brueghel brothers, Peter de Hooch, van der Meulen and Franz Hals. The myth of Flemish painting is a myth of strength, fullness, and solar joy. Each painter I mentioned participates more or less in this myth, but Franz Hals especially expresses its social force. His technique is close to that of Rubens with a *je ne sais quoi* that is less luminous, less radiant, less solemn, and perhaps smokier. Smoke. The painting of Franz Hals sinks into the smoke of a hundred pipes, into the sulphurous residues of a great fireworks display on Carnival Day. Brueghel the Elder manifests the obsessions and larval anguish, so to speak, of the Flemish soul pursued by the infernal terrors of its old racial unconscious. Franz Hals embodies the joy of surface, laughter, and noise. The painting of Franz Hals laughs in a range of ashen azure, salmon, acid greens, sometimes screaming pinks and dark garnets that are always similar to clouds of coagulated smoke. This painting style laughs less than that of Jordaens – for these constitute real laughter – but represent powerful images of the life of peasants, kings, nobles, and the bourgeois, with a vague tinge of crepuscular melancholy here and there. Rubens is the jubilation of the flesh, a banquet of voluptuousness in the radiations of great solar magic. Jordaens is the artificial and disguised gaiety, the theatre transported into the familiar life. Franz Hals is the nostalgia of latent pleasure, the desolation of inner life amid dynamic scenes of pathetic outer life. In Franz Hals's paintings, the shadows of an early twilight rise in the heart of the sun of life.

The painting reproduced here is special in that whereas painters usually conceal their technique, Franz Hals shows his, but each visible brushstroke carries the tormented trembling of his life.

A Technician of Stonework: Monasterio[lv]

I apologize to Mexican artists. There is no Mexican art in Mexico. Nowhere have I found that dazzling touch, that unmistakable outpouring that distinguishes the works of a race, which captures the essence of a continent, and on which it is perhaps about time for Mexicans to start developing their own identity after four hundred years of European influence – or, more accurately – *fascinated domination*.

If the 1910 revolution is to have any meaning, it is not only because it has freed the oppressed classes from capitalism's hold, which is still present today, but because it has also awakened the Mexican race's long-forgotten unconscious. However, how many contemporary Mexicans have understood the necessity of liberating their unconscious?

The young sculptor Monasterio demonstrates through his carved stones that he has felt the intellectual oppression of Mexico, and certainly, one feels that something is in gestation in his stone. However, Parisian sculpture's fashionable fine art styles and speculations still taint the *form*.

The Parisian school, however, is more aware than anyone else that the white world's strength has run out and that we must look to the arts of the past for fresh inspiration.

Monasterio's technique is powerful. He makes the stone take flight with vast strikes, discovering under the stone forms of rounded life, bodies without angles where a simple circular force that I am unaware of shines forth. This large and expansive approach, which is more planned than accidental, is something I had already seen in

Parisian sculpture. The influence of African sculpture, particularly some Hittite or Assyrian bas-reliefs, has permeated modern French sculpture to the point of slavish replication.

By imitating this stylization, Monasterio replicates, through Parisian sculpture, the forms of Assyrian stylization: it is a stylization of the second degree. And all modern Mexican paintings and sculptures bear the stamp of this second-degree stylization.

But it must be acknowledged that they enjoy the providential good fortune of having the main sources of all stylizations on their territory. The Toltec, Tarasque, Maya, and Tontoacan sculptors worked with a similar spirit of generous mortification of the forms. By imitating the arbitrary stylization of Paris, Monasterio rediscovers through his old racial unconscious the resurrected *necessity* of this same stylization. This leads to the conclusion that the stylizations of Monasterio, which at first glance seem to be the result of a technical artifice when examined closer, can be seen to be alive with the force of atavistic inspiration which, to a certain extent, justifies them.

There is, without a doubt, a skilled technician in Monasterio, a man who knows full well the difficulty of stone carving and whose works show movingly the feeling of having overcome this difficulty: we feel in his works the *han!* the breath of a man who, by dint of work and pain, has managed to dominate nature but who, through mastering it, wanted to erase all traces of his torture to offer us an agile work that is light, balanced and round. The sculpture opens like the doors of a very old triptych, presenting us with flattened and enlarged forms, the forms of condensed and opulent humanity seeking to spread itself out widthwise. The bodies are heavy and powerful, and as if barely detached and disguisable from the mass of nature that offers them all its force. Yet, thanks to these forms, they could be described as inhuman since they lack muscles and nerves; for they are like the petrified sketches of a form that is *working its way* toward the human, such that they are learning to support the soul.

But it is precisely the confused, material, hardly roughened soul of these bodies which shows that the renowned technician is still looking for inspiration.

It is true that, for the moment at least, we can only see in him a *refined craftsman* of stone; I am still waiting for the poet in him.

When Monasterio shows us an undressed man lying under a tubular factory manifold crushing him, I admire that through his forms, the undressed man evokes in me an almost divine humanity that crawls around in the outlines, in the bas-reliefs and on the facade of certain old Mayan temples, in the vestiges of Toltec or Totonac architecture. It is this racial influence that inexorably shapes Mexican artists. If I have any criticism for them, it is that they do not relentlessly follow the originality of this inspiration with an obstinacy that ought never to tire.

Nonetheless, despite stylization, the tubular factory manifold still stands as a representation of an antiquated symbol, the ideology of *bias*, which has nothing to do with the sculpture itself; it suffices that the reclining man is a proletariat and that shackles enclose his feet.

In my opinion, the problem that arises is not that the proletariat has chains on his feet – chains that must be broken – but that modern man has managed to be the victim of a civilization he invented.

Another sculpture by Monasterio depicts a Venus transformed into a machine. The tragedy is that he avoids the issue of love turned into a machine. He ought to have stopped and insisted on this issue. From a merely human perspective, Monasterio's sculpture of a body almost entirely replaced by tubing is a dreadful torture. Still, he forgot to depict this torture on *a higher level*.

Monasterio calls it a Surrealist sculpture, forgetting that Surrealism never exalted the machine. Surrealism mixed the appearance of machines with all the external appearances of a world that does not deserve to exist. Surrealism looks for a superior reality and, to reach it, destroys forms, transient forms, in search of what, in the language of the ancient Vedas, we call the *Unmanifest*.

The Venus of Monasterio appears to fit in with the machines perfectly. Still, it is important to remember that Futurism is the art form that exalts this same conquest of the machine, speed, the modern world, and all its amenities. Later, Surrealism came to overthrow the kaleidoscope, which was frenetic, pointless, glistening, and had lost its way.

Futurism is thoughtless; one finds only hectic representations of forms, whereas Surrealism seizes *manifest* forms to extract the *Unmanifest*.

The imbeciles said that the Surrealist movement was destructive.

Undoubtedly it was destructive but like any transient and imperfect form, it seeks to go further than these forms toward the occult and magic presence of a fascinating unreality.

Monasterio's intermediary art, whose technique is perfect, lacks this absolute reality. However, he deserves that his art, which is still in full gestation, manages to become fixed and inspired, just as the current Mexican art, which is still larval and impersonal, deserves to find the ancient solar inspiration of the great artists of the past.

P.S. – I am aware that when I mention the impersonality of Mexican art, some individuals may respond, Diego Rivera. It is undeniable that Diego Rivera's frescoes have the beginnings of personality. Apologies, but this embryo is still illiterate. Moreover, it is certain that Diego Rivera lived and worked in Paris. We are far from the powerful solar fulguration of the original Mexican art.

Moreover, it is also clear that Diego Rivera is a materialist. When there is no sense of transcendent power, painting, like other art forms, exhibits a *block* in inspiration and an *inner opacity* to the shapes.

The shapes of Monasterio are closed, yet they are not opaque. One perceives in them what appears to be the hope, call, and echo of a superior light, which, furthermore, has nothing to do with the light that arises from the incomprehensible mysteries of nature – mysteries that the ancient Mexican painters seemed to have scrutinized.

The Painting of Maria Izquierdo^{lvi}

I came to Mexico in search of indigenous art, not the imitation of European art. While imitations of European art in all genres abound, no authentic Mexican art can be found anywhere.

Only Maria Izquierdo's paintings bear witness to a truly Indian insight. In other words, Maria Izquierdo's sincere, spontaneous, primitive, and disturbing painting was a revelation among the hybrid manifestations of current Mexican painting.

However, some clarification is needed: while her painting is spontaneous, it is not entirely pure; here and there, in certain works, the direct influence of modern European art can still be found. This is the danger: as it develops, Maria Izquierdo's pictorial practice is becoming increasingly influenced by modern European techniques and, in some paintings, even by its spirit. And this is all the more regrettable.

The Indian spirit is disappearing; I fear that I came to Mexico to witness the demise of an old world when I thought I saw its resurrection.

My emotion was all the greater to see, in the gouaches of Maria Izquierdo, indigenous characters trembling naked among ruins. They perform a kind of dance of the spectres: the spectres of a life that has been lost.

Additionally, Maria Izquierdo's artwork frequently incorporates European techniques and this civilization's mechanistic culture. However, she uses these European machines and aircraft in the strangest ways.

The hieroglyphic process of the Indians is well-known; it consists in placing in front of the mouth of either a speaker or singer the imaginary sign of the voice or speech. It looks like an inverted spiral staircase, a circular coil of lines. In one of Maria Izquierdo's oil paintings, a naked Indian woman sings in front of an open window while the fumes of a nearby factory rise in spirals in the air, outwardly making circles in front of the Indian woman's mouth. The swirls in this painting are breathing, being the singer's very animated breath. Maria Izquierdo uses the fumes of Europe as if she were going to eliminate them in the painting, which carries the germ of a dual idea. Although she does not fully unravel this concept, she is so strongly influenced by the spirit of the Indian race that she even unintentionally repeats its voice.

I infinitely prefer those paintings without a trace of the European spirit.

In Maria Izquierdo's painting, it is possible to establish innumerable subdivisions that correspond to all the influences that the painter has undergone in the trajectory of her already very important work.

There are hybrid paintings where the racial spirit is preserved, as the one I just discussed.

There are also works of art where the techniques of contemporary European art can be seen clearly and where the mannerisms of Derain, Picasso, Kisling, Coubine and Kremegne express themselves from underneath the surface.

Before my eyes is a beautiful nude sitting on a chair, this artwork contains echoes of the random deformations typical of Parisian art, particularly on the right arm and one side of the back. Yet, Maria Izquierdo discovers a 'necessity' for such deformation in contrast to the Parisian deformations, which are purely arbitrary and have no connection to reality. Some of the tortured, unquiet, and I would even dare to say the metaphysical mind of the Tarascan race has passed over into this deformation. I do not want to sound grandiose, but this arm and this back, which seem to move, and whose parts seem to vibrate to form the arm and the back of a real man, guide us to a crucial geometrical issue. Irresistibly, we think of the architecture of man. And this is the exact goal of painting, of art as viewed from within painting, of art as examined in its purest form: to *inevitably* present before us a crucial issue and to lead us to this issue *dynamically*.

What is so beautiful, so precious in this painting, is the hand. A hand without deformation that has a particular structure to it, and which seems to speak to us like the fork of a fiery tongue. Green: like the darkest part of a flame, which carries all the agitations of life. A hand to caress and make graceful gestures that live formed in the red shadow of the canvas. The whole painting is coloured like the colonial stones of Mexico, the dark colour of fire. All of Maria Izquierdo's paintings develop the colour of cold lava, the volcano's penumbra. This gives it its disquieting character, unique in all Mexican painting; it reflects a world in formation, a world still in fusion. Its ruins do not evoke a world in ruin; they evoke a world in the process of being remade.

Without a doubt, Maria Izquierdo does not escape the reproach of aestheticism; one finds in her work, here and there, undressed lamenting virgins in front of a crucifix. Here is the amalgamated side of the current civilization of Mexico: a type of pagan Catholicism which, behind the Latin cross of Christ, tries to find the cross with the equal branches of the old geometrical palaces of Uxmal, Mitla, Palenque or Copan.

Maria Izquierdo, provided she takes the trouble to appreciate her strength, can revive, in front of a nomadic group of naked, red-faced Indians, the natural cross, the scientific cross of the ancient solar culture that carries its gods as banners.

P.S. – The Indian spirit has its own set of synthetic laws. Its allegorical force is so potent that it unconsciously leaves behind a complete system of the world and its life wherever and whenever it speaks.

Undoubtedly, Maria Izquierdo is in communication with the true forces of the Indian soul. Her drama is carried in her and consists of needing to know its sources better. To safeguard her nature, she must make a considerable effort in favour of purity, and this effort will immediately find its reward. One of Maria Izquierdo's horses immediately evokes all the horses that, during the Conquest, impressed the minds of the old Mexicans. There is totemism in Maria Izquierdo's painting. One can confuse her wild horses with the evil spirits of the earth. And this totemism produces a kind of millennial animism; I also find it in another of her paintings that I remember now: some animals galloping and circulating from one part of the canvas to another, and in the centre, a moon shines like a bull's eye on a wall. For almost ten thousand years, the religion of the bull's eye on the wall has been practiced by a sect of thirty thousand people on the borders of Eastern Siberia, between Russia and Mongolia. Without knowing it, Maria Izquierdo has rediscovered, in this painting, the very soul of a very old human concept.

Maria Izquierdo^{lvii}

Inspiration, that powerful atavism of the race, abounds in the art of Maria Izquierdo. Forms and colours are born under her brush with a kind of inner vivacity that is a mark of her predestination. The characters enter in the form in which they had previously lived; the colours unite with the vibration of the solar spectrum in such a way that they correspond to each other in a more than strange harmony: a red and a blue perform the miracle of sending back to each other their mystery, the mystery born of colour.

Two Notes

Maria Izquierdo's paintings[lviii] prove that the red spirit is not dead: that its lifeblood still bubbles with increased intensity precisely due to this long wait, this incubation, this maceration.

*

The concrete red soul speaks. Without exaggeration, it can even be said to *roar*.[lix] Maria Izquierdo is the only contemporary Mexican painter to have felt that part of the genuine Mexican soul that is furious, whirling, and that sweeps one away and tames lions effortlessly as if by playing. The paintings of Maria Izquierdo transport us to the fantastic era when lions roamed freely within the walls of a sacred city, more animated, intellectual and lucid than humans.

Mexico and the Primitive Spirit: Maria Izquierdo[lx]

If the Sensible is known through objects, objects are known through dreams. In the waking state, everything that exists is dead; objects do not reveal their face. One must be asleep for objects to talk. Only men of the modern era think that the time has long since passed when objects talked without being questioned.

They say that the primitive mind cannot see what *is* because nothing, in reality, exists for it, reproducing what it supposes by brush or pen, and what it supposes is always to the measure of its unlimited imagination. But the imagination is linked to knowledge, and knowledge to Unity. Great imaginations are not those which make the Sensible flow in the multiplicity of its aspects but those which, amid the Sensible, move with that kind of alchemical virtue which belongs to the state of sleep.

For those who understand figures and their peculiar workings, sleep transports us to a time when objects had to talk because man's consciousness when awake resembled that of a muzzled animal.

The primitive, not feeling distinct from what is, cannot believe that something lives outside of him, and he has no sense of ownership; in turn, the things that are cannot have properties that belong to them since they participate in all that is; so that the sense of the eternal altruism of things brings us back to a sense of unity via a kind of alchemical transmutation.

But by saying unity, one also means knowledge, since 'to know' means 'to rise up with'; and in sleep, the figures of moving objects have, with their singular properties, the properties of all other objects. Objects do not form the real but are the real *en voyage*, and in dreams, it is the properties of the objects that travel; and passing their forces from one to another, they teach us the whole of reality.

Thus, with the loss of their singular qualities, objects teach us reality; consciousness, by showing us what is, only kills the things that speak; for it is always necessary that an object cease to be itself to teach us what it is *in reality*. The absurd words of dreams are the words of a reality *en voyage* which has just begun to speak.

To let the self be sacrificed is to enter a whispering reality; it is to allow all the objects of the Sensible to use their properties truly. In reality, the way to engage with all others is to give up single properties. The richness whose qualities the stern consciousness of contemporary man does not suspect is furnished by the primitive altruism inherent to an unrestricted abandonment of oneself.

What does the dream do but take away from the speaking ear the property of receiving something that the sounds of the world give it and, in turn, become capable of emitting concerted sounds?

If a colour, which can evoke a marching army, can also explain how a dream functions, it can also explain how something's extreme particularity might, by that particularity, draw us closer to the unity of what is.

This is how the Primitive broke down the barriers that currently separate us from the knowledge of objects.

If everything is in everything, only the primitive mind has allowed human consciousness to enter into the variety of objects through the metamorphosis of an object.

And the dreams through different times take us back to when, under the shock of human spontaneity, the whole of Nature became bewitched.

We now understand by what mechanism of natural sorcery the so-called primitive or sacred spirit has been able to infuse everything it touches with a world of infinite and contradictory qualities; and how nothing it proposes to us seems in reality what it is.

'This lion believes he is a man,' Rimbaud says, 'but I'll teach him that it's nothing but a yapping pug.'[lxi]

Maria Izquierdo's lions, on the other hand, are like the volcanic craters from which they were born.

In Mexico, there is a plant-principle that lets one travel through reality; through it, an infinitely stretched-out colour spreads itself to the music from which it emerged. This music invites down howling beasts that sound like hammered metal.

I have brought back Maria Izquierdo's gouaches because they at least partially embody this spirit. Of course, this spirit is not pure. If there are still odd pockets of this sacred spirit in Mexico, one should not look for them in the cities since this ancient spirit is Indian, and the modern, mestizo Mexico is doing all its power to eradicate it. Because the mestizos of the cities, who have to struggle between two bloods, are determined to destroy in themselves whatever remains of the red spirit, if they do not kill their red blood first. And all of this results from their sickening fear of not being of their time.

Although of pure Tarascan race, Maria Izquierdo lives in Mexico City. And we know that for Mexicans, all that which is of indigenous culture, all that system of concrete exchanges between man, with his senses turned inside out, and the world injected with forces that cross him from all sides, all that which for some of us is part of effective magic capable of regenerating us, appears to the mestizos of the cities as something as outdated as the myths of ancient Greece, or the magical tricks of an old Babylonian priest.

And the conflict between these influences can be seen in Maria Izquierdo's artwork. Modern painting is sweeping Mexico City thanks to artists like Derain, Masson, Salvador Dali, Chirico and Matisse. Although Maria Izquierdo was Indian, she was concerned about what she might contribute to it.

In her gouaches, we see lost architecture, statues on dead earth, and stones that, in a cellar light, take on the air of human organs.

But here and there, the inspiration of her race is the strongest. It knows what hazardous spells modern painting is made of and that these spells evoke illness, not health. For the painters I have just mentioned, what do they do but mindlessly bring back the forms that rise from their troubled Unconscious?

Certainly, we all feel confused here in Europe that the outer world is over and that it is time to return to something else. What we can no longer find in the waking world, we look for in dreams. And it is by drawing from the life of dreams, where their psychology disappears, that the artists of today bring back those figures, those figure-signs, which have such strange kinships with primitive productions.

They have rediscovered the old spirit, which wants reality to obey the forms of an invented intelligence. And it is man who magically invents them. And the world is what he makes it. They have given up on art that does not serve. But what they find, is that they are the first to claim that they do not understand.

This is because today's art-inspiration is an art that has lost its connection to science. When the ancient artist painted, he painted as one exorcises; and he traditionally knew the gestures that allow one to dissociate from what is. Art was an open hunt whose path was anxiously followed. Every time an artist operated, it was clear that the world did not remain inert, and something of the collective life was whipped up each time.

Now it seems that life has turned, that we have returned to those same regions of consciousness where the mind directly invented forms to refresh reality. But with the past forms, the painters undoubtedly managed to command everything that moves. In contrast, today, these same forms, which the collective Unconscious has resurrected, may exorcise us, but this is because they command us, and we no longer know how to command them.

If, even in Mexico, the primitive spirit is in decadence, it is all too obvious that Indian artists can only be themselves when they are truly inspired by it, instead of, as Maria Izquierdo sometimes does, reproducing European images that are only the reminiscence of the pure forms that revolve in their unconscious.

The Indian spirit, when it survives, obstinately continues to produce those symbols, those form-signs that astonish us.

I have seen in magical dances women with their children in their arms making the gesture of embracing the sun, and they know atavistically the cypher which makes this embrace effective.

Ancient rites and virtues rest in the mountains of Mexico, where man systematically burns the trees in the form of signs. These signs are identical to those used in all traditional magic, and Nature, too, sculpts them into the shapes of the rocks with an obstinate and mathematical rigor as if in response to man's ever increasing cries for help.

Thus, we see that Mexico, when it remains true to itself, has nothing to receive from anyone but has everything to give.

The Indian soul, aware of secret alloys, has no use for these shards of lost reality in which the modern mind anxiously looks for signs of something other. Maria Izquierdo draws on her unconscious race to bring us her lions, which the human soul ought to adore because they are a part of all the Kingdoms in which Nature has observed itself.

Maria Izquierdo's painting explains, with a coloured vibration in which unusual figures plunge, why these objects are made to go together: a man, a horse, a colour, a crater. Objects attract each other due to their particularities; they are only artificially separated. If the last Mexican Indians no longer know how to consider what they possess with the spirit of ownership, if they do not know love in duality, if they no longer see what they are separated from, it is because they have never lost this unique spirit which reduces the world to a single movement; it is because they still have that spirit of death which made the life of ancient Mexico; and that, detached from all accidents, from all the passing aspects of the Sensible, the Indian, who knows how to kill what passes by, rejoins life in its totality.

IV

Havana[lxii]

The Eternal Betrayal of White People^{lxiii}

Tired of being gods, men periodically remember they are men and take to exalting this condition of being a man as if it were superior to the gods'.

I am not sure if it has already been observed that, throughout history, the instant when men recognize themselves as such and nothing more, civilization, in its turn, breaks down as if the support of the exacerbated imagination of men were necessary for the life of the world to live up to its destiny.

The crises of humanism, with remarkable parallelism, always correspond with crises of civilization. The coincidence, it must be said, is strange. When the state of civilization is already desperate, insofar as the idea of culture is facing total regression, men, it would seem, take to speaking of humanism as if man had the power to escape nature, as if the prevailing anarchy had not been caused first and foremost by this narrow and degrading idea of man that, over the centuries, has constantly been camouflaged under the term humanism: from the humanism of the Renaissance to the materialistic humanism of today.

Humanism has always signified that man reduces Nature to his own size and makes 'man' a species of common measure, both physical and moral, to which all things in the world should continually refer.

And this is always the moment when the cult of that specific faculty of man is propagated: reason, and when the human dual perspective of morality and psychology extends its cruelty in all directions.

It is disconcerting to realize that outside of man, morality does not exist and that the materialist point of view that seeks to make human reason a sort of universal master only achieves subjugation, the subjugation of man in front of nature since man is made a slave to his own morality and becomes the prisoner of the taboos he created.

This moral conception of nature and life – according to which man senses his own life as distinct from Nature – corresponds to a dualist notion of things. And humanism has always been born during periods which separate spirit from matter and consciousness from life.

Such a conception is European. Through the centuries, the white world has always made a specialty of this.

Each time there is a religious war in Europe, they are always waged against the eternal unity of the spirit. The Albigensian Crusade was waged against the partisans of unitary life, whilst, during the religious wars in India, it was usually the partisans of the duality of life and of the pre-existence of matter, which invariably finished by being crushed.

Throughout the ages, the Hindu world has manifested an ineradicable belief in the monist conception of man, nature, mind and life.

And the heretical Buddhism was extracted from India by the Brahmans over the course of several wars lasting two to three centuries.

Buddha, the great Buddha, was a traitor. He is considered a traitor in India, and the Brahmans are not afraid to declare it.

It was not during the Renaissance of the 16th century that the unenviable childishness of man's debasement and this anarchic idea of life properly returned. In Greece, too, during the 4th century BC, a school of philosophical sceptics reduced life to the measure of man, qualifying the divine myths on which the authentic Greek civilization built itself as puerile fairy tales; these very same myths whose magical and subterranean life aided ferment the dramas of Aeschylus.

From Aeschylus to Euripides, the Greek world follows a downward curve. What is taught in school is that thanks to Euripides, man could make a more just and rational idea of Nature. The truth is that Euripides destroyed the conscience of nature with his paltry and humanized conception of life. The ignorant speak about the eternal culture of Greece, and they place Aeschylus, Sophocles and Euripides on the same level without understanding the world that separates them; that these three names represent the three stages of a disastrous decline, leading *man to abandon his powers*, from century to century.

The term 'humanism' signifies nothing more in reality than an *abdication* of man. In the ancient myths, man is equal with the Nature that he synthetically understands; but as soon as his analytic spirit is born, man imagines being able to penetrate nature and dissect its secrets in the same way that a surgeon dissects a muscle or separates the organs from a body. Just as the surgeon ceases to listen to the body, man loses contact with Nature, for it is only through instincts that we can penetrate Nature's soul. Say all you want against instinctive knowledge; it is nonetheless instinct that made all the greatest of man's inventions possible. It is man's *limitless imagination* that has always nourished civilizations. Each time the rational mind reappears, this appearance indicates that a world will die. Since there is a defect in the white race, which periodically pushes it to deny that the understanding of the world cannot be limited, and while it perhaps gathers clear knowledge, it is also inauthentic because it is only based on dead objects, the scattered and inanimate parts of Nature.

Today's conflict is between the exact and dead occidental knowledge and the confused but eternally alive knowledge of Oriental monism.

P.S. – We must not confuse the high metaphysics of the Orient, as it has been handed down to us since the 8th century AD, in the written versions of the Vedas (a metaphysics in which spirit and matter form an indestructible whole, reflected in turn, in pieces, in the world of Sangsara, or the realm of universal illusion), we must not, I repeat, confuse this high metaphysical monism with the falsification of it offered to us by the English theosophy of H. P. Blavatsky and Annie Besant. The theosophical school is English and represents the effort made by the intelligence service to poke its nose right into the doctrines of the Orient.

Theatre in Mexico^{lxiv}

There are two, possibly even three, worlds in Mexico.
1. The Indian world, some would claim, is on its way to disappearing. These 'some', finding it disturbing, are the very same who strongly push for its disappearance. Insofar as they have remained pure, the Indians resist the Occidental way of life; which is to say, they refuse to let themselves be industrialized.

During dances recently performed in Pachuca, a small town in Nahuatl, by a group consisting of Nahua and Mixteco Indians, the dancers appeared painted and tattooed in accordance with their traditions. They numbered three thousand in total. The colours they were wearing were outstandingly splendid. And the industrial paint merchants, who expected to do good business, got nothing for their troubles. This is only one of a thousand examples. They danced for 48 hours straight, each Indian rising from group to group, screaming like the animal under whose sign they were born, etc.

For others, the Indian world is strong enough to resist the civilizing thrust of both the United States and Europe, and the number of Indians in certain tribes, far from diminishing, is growing. However, there is no official agreement on this point, and the numbers of pure Indians surviving in Mexico vary from 200,000 to 3,000,000 and even 7,000,000. Some even calculate up to twelve million. These 'some' are those for whom the sense of purity escapes. In any case, the fact that Indians from all parts of Mexico gather periodically to celebrate their gods proves that the Indians have not capitulated. And it makes even more sense when Indians from races that were once rivals gather, as happened in Pachuca, which proves the ranks of the true Reds are swelling.

2. Next to the Indian world, the mix of métis and Creole (these are the descendants of the White people). They are more or less North Americanized and believe themselves to be superior White people. For most Mexican Creoles, the Indians are still barbarians, and their outlandish rites are reminiscences of a bygone era.

3. And finally, there is the Indian soil, which constitutes a world apart without any relation to the world of the métis and the Creole people and which remains related to the Indian world only inasmuch as the Indian world remains faithful to itself. And what I am saying here is not an allegory. The Indian soil has its own life and breath. And you would have to be even less than a man not to notice it.

The soil returns bright columns of dust to the sky, and the sky throws sulphurous thunderbolts upon the earth. The jagged and winding mountain ranges perform a unique dance. Curtains of light spread out. From one minute to the next, the kaleidoscope of the painting changes before our eyes: all is landscape and movement. There is no colour but some coloured vibration which, kilometer after kilometer, meanders into a melody of mirages that the Mexican soil never tires of creating. According to me, such soil, which has not stopped shivering with poetry for centuries, a poetry whose magnetism is still alive, has nothing to do with the civilization trying to rule over it. This soil is a real theatre, and only the Indian traditional rites still represent theatre, not the imitations of dances and shows exported from London and New York music halls.

But, in the same way, that three worlds share today's life in Mexico, there are also three worlds in Mexican theatre.

1. The world of the perpetual theatre of the mirages of the Indian soil.

2. The world of the Indian theatrical rites.

3. The world of the White theatre in Mexico is nothing more than a simulacrum between the real white world of the United States and Europe and the world of Indian theatre.

I have seen here in Mexico, in the Palace of Fine Arts, a mix of Russian, Spanish, Tibetan and Mayan dances.

The Mayan gods danced in a thousand-year-old half-light, the everlasting moon ruling over their primitive emotions, when, suddenly, the present world entered, in the guise of a Creole woman, to defeat the shaky and terrified gods.

The subject of this ballet represents the official spirit of Mexico, which believes it is destroying old superstitions by suppressing

Indian rites, and which cannot see that it is losing that primitive and fertile force simultaneously. A force in which our civilizations must renew their vital energies once in a while.

In a world where the white civilization has failed and is proving toxic in every way, it is no time to destroy the sources that could prevent us from losing hope.

Translated by François Audouy in collaboration with Paul Allain (special thanks to Aimee Quantrill).

La Corrida and
Human Sacrifices^{lxv}

I became friends here in Mexico with a young academic. He's a blue-eyed man, unafraid of yet another paradox. I see in him a zealous Indian supporter and, more than his paradoxes, it's his Indianism which interests me. And even if my friend is a Creole, he possesses, besides his dazzling European brain, a real Indian mystique. Tell me, I ask him, about bullfights and he immediately speaks about human sacrifices. The other day, you drew the strangest of all parallels between those two violent activities.

I will tell you, he replied, about bullfights and human sacrifices, but I will also tell you about the theatre. Indeed, I am not sure if you have noticed how theatrical these two activities are, how they both participate in a remarkable way in that innate need for representation, and representation even to the point of a crime, which is one of the most powerful and active provinces of the human soul.

Just like the ancient human sacrifices, bullfights are theatre, but there is a theatrical element in the *corrida* that no spectator has perceived for a long time. Besides, here in Mexico just as in Europe, everyone has forgotten that treacherous aspect of theatrical representation that turns the spectator into an accomplice and not an actor. Theatre is a superior form of Alchemy. It evokes, we might say, that philosophical part of Alchemy.

According to you, I asked my interlocutor, what is this 'philosophical part of Alchemy'?

He answered (forgetting he was a Creole), when it comes to anything that concerns the Middle Ages, you other Europeans, you wander in the dark. People talk about the night and the darkness of the Middle Ages, but they would be better off talking about that night you were plunged into regarding everything that relates to the Middle Ages. In your eyes, alchemy is limited to that primitive and coarse form of European Alchemy, for European Alchemy is nothing but a degraded interpretation of the low forms of Alchemy. You learnt secrets from the alchemists of the Middle Ages, who were striving to obtain gold, which is where modern-day chemistry stems from; but beyond these alchemists' secrets lays the philosophers' Alchemy, what I called a moment ago the philosophical part of Alchemy; for there is the goldsmiths' gold, and then there is the transcendental gold of the philosophers, and the former is only, we might say, a projection of the powers of the latter in the fields of the senses and of usefulness.

And one could say the same about the theatre. When it comes into action, it takes possession of everybody's brains. It captures the crowd's feelings, decants them, sieves them, and sublimates our basest instincts. A real theatrical presentation, in fact, acts out a crowd's psychoanalysis; it frees them by casting light on them and releases them from their repressions.

It is this psychological usefulness of the theatre that modern crowds have forgotten about. They see in it nothing but a pointless game, whereas a real theatrical representation is an act, an act of a superior kind.

The same goes for bullfights. They contain a theatrical device. It is a drama in three or four acts: presentation, action, and death. The torero plays with death and makes this known. He performs in front of the bull, some kind of death dance. He could kill the bull straightaway. He plays with the crowd's expectations and with the bull's impatience.

However, this is not everything; this is not where the real drama lies. The drama lies in the arousal of instincts. It lies in what is at stake in any performance: the heightening of human feelings. The purpose of a tragedy, when it shows us its passions when it presents its drama to us, is that it externalizes the spectator's passions and their suppressed dramas. It is not only the actor's fate, the fictional character's fate, which is represented on stage every night, but it is the fate of the spectator themselves.

Without this identification, no performance is possible. Regarding the spectator who does not believe that it is they who are at stake, that it is they themselves who are to be sacrificed onstage, it could be said that they are a bad spectator, or that the drama is fake, or that it is detached from human feelings and that the actor is bad.

The wonder of the theatre, my young interlocutor, carried on, and what makes it a superior art form is that the drama, when acted out, does not really happen. The act which is being represented does not happen in real life.

The actor who is about to commit a crime does not commit it in real life; he, therefore, keeps intact those powers which are needed for the crime. The real criminal, on the other hand, is a bad actor from a theatrical perspective, as he ends up wasting his power. The passion he has expelled extinguishes itself by discharging into crime. Therefore, materially it no longer exists. The criminal in real life is an actor, possibly, but a deflated one.

And as far as real life is concerned, the actor is a refined criminal since he has managed to keep intact the malicious powers of his passions.

During a corrida, the crowd's passion reaches a climax, but due to the torero's fatal gesture, that passion performs an act and is thus discharged. You only have to look at people leaving the bullfight: they are the real deflated criminals. Their passion has been satiated by blood. And since blood has been shed in real life, we can say that a useless tragedy has taken place.

The miracle of the theatre, on the other hand, is that it allows powers to be born, that it creates a mysterious alchemy of passions, but far from losing them, it holds them since no act has actually been performed.

I am now coming to the nub of my subject. Just like tragedy, and contrary to bullfights, human sacrifice is an action which conserves.

From the perspective of both the sacrificed man and the crowd, it produces a sort of double transfiguration. The crowd expels its passions, its death passions, its life passions, its cruel vices, its bloody lusts.

The power of all these bad passions reaches its paroxysm, and we might believe that they are lost since blood is shed, because a man is really killed. It's true, but one must not forget that it's not a bull who is sacrificed here but a living man, a thinking man, a suffering man. The bull is just an animal. The man is an animated, trembling spirit. Whereas the bull only gives its blood, the man gives a soul – in other words, it is a thinking act.

During corridas, the sacrificed bull leads the crowd's passion towards the earth, where they lose themselves in its blood. There is a lost power here, an open chain that will no longer close. With a man's sacrifice, through a sort of magical identification, the crowd sheds its own blood, but the sacrificed man gives his soul back to the crowd.

Because – and this is the miracle of the theatre, that it reproduces the tragedy of human sacrifice – the human sacrifice is consensual, willful. The man who is forced to die accepts his death trembling. He turns his death into a useful act; he offers up power by dying. It is power against power, and the lost power is balanced by the power offered. The chain of the act is closed. The double stream of reversed passions, the crowd's passions and those of the sacrificed man have led to a form of magical transfiguration.

Sacrificers and spectators come out; we might say, improved, as they might after the performance of a sacred drama and, exulted too, the victim's soul accompanying them. My young Mexican friend concludes: between the pointless barbarity of the Spaniards' bullfights and the highly subtle magic of the Aztecs' human sacrifices, one reveals the highest degree of civilization, which one eventually results in some kind of gain from a useful act?

Are you able to tell me?

Translated by François Audouy in collaboration with Paul Allain.

Red Paint^{lxvi}

The Red civilization has now been extinct for three or four centuries. And the Red soul has returned underground.

Here and there, however, the Red culture still flickers even if it has been well covered by the additions of European civilization.

Maria Izquierdo's paintings prove that the red spirit is not dead: that its lifeblood still bubbles with increased intensity precisely due to this long wait, this incubation, this maceration.

European art lacks substance. Very skilled technically, masters are well known for the art of accommodating styles, of tying external lines into figures which are more or less copied from the high traditions of ancient art – an ancient art which has been close to and is today Assyrian, Egyptian, Hindu, Chinese, Balinese, Persian but also pre-Columbian – French painters, however, suffer from a lack of inspiration.

And inspiration, inspiration which is a powerful racial atavism, is plentiful in Maria Izquierdo's art. She is not one of those painters famous for their ability to see and paint. Such capacities are minor for a truly inspired painter. It cannot be said about Maria Izquierdo that she paints. Shapes and colours are born under her brush with some kind of intimate liveliness that marks her predestination. Characters appear while keeping the shape in which they lived before; colours unite to the vibration of the solar spectrum so that they answer each other with the strangest of harmonies: red and blue perform a miracle of throwing their mystery at each other, the natural born mystery of colours.

This is no invention of shape; these are no inventions of colour. This is an invention of a past, buried life that finds its shapes, its situations, its space with primitive ingenuity. Maria Izquierdo finds within herself the memory of ancient spells, of ancient dramas, of ancient tragic conspiracies, of ancient massacres.

A fabulous, mythical life streams from her paintings, radiates from her brushes. And this life is gifted with its own natural born shapes, coarse, winged and bold. It unveils naive shapes, the brutal, childish, violent colour that it needs. All the ages of Ancient Mythology are here, along with its tempests, its haunting mystery, its tormented clouds.

Friends of man, tamed lions burst like suns under the ramparts of an enchanted city.

Today's painting needs an infusion of mythical blood. Maria Izquierdo can provide it because, in her paintings of contemporary life (a girl undressing behind an open window), an old ash tree shines with its shapes and colours, while the rays beam out from an oblique sun whose centre is nowhere to be seen.

Translated by François Audouy in collaboration with Paul Allain.

Indians and Metaphysics^{lxvii}

There are more than a hundred Indian races in Mexico living on the margin of modern civilization and who reject that civilization.

They have been rejecting it for four centuries now and throughout that period, our civilization has had enough time to fall to pieces.

If it is true that there are still some Indian tribes that have not mixed with white blood, very few have escaped the utterly utilitarian and self-serving virus of today's world, very few have preserved their rites of Nature in their pure form, as they were originally celebrated.

Materialism, whether scientific or not, as well as the Jesuits, have undermined the very roots of the old Indian beliefs and, by doing so, have cut off – it has to be said – some astonishing communications. Here and there, however, the ancient sun ritual persists in all its powerful and magical liveliness.

When I first arrived in Mexico, the Tarahumara race was presented to me as one of the last to have kept the imprint of the past.

Up in the remotest peaks of the Sierra Madre, in the midst of their multiple horizons that stretch to infinity and occupy vast backdrops of terraced views, the Tarahumaras still perform the metaphysical sun ritual based on the numbers-principles. Through the creative peyote dance, they celebrate Man and Woman's eternal tearing to pieces, whose principles were gathered together by Nature in the guise of the sacred root.

I stayed for some time with this strange and anachronistic race, observing their great virtues, which seemed to me to be the direct consequence of that special anachronism.

Today's white world is not aware that its painful disorder is a civilizational disorder.

Those who have rightly raised the problem of the modern world have been seen as philosophers, in other words, know-it-all-reasoners who no one should listen to; however, the modern world is currently ruled by politicians, and when choosing between an inspired philosopher and an ignorant politician, the world should not hesitate.

White civilization has gone astray, and, to remedy this, the only solutions are archaeological, in other words, resolutely turning our backs on current events and breaking away from them. A philosopher can still say that safely (whereas) a politician cannot because politics has always been nothing but patching up.

As opposed to the ludicrous efforts attempted by the modern world to mend a life that is brutally torn apart, the pure uncivilized Mexican Indians present an image of some kind of peace based on the highest philosophical principles that have remained unchanged for centuries.

Nonsensical and unlikely as it may seem, I have to come up with some truth or other.

It is not just the Indians' life; it is also their race that is based on certain principles. And a race-principle is a race which is closer to certain mixtures, to some physical sources from which the life of Nature began.

A race that has preserved its original cohesion also keeps its physical strength and original acuity, in other words, the strength and intensity of its spirit. These truths may be old-fashioned, but they are truths all the same.

And the strength of the human spirit creates order.

Disorder is always the result of weariness, a sort of dissociation in the principles where the Male and Female of Nature lead a separate, antagonistic, and unthinking life.

These are the simple and original ideas that the life of the Tarahumara race has brought to my mind.

I can say that by going up there where the Tarahumara Indians live, the scale of human life changes completely, and with them, we enter into a truly metaphysical world; because what is at stake here is elevating the level of human thought.

Yes, all races have their own origin; when taken in their strength, those races that have not lost the secret and the extra-human tradition of their origins attest in their conception of life itself to that extra-human origin, showing it in their organization and their order based on the most sublime hierarchies. For them, there is no class system; therefore, the pure Indian races from Mexico continue to reveal to us an image of real hidden fraternities.

Translated by François Audouy in collaboration with Paul Allain.

V

Three Texts on Mexico

Awakening of the Thunderbird^{lxviii}

It is a fact that civilization awakens us. A civilization that has missed its goal is one where men slumber while the sky trembles.

This is why, much more than the Italian–Ethiopian war, what is happening in Mexico is vitally important for civilization.

The Renaissance of an Inspired Race

The Indianist policies of the present Mexican government do not only indicate the awakening of indigenous nationalism.

It is not a state policy; it is the policy of a race. It is not only a nation that is forming but a true civilization that is being born.

A Planned Civilization

This renaissance of civilization is conscious. If one speaks here, in Europe, of a planned economy, then, in Mexico, we can speak about a planned civilization.

It is necessary to insist that this renaissance is not artificial. Mexico is a reaction against Europe. It wants to rediscover its tradition. This does not mean that it is superstitious of the past.

12 against 5

Race there has been conserved at over two-thirds pure and one-third mixed.

On one hand, twelve million Indians live there and await, while on the other hand, half, five million Spanish métis, possess the land, the privileges, and the country's wealth; they hold onto all the reins of power. But the twelve million Indians are terrifyingly strong. They are patient. They are the strength of silence. Their patience is millennial, and the silence of the Indians is terrifyingly eloquent. We seek to describe this silence and to speak about all that it hides of consciousness and lucidity. One day soon, which is ever near, the five million métis will be overturned by this silence.

The Mexican Revolutions

For those in France, it is crucial to understand that the five million Spanish métis, rather than the twelve million pure Indians, are responsible for the impression of new Mexico's instability, insecurity – of a world that is constantly changing.

In Mexico, like elsewhere, it is the White man that perverts the race.

The revolutions in Mexico are a revolt against the state of things. As long as the government does not belong to the true Indian race, Mexico will remain in revolution.

This has already been said, but what has not been described is that the new social state dreamed of by the true Indian race will impose a new spirit.

In the Country of the Blood that Speaks

Once again, the blood of the old Toltec-Maya race has begun to speak.

Under the guidance of its painters, poets and intellectuals, which constitute a living and even virulent elite, the whole of Mexico is beginning a fantastic journey through its own blood.

Because the blood of race speaks, it is by following the inspiration of blood and race that the Mexicans seek to restore their civilization.

If, over the facts and oppressions of history, now is the moment that Indian blood speaks, we propose questioning this blood and deciphering its mysterious language.

Symbolic Journey through Indian Blood

We will search throughout the whole country for the vestiges still alive of the ancient Mayan civilization.

And in all the areas where modern progress has not yet definitively begun, it will be Indian blood itself that will question us.

Persistence of Ancient Magic

And we believe this pure blood to be magical, which is to say, we believe it to be magical.

Mexican Paganism

We will be copiously developing Mexican paganism. We will describe the dance of water, fire, maize and snakes. According to the Mexicans, the Earth has a black sun at its core, and snakes that crawl across the surface of the planet take part in its spirit. These snakes are the subjects of this black sun.

Descent of the Gods

We will make the Gods descend. We will describe them in their day-to-day attitudes. We will say how the Mexicans go about making their Gods appear.

We will describe how the Gods enter, one-half red, the other black with blue-feathered feet and hands, and we will show in the middle of the dances the red of fire, which, through concentric movements, slowly wins out over the blackness of the night until it is eliminated.

And after this, the feathered feet reach up to the high parts of the air as if in a sort of tired theatre. And thus, after some time and patience, the complete myth is finally represented.

The Totemism of the Mexicans

We know more or less this magical process which consists of linking the fate of an individual, a clan, a country, or a sect with an animal's life, the life span of an animal species.

When in Mexico, we will research the persistence of totemism, insisting on the point that Mexico is the only country in the world where this identification was carried out on a large scale, that they took from it a system of life and culture and that their kings, magicians, initiators, priests, having become birds or snakes, figure in the foreground of their rituals, their myths and as a consequence their magic. Not only is totemism acknowledged, it is right out in the open, and right until the hour of the colonial conquest, it constituted the base of Mexican civilization, as a belief it was greatly valued, as a sort of State institution.

Through this identification and symbolism that is not imaginary but real, the Mexicans confess and proclaim the presence of living forces, the violent blood, and the active and magnetic fluids they have drawn out and can still draw out of their exchange with animals.

However, this belief must be collective to be efficient: entire crowds must now and then link together.

It is not certain that modern-day Mexicans can still give birth to a collective totemism.

A Source of Primary Inspiration

Whatever the case, it would appear almost certain that the earth and the air of Mexico possess sources of primary inspiration.

Ancient theogonies prove it with exalted, furious images – the superabundant metaphors of their poems where animals emerge.

The air that skins bodies and forces organs outside of themselves twists the images of the great Mexican poets.

The Secret of Indian Blood

There is the blood that speaks and that which spills, and both are, in reality, the same.

Blood speaks in tortured images, which, in turn, have become torturous.

It speaks of human sacrifices.

All this proves that the ancient Maya knew how to sound for it since it suggests the presence of a hidden force that emerges when summoned.

Mexicans and War

Since we are talking about blood, it would be apposite to speak of war, for we have not yet spoken enough about the fact that in Mexico, human sacrifices were a means of exorcising war, of driving away blood with blood.

Magic and the Theatre

In the face of the havoc that ensues from the modern scientific spirit and the impossibility of starting from scratch, the old civilization of the bird arrives as if all of a sudden, flying over with an intense desire for space and freedom. We will ask the painters, the poets and all types of intellectuals if they do not believe that the theatre, which uses symbols and allows for all types of allegory, is not the last religious and sacred means left to us that might resurrect the magic chain in the crowds, and if it is not the preferred method for the poetic and fluid emission of forces that are contained in metaphors, gesture, signs and allegories.

Mexican Hieroglyphics

An important idea, and one that could be resurrected, is the contempt for art.

In the sculpted and painted imagery of the Mexicans, art does not exist. Beauty neither. This is a European and modern idea. Pleasure in front of beauty does not exist. Forms and lines are not beautiful; they are useful and serve a purpose. But their purpose is neither to eat, drink, nor promote the comforting material commodities of life. They serve to capture forces or to make capturing forces capable. One cannot separate them from magic.

They have lifelike content, which announces a certain science. The Mexican hieroglyphics are at once an art form and a language, and they must be understood in several ways.

Mexico and Justice

All theogonic civilizations had an antisocial idea of justice.

And if there was no theft in Mexico, it was for reasons other than the fact that everyone had enough to eat.

We will try to let it be understood that a social state where the individual is perpetually sacrificed to the masses accepts and rejoices in it.

For the Mexicans, latent heroism stems from contempt for the human persona.

An entire social order follows suit, notably concerning war, property, and love.

The ancient Mexicans did not know individual love, a European and Christian idea.

It is important to know that the new civilization, if it is born, proposes to make love.

Music of the Invisible

We will look for what remains of ancient music in four tones, and which possesses up to sixty million notes.

We will describe the instruments, such as those whose cries reverberated from mountaintop to mountaintop and drowned out the sound of the sea.

A Metaphysical Life

We propose going even further.

We will assess to what extent the nascent civilization insists on becoming aware of the metaphysical spirit behind the myths and the forms of the ancient gods and which living forms it believes it can presently offer.

If the Indian blood means something, it is in its ability to resurrect and capture this metaphysical spirit. Not resurrecting this reality would be like reducing the gods of this old Mexican pantheon and the sun cult to nothing more than a carnival.

Suns turning like vast teethed wheels, the Snake god meandering and its abstract circumferences, the god of Fire, the multiple Water gods, the god of Thunder, the Snake-Woman, the Thunderbird, and the old, old god responsible for all creation, all of this roaring imagery, that drips and slides with the force of a primitive flood, all of this is for us more or less sacred and ritual; it all slips, thunders, rolls and drips in reality. Because the Mexicans did not know of a detached creation, an image contemplated and detached from the mind, as if there were the image on one side and life on the other. Everything that is spirit is blood, which is to say, a living operation. That which is thought is created; actuality and thought communicate, and we might even say that actuality forms thought.[lxix] Out of mind and matter, the Mexicans only knew the concrete – and the concrete never tires of working, of drawing something out of nothing.

Mexico and Madness

For the Mexicans, the madman is he who has found the divine and who has returned to nature; he whose unconscious has discovered the movement of nature. For them, the madman is on the side of truth, and truth, like death, does not scare them.

To finish, we will demonstrate how the ancient civilization of Mexico knew how to tame celestial catastrophes and to recognize in madness and terrestrial crimes the spoken words of a mysterious unknown.

This is the secret behind Totemism, astrology, and bloodshed in a pure, detached, and ritualistic manner that served to save greater blood – the secret from which the Thunderbird will be born again in the discordant and shattering sound of volcanos.[lxx]

Mexico and Civilization[lxxi]

It[lxxii] is perhaps a baroque idea for a European to go to Mexico in search of the living foundation of a culture, a notion which seems to be crumbling here, but I must confess I am obsessed with the idea; in Mexico, connected to the soil and lost in the molten streams of lava, vibrating in Indian blood, exists the magic reality of a culture, that would not require much to materially reignite the flames.[lxxiii] And it is not by chance that speaking of Mexico brings me to the topic of fire. If all of civilization began with fire, then, all Mexican reality is fueled by the notion of fire from below and for life. Fire, the image of civilization, persisted in Mexico throughout the ages and more than just as an image; it actively incorporated itself into the myths through which the civilization of Mexico manifests its vivacity.[lxxiv]

Earth,
water,
sky,
fire,
I invert a sort of hierarchy,
I take the list of elements in order of value opposed to that which Heraclitus gives us;
fire,
sky,
water,
earth,
I take the list of elements that conform to Heraclitus's hierarchy;
I set free this philosophy in action; I reconstitute these four mythical images: and all of Mexico is laid bare between these four images.

Not as they are elsewhere found. I am certainly not remaking an elementary alchemy. Nonetheless, all existent matter passes at a given moment through these four points, the same way that modern physics has discovered energies and principles that describe in a clear language that which the ancient alchemical symbols described;

and to mercury corresponds movement
to sulphur   >>   energy
to salt   >>   stable mass,[lxxv]

in the same way, the activity of the principles manifests itself in Mexico in images of its perpetually renewed powers.

If there is culture, then it is lively and burns organisms. Because there is no culture without the hearth [*foyer*]. Considering what is left of it, the earth and air of Mexico seem to hold the means to endlessly renew the living hearths of culture. This is why the old Maya-Toltec culture might still interest us today.

Although the old Indian race has been driven down and covered over, the steady irrigation of nerves that runs beneath the Mexico of the Conquest is still present today; time has not been able to extinguish it.

And there where material progress, or the conquest of an entirely external perfection, in which neither our human heart nor our human body has been able to participate, where everything that relies on and is *refined* by comforts, to the *exclusion of all internal progress*, there we can say that true culture has ceased to develop.[lxxvi]

As our progress advances, as our hold over external nature wins us measurable deserts, the sky escapes us.[lxxvii] This expression is not just an image without consequences for reality.[lxxviii]

We know nothing of the Mexican civilization – a good occasion, without doubt, to dream hypothetically.

Lawrence had his idea; nothing prevents us from advancing ours, of presenting this idea of a mass culture which cuts down individuals. A Culture which is a vast and tenuous impregnation. Because the danger of myths, no matter how high and tenacious they are, is that they can be snuffed out.[lxxix]

And the Myths of Mexico, as far as we can see, still reignite in us, in each one of us popular ideas, of birds of prey in need of flight.

A civilization where only those deemed cultured participate, which possess an idea of culture as detached, and which anyone can shake up if they read the books, is a civilization that has broken with its primitive sources of inspiration. Since it knows a duality of culture, a dualism in reality, a civilization where the body is on one side and the mind is on the other, and it risks seeing the link that connects these two dissimilar realities become detached in a short period of time.[lxxx]

In Europe, there are no longer myths which collectives can believe in. We are all waiting for the birth of a valid and collective myth.

And in Mexico, insofar as it is being reborn, it could[lxxxi] teach us once again to bring these myths back to life since Mexico is ready awaiting for myths to be resurrected.

But inversely to what has occurred for us, the time has not yet come for them to see their old myths die.

The Spanish Conquest destroyed in the space of a day the Myths of which the forces had not yet finished growing. It extinguished gods that were still being nourished by its subsoil, extinguishing them when they readied themselves to transform. The barbarous and non-evolved appearance of the ancient Mexican pantheon of gods demonstrates that their notion of god had not yet been humanized. These gods I am speaking of, who belong to a culture made of lightening, are of the Maya Toltec culture that has now returned to the soil, that the undergrowth of Mexico absorbed into it from one day to the next, these gods could once again see the light of day because the new Aztec culture did not elaborate on them enough (and if one finds this all to be fantastical, absurd, fanatical, imaginary and unreasonable, then do not forget that I have been careful enough to say at the beginning of this dream, that I am precisely dreaming), I believe that they are preparing themselves to be reborn but of a life even more rapturous and concentrated.

But these god-links of the earth, that exist so that the water and the sky were reconciled, these god-emanations of fire from the earth, and water from the sky, of water taken from the sky that socked the plumage, these gods iridescent with life, quakes of the water of life bent by the wind from the sky, that play in the four sounding corners of the atmosphere, in the four magnetized notes of the sky (and I know that for an Indianist scholar all of this is nothing but waffle and this by the way is what separates all true scholars of life),[lxxxii] these gods are the non-extinguished vibration,[lxxxiii] and which speaks to the ear of the soul, to the heart of the spirit.

These gods are a source of life, evidence that life has not yet been extinguished. A civilization that loses its gods and now only appreciates the material comforts is one where the representations of these gods have lost all contact with the real. However, gods connected to the real are never disposed of their power, that, or life perishes with them. When gods become mere effigies, it is because their symbolism is transitory and illusionary; there is no force human or inhuman that could ever dispose of those gods that signify the created, which are the spasmodic manifestations of being and an aspect of the spasms of this being.

This means that since they were and still are the active natural forces, the Mexican gods never lost touch with their force. – This is what gives us hope in the Mexican civilization. It is an image of the world, the revelation of a system of forces that knew the balance between two worlds (and in their most intimate and hidden relations).

Paracelsus, who is currently having a resurgence, was the first to develop such a tenacious reality concerning the relation between the macrocosm and the microcosm.

Yet the civilization of Mexico lives on a nightmare of organs.

It is a tantalizing idea, fertile in obsessions of all sorts. Fertile and difficult,[lxxxiv] perhaps, but close to all forms of sensibility. Outside of this organic burn, it does not seem that any Mexican individual can escape, or even wake up. We mean that for the Mayan race, whose blood has now begun to speak, the means of existing and re-entering dreams, in an inexhaustible abundance, have the characteristics of a mythological force whose bite has never tired. – Neither the images of their thunderous poems that make their organs blossom on outside and return to them sensibility like a glove, nor the hieroglyphs of their gods, always armed, have exhausted their nervous grip; the same blood continues to speak. We search in vain among us for some poem where blood speaks, some image, some statue where a violent allegory expresses itself. Our world has lost its magic. If magic is a constant form of communication that moves from the interior to the exterior, from actuality to thought, from the thing to the word,[lxxxv] from matter to spirit, we could say that we have for a long time now, lost this form of striking inspiration, of nervous illumination, and that we need to refresh ourselves in these still living and unaltered sources. It is certainly worthwhile to redistribute land and to ensure that wealth can continue to circulate, but we know that in Mexico and while the indigenous people reclaim their lands once dispossessed, an active school is also looking for its gods, and it is not beyond imagination to say that they will rediscover them on earth. We mean that it will be through these black forces that the new civilization of Mexico will begin.[lxxxvi]

Before finishing, we would like to draw a table of the Mexican civilization so far as it can be reconstructed.[lxxxvii]

It is certain that no matter how few we are, in Europe, civilization is currently searching for itself,

And if it is true no trace no conversion to European civilization,

but we should help through attempts to discover their ideal life there

and here all the paper,

but look at Massignon's letter.[lxxxviii]

The Force of Mexico^{lxxxix}

The Hindu Vedas bear witness to the oldest known civilization,
   at first sight, the nascent civilization of man seems to have reached its apogee,
   apart from this, there's a *restlessness* on the outer edges of History, a point where legend and reality, the natural and supernatural, the explained and the unexplained, meet.
   A restlessness that does not translate in the same way for poets as it does for scholars.
   This restlessness recalls Minos, Mycenae, Mitla, and Copán.
   What's there to say?
   This means that Hindu civilization, the Chinese civilization, the Egyptian civilization and the Greek civilization of historical times represent the civilization of humankind, but that in Mycenae, in Crete at the time of Minos, in Palenque, in Mitla and Copán, a disturbing form of humanity seems to have evolved that despairs historians and archaeologists but gives poets a kind of fabulous nourishment.
   This also means that the humanity I am talking about borders on inhumanity in many ways.
   No matter how fabulous and disproportionate it may seem, the Egyptian humanity of epic times remained within the organic limits of man.
   But what is most important, and most worrying if you like, is that we cannot help feeling a kind of strangeness about the actions, the spiritual and physical behavior of the men of Mycenae, the archaic city of Mitla, Palenque and Copán.
   History tells us nothing about them since they lived and acted in ante-historical times. But there is something more.

The caveman is prehistoric, obtuse, psychically speaking, *still to be born*, but in the end; he shares the qualities and embryonic virtues of the human; the other man, that of the evolved but unknown civilizations to which no date can be given, seems to have leapt not only out of history but also out of the human.

Thus, the historical Egyptian civilization and the ante-historical Mayan civilization (although archaeology has made ample use of them) seem to stem from a common philosophical basis.

And yet the Egyptian civilization exudes security and balance. In contrast, the multiform civilizations of Mitla, Palenque and Copán exude balance in terms of form. Still, in terms of soul, origins and the foundations of inspiration and living creation, they exude the unusual, the insecure, and *restlessness*. There is something, one might say, unnatural about them.

You could say that this is a vision, a poet's perception, that, in reality, corresponds to nothing.

Yet dates have been set for the Egyptian civilization, but no date can be set for the Mayan civilization, which seems to share an identical inspiration.

No one has yet agreed on whether it goes back 10 to 18, 25 or 50,000 years.

There are myths in the epic history of Egypt. Still, they are refined, balanced myths that fit within the framework of man's reason, within the dimensions and perspectives of his *organic humanity* . . . .

*

France is an old capitalist, bourgeois country.[xc]
I came here to escape the capitalist spirit of France.

The life of the world is sick. But few people understand what I mean when I speak of the life of the World, and of a collective illness that would affect it.

Yet this is a fact of vital essence and importance.

*

Children's solutions: simple solutions.[xci]
With the highest culture goes stench, and the spirit walks with filth: F. d'Assise. Benedict Labre. Hermits. Clean people benefit for

a time from the macerations of the afflicted filthy. To clean is to dull. Everything pure smells bad. Culture functions well enough without civilization. And too much civilization is *destructive* of high culture. But civilization is the fruit of a distant and soon lost culture.

There are primitive Forms of civilization, which are then the organization of the immediate fruits, taken as they are, of a culture, still grasped in its Principle.

*

Hygiene and asepsis,[xcii]
the modern science invention that has made the wonders of surgery possible, this is nonsense: it is not a question of saving men, but of saving the right men.
There's no universal plan in the thinking of all these carers of *meat*.

*

This is not a written theatre[xciii]
but ciphered, in signs, in hieroglyphics as in the origins.
A theatre that wants to make Man into a great statue and an Elemental force, with the technical and organic use of breath
    over and behind the head
    at chest level
all the kabbalistic numeration of breath
NAMES.
    And shouting through anger
    action through anger
and what religions term Gods, which we must reclaim from religion to use as true Men do. –
religions have their rites,
we have the theatre from which religion emerged,
since there is a force there, why neglect it? Why lose it?
I looked for a language more essential than the language of words, and which, passing through the whole organism, brings Man back to the central unity of these forces
    and what they understand

but where do words come from if not from a dance of speech, and the rational meaning only came afterwards? It is a language essentially made for the masses.

The cultural idea is as follows:
Take back from religious rites the forces they hold and release them naturally onto the masses through theatre

NOTES

i *The notes below are for the most part translations of the notes produced by Paule Thévenin for* Messages Révolutionnaires. *I have altered them to make the most sense to a reader who is fully aware that the translator is not Thévenin. Since Thévenin's notes are rarely surpassed in quality, translating these notes into English was the best way to transmit the work Thévenin undertook for* Messages révolutionnaires, *supplying the reader with notes about each text. For the newly found texts, notes have been added. I have also added notes where the text was an addendum to a* Tome *of the Œuvre Complètes. In the revised and augmented version of* Tome VIII, *there are additional notes where Thévenin has indicated slight alterations to the transcriptions. These have not been translated because the French transcription has not changed since. The style of the notes has been amended to that of Bloomsbury Publishers. Lastly, all translation of Artaud's own notes and other texts in French have been translated into English so that the reader might navigate this additional material more easily.*

The title, *Messages révolutionnaires*, was given by Antonin Artaud in a letter to Jean Paulhan on 21 May 1936. Here, he announced that a Mexican publisher had offered to publish a volume of 'all' [his] texts on the indigenous culture of Mexico. According to the information we have been able to gather, in October 1936, to provide Artaud with some money for his return journey, Mr José Gorostiza, who became Director of the Nuclear Energy Commission in Mexico after the Second World War, acted as an intermediary to negotiate the acquisition of the rights, to publish the texts that had appeared in Spanish translation in the Mexican press since April 1936.

Circumstances did not favour this publication. It was not until 1962 that Luis Cardosa y Aragón began a systematic search of the publications that had appeared in Spanish during his stay in Mexico, compiling them in a volume entitled *México* (Universidad Nacional Autónoma de México). Most of the texts that make up *México* appear in *Messages révolutionnaires*, except four texts: the

'Montagne des Signes', which opens *D'un voyage au pays des Tarahumaras*, the 'Pays des Rois-Mages', 'Une Race-Principe', and the 'Rite des rois de l'Atlantide', which has a more appropriate place in the *Tarahumaras*. Unfortunately, for a large part of these texts, the French original has not been located, and we have had to resign ourselves to making them known in a 'retranscription' from the Spanish, which Artaud had foreseen since, in the same letter of 21 May 1936 to Jean Paulhan, he wrote: 'This book will be entitled in its entirety *Messages révolutionnaires*, and it would nonetheless be necessary for Paris to have these Messages translated into French to make them known.' (V, 205)

ii　These three lectures were given, under the patronage of the Department of Social Action of the National Autonomous University of Mexico, on 26, 27 and 29 February 1936, in the Bolivar Amphitheatre of the National Preparatory School. They were announced on Sunday, 23 February, in *El Excelsior*. The article briefly summarized Artaud's literary, theatrical and cinematographic activities. Information was provided about the 'Théâtre de la Cruauté', obviously taken from the brochure *Le Théâtre de la Cruauté* (Second Manifesto), published in 1933 by Denoël. It ended with the programme of the three lectures, which Artaud most probably wrote for the Mexican press. Fortunately, we have the original French text of these three lectures, which Artaud sent from Mexico to Jean Paulhan. Artaud arrived in Mexico City on 7 February 1936, so there is every reason to believe that these three lectures must have been partly written by then. He must have begun this work a few days before his departure and continued it during the crossing: 'Surréalisme et Révolution' refers to a tract dated 5 January 1936, and he had embarked from Antwerp on the *S.S. Albertville* on 10 January.

The conference programme is as follows:

– *Wednesday, 26 February, 7.30 pm,*
　1. – *SURREALISM AND REVOLUTION.*

In this lecture, we will describe the new state of mind of the French youth. We will say what they think about both Surrealism and the Revolution. We will endeavour to define what the social state of mind of Surrealism is, and we will say how it has evolved. We will talk about Karl Marx and Lenin's historical and dialectical materialism. We will try to define the situation of French intellectuals regarding the proletariat and the social problem as a whole. We shall describe young people's anxiety in the face of all the questions shaking the world.

To conclude, we shall say what the new idea of man is emerging in France. A certain humanism that is no longer that of the sixteenth century.

> *– Thursday, 27 February, at 7.30 pm,*
> *2. – MAN AGAINST FATE.*

By fighting against the ancient idea of fate, expressed in terrible and humiliating myths, modern man is becoming aware of his strengths and wants to show that he no longer fears fate. We will examine examples from medicine, philosophy, physics, art and theatre.

> *– Saturday, 29 February, 7.30 pm,*
> *3. – THE THEATRE AND THE GODS.*

Contrary to the idea taught in schools that the theatre is the offspring of religions, we shall try to show, by means of examples, that religion is born from the ancient and primitive rites of the theatre. In a theatre conceived in this way, man was not separate from nature, and the so-called gods were the subtle natural forces that modern man could still harness. This will allow us to talk about the gods of Mexico and compare them with those of the Vedas, the Zend-Avesta, etc.

From these three lectures, we will draw a new idea of culture, as the French youth believes it should be constituted in today's world. Dramatic interpretations of scenes from tragic theatre will accompany these lectures.

iii   Text based on the typed copy sent by Artaud to Jean Paulhan; this copy is nine pages long and contains major corrections and additions by Artaud himself.

iv   This pamphlet, written by Georges Bataille, ended with the following words:

The following will speak on Sunday, 5 January: /Georges Bataille, André Breton, Maurice Heine, Benjamin Péret:

As the victories of Nazism spread and the progress of fascism in France intensified, the movement Contre-Attaque: Union de la lutte des intellectuels révolutionnaires *was founded to contribute to a sudden development of the revolutionary offensive. Without renouncing any available means of action, it is in particular by expressing new ideas and directives, responding to new, unforeseen circumstances, that* 'Contre-Attaque' *will try to contribute to the decisive struggle whose only possible goal is the seizure of power.*

In addition to the Surrealists, other sympathizers, intellectuals and former Surrealists signed the manifesto of this movement, whose main driving force was Georges Bataille. However, the Surrealists withdrew before the first (and only) *Cahiers de Contre-Attaque* appeared (May 1936).

v   Alexandre Saint-Yves d'Alveydre (1842–1909). The complete title of the work is published with the subtitle (posthumously): *Les Clefs de l'Orient / les Mystères de la Naissance / les Sexes et l'amour / les Mystères de la Mort / d'après les Clefs de la Cabbale orientale / Avec sept dessins de Richard Burgsthal.* (Published by 'Les Amis de Saint-Yves' at the Librairie hermétique, 4, rue de Furstenberg, Paris, 1910.) In the last chapter, 'Les Mystères de la Mort', we find the passage to which Artaud refers: 'Let us dare to say it: yes, the Father is destructive, by the very fact that he is the creator. Sometimes a terrible God, always Almighty, not over Nature, but through it and over the sons of Man and through them.'

vi   It should be noted that the exact date of 10 December 1926 given here by Antonin Artaud as the date of his expulsion from the group by the Surrealists does not coincide with the date given on several occasions: November 1926 in *Au grand Jour*, November 1926 in the history that opens the special issue: 'Surrealism in 1929', of the Belgian review *Variétés* (June 1929).

vii   The document does indeed say *Egyptian Book of the Dead*, although it is Thibet that has just been named twice. As Artaud underlined these words in ink, it cannot be a copyist's error. By this, he must have meant the anteriority of the *Ancient Egyptian Book of the Dead*, which he attached more importance to than the *Tibetan Book of the Dead* (cf. in *Tome VIII*, letter of 26 August 1934 to Henri Poupet).

viii   An account of this lecture that appeared in *El Universal* on 28 February 1936 suggests that Antonin Artaud improvised during his lecture. The report states that Antonin Artaud had mentioned Soupault, who was not named in the text sent to Jean Paulhan. The author of the note, who was impressed by the lecturer's gestures, attitudes and intonations, cites the following sentence as having been particularly applauded: 'The French youth sees corpses in those who only write propaganda.'

ix   Text based on a typed copy of six pages sent by Antonin Artaud to Jean Paulhan and with corrections in his own hand. Under the title, 'El Hombre contra el destina', the Spanish translation was published in *El Nacional* in four issues: on 26 April and 3, 10 and 17 May 1936. Luis Cardosa y Aragón reprinted this translation in *México*.

x   The error in the copy that Antonin Artaud had not noticed, which gave the centrifugal force the movement that goes from the outside to the inside, and the centripetal force that goes from the inside to the outside, has been corrected.

xi   The report on the conference, published in *El Universal* on 29 February 1936, states that Artaud illustrated it with examples drawn from philosophy, medicine, theatre and art.

xii   Text based on a ten-page typed copy sent by Antonin Artaud to Jean Paulhan, with corrections in his own hand. Copy signed and dated by Antonin Artaud: Mexico, 29 February 1936. The first part of 'El Teatro y los Dioses', translated by José Ferrel, appeared in *El Nacional* on 24 May 1936. The following note accompanied this publication:

> *From who knows where, a sensitive, intelligent, lively and cultured man has arrived in Mexico City: Antonin Artaud, whose activities immediately made him famous among our writers. He supports several theories that he expounded in a series of lectures that should have been listened to more attentively and deserve to be published. One of them,* 'L'Homme contre le destin', *was serialized in this supplement's* 'Théâtre et Cinéma' *pages. Today, in the* 'La Vie littéraire' *section, we present the first part of* 'Le Théâtre et les dieux', *which will be of interest to all friends of* El Nacional.

xiii   Already quoted, but reversing the order of the suns, in *Héliogabale ou l'Anarchiste couronné*. VII.

xiv   It was through the work of George Soulié de Morant that the techniques of Chinese therapeutics were revealed. The success of this therapy had struck George Soulié de Morant during a cholera epidemic that raged while he was French Consul in Shanghai in 1932. Artaud contacted George Soulié de Morant to try acupuncture treatment, hoping to relieve his ailment.

xv   Allusion to the 'International Writers' Meeting for the Defence of Culture' organized in June 1935 by the French Communist Party, which Antonin Artaud could not attend. (Cf. VIII, 278)

xvi   The point here is an analogue of the centre of the void. In the lecture found by Alberto Ruz Lhuillier, Artaud specifies that the central point represents the void. (See VIII, 242)

xvii   In this second part, we have collected texts by Artaud that appeared in the Mexican press in 1936. With the exception of 'Théâtre

d'après-guerre à Paris', they appeared in the daily *El Nacional*. They
were all gathered in *México* by Luis Cardoso y Aragón, except the
'Lettre ouverte aux Gouverneurs des États du Mexique'. The original
French text has not been found. This posed the problem of
'retranscription'. These publications were Antonin Artaud's main
source of income in Mexico, and he had to get his copy in on time.
Translations of the Spanish texts were often made at the last minute,
around a coffee table whose napkins could even be used as paper,
and immediately affixed to the newspaper. The various translators,
Samuel Ramas, José Ferrel, José Gorostiza, Luis Cardoso y Aragón,
Xavier Villaurrutia and Enrique O. Henriquez, did this work out of
friendship so that Artaud could extend his stay in Mexico.

Thévenin writes the following justification for the transcriptions:
*Therefore, some errors may have crept into these translations,
which the transcription may reflect.*

*Nonetheless, the texts represent such a special stage in Artaud's
work that restoring at least their content was justified. Indeed, it
would be futile to believe we could find the writing conveying it.
For some texts whose French original has been found, we have been
able to compare the Spanish translation with the original itself. In
some cases, the Spanish text follows the French text fairly closely;
in others, it departs from it to such an extent that if we translate it
literally, the sentences we end up with have nothing to do with
Artaud's original sentences. There's neither a cut-up version nor an
abundance of notes to work with. In the latter case, the French text
may have been reworked after being dictated to the translator.*

Since the first French edition of Messages révolutionnaires, *
another text from this period has been found by its translator,
Alberto Ruz Lhuillier: 'Je suis venu au Mexique pour fuir la
civilisation européenne.' This has been added at the end of this
section.*

*In addition, the Spanish texts from México have been collated
with that of the first publications in* El Nacional *or the* Revista
de la Universidad de México. *This operation brought to light
several errors which had occurred when the text was transferred
to the volume and which have been corrected in this edition; for
some, moreover, simple common sense had already led us to
rectify them.*

xviii Text of a lecture given on 18 March 1936, in the salons of the
Alliance française (a venue that explains its panoramic and
informative character), under the presidency of the French
ambassador to Mexico, Henri Goiran. The conference had been
announced in the press under the title, 'Le Théâtre après la guerre en

France' (*Excelsior* and *El Universal*, 18 March 1936), but it was under the title, 'El Teatro de postguerra en Paris', that it was published in June 1936 in the *Revista de la Universidad de México*.

xix Lugné-Poe created August Strindberg's *Créanciers* on 21 June 1894, at the Nouveau Théâtre (revived at the Maison de l'Œuvre on 22 October 1920); Ibsen's *Les Revenants* premiered at the Théâtre Libre on 29 May 1890; Ibsen's *Hedda Gabler* was first staged in Paris by Albert Carré at the Théâtre du Vaudeville, on 17 December 1891; the play was later revived by Lugné Poe, who had placed the Maison de l'Œuvre under the sign of Ibsen: Ibsen cycles were regularly staged, alternating the Norwegian playwright's works. Crommelynck's *Le Cocu magnifique* premiered on 18 December 1920 with Lugné-Poe and Régina Carnier. Gabriele d'Annunzio's *La Gioconda* (first performed in 1905) was revived on 15 January 1923, with Suzanne Desprès as Silvia Settala.

xx *Le Désir*, by Jóhann Sigurjónsson (1880–1919), was staged in 1920 at the Comédie des Champs-Élysées by Arsène Durec (1880–1930). Arsène Durec started out working with Sarah Bernhardt. He later turned to directing. His ingenious lighting design helped pave the way for Copeau and the Vieux-Colombier.

xxi *Le Paquebot Tenacity*, by Charles Vildrac, 5 March 1920; *Saül*, by André Gide, 16 June 1922; *La Nuit des Rois ou Ce que vous voudrez*, by Shakespeare, 19 May 1914 (revived 22 December 1920); 'La Princesse Turandot', by Carlo Gozzi, 2 February 1923; *Les Frères Karamazov* (adaptation by Jacques Copeau and Jean Croué, based on Dostoyevsky) premiered on 5 April 1911 at the Théâtre des Arts, revived at the Vieux-Colombier on 28 November 1921; *La Mort de Sparte* by Jean Schlumberger, 23 March 1921.

xxii In fact, Dullin had taken part in the premiere of *Les Frères Karamazov* at the Théâtre des Arts on 5 April 1911, directed by Arsène Durec; in March 1913, he reprised his role, but at the Vieux-Colombier.

xxiii *Les Amants puérils* by Crommelynck (who played one of the roles, with Marguerite Jarnois playing Marie-Henriette), 14 March 1921; *l'Annonce faite à Marie*, by Paul Claudel, 2 May 1921; *Le Simoun*, by H.R. Lenormand (with Dullin in the role of the Prophet and Firmin Gémier in that of Laurency); 21 December 1920, was the first performance of the Comédie Montaigne Gémier.

xxiv *L'Occasion*, by Mérimée, 2 March 1922, Salle Pasdeloup; *L'Avare*, in the repertoire since the company's foundation, was revived at Théâtre Montmartre on 18 October 1922; *La vie est un songe*, by Calderon, 20 June 1922, Vieux-Colombier; *Antigone*, by Sophocles, freely adapted by Jean Cocteau, 20 December 1922; *Volpone*, after Ben Jonson, by Stefan Zweig and Jules Romains, 23 November 1928; *Les Oiseaux*, by Aristophanes, freely adapted by Bernard Zimmer, 26 January 1928; *La Paix*, by Aristophanes free adaptation by François Porché, 22 December 1932.

xxv In fact, Jacques Copeau's first performance at the Fondation du Vieux-Colombier on 23 October 1913, included: *Une femme tuée par la douceur*, by Thomas Heywood, adapted by Jacques Copeau, and *L'Amour doctor*, by Molière. Molière's *Les Fourberies de Scapin* premiered at New York's Garrick Theatre on 27 November 1917, at the same time as Jacques Copeau's *Impromptu du Vieux-Colombier*. An error must have crept into the Spanish translation, which lists the last play in the Vieux-Colombier cycle as *La Célestine*. However, this cycle ended on 15 May 1924, with a final performance of *La Maison Natale* by Jacques Copeau, which premiered on 18 December 1923. This is what Artaud says two paragraphs above: *The theatre was closed, and the company dispersed. It was not until September 1929 that the Compagnie des Quinze was formed, which moved to the Théâtre du Vieux-Colombier, whose stage had been restored by André Barsacq.*

xxvi Here, too, the Spanish translation is surely at fault. The translator understood this: Jean Cocteau recounted in his book *Anecdotes*. However, no work by Jean Cocteau bears this title; on the contrary, it was in *Picasso* (collection 'Les Contemporains', Paris: Stock, 1923) that he recounted Picasso's invention of the set for *Antigone*:

> *On the eve of the dress rehearsal of Antigone in December 1922, actors and author were seated in the Salle de Atelier, at Dullin's home. A canvas, the blue of laundry balls, formed a rocky background for the Crèche. There were openings to the left and right; in the middle, in the air, a hole behind which the role of the chorus was declaimed with a megaphone. Around this hole, I had hung masks of women, boys and old men, painted by Picasso, and those I had made from his models. Beneath the masks hung a white panel. It was a matter of clarifying on this surface the meaning of a makeshift decor that sacrificed accuracy and inaccuracy, equally costly, to the evocation of a hot day. Picasso walked back and forth. He began by rubbing a stick of sanguine on the board, which, due to the unevenness of the wood, became a marble. Then he took a bottle of ink and traced motifs to masterly effect. Suddenly, he blackened a few voids, and three columns appeared. The appearance of these columns was so sudden, so surprising, that we applauded. Once in the street, I asked Picasso if he had calculated their approach, if he was going towards them or if he had been*

surprised by them. *He replied that he had been surprised, but that one always calculates without knowing it, that the Doric column results, like the hexameter, from a sensitive operation, and that he had perhaps just invented this column in the same way as the Greeks had discovered.*

xxvii *Maya*, by Simon Gantillon, 2 May 1924, Studio des Champs-Élysées; *Le Dibbouk*, by Shalom An-Ski, French version by Marie-Thérèse Koerner, 31 January 1928, Studio des Champs-Élysées; *Crime et Châtiment*, adaptation by Gaston Baty, adapted from Dostoyevsky, 20 March 1933, Théâtre Montparnasse.

xxviii During the 1921 season, Rolf de Maré's Ballets Suédois created *Les Mariés de la Tour Eiffel*, by Jean Cocteau, music by Les Six, set by Irène Lagut, costumes by Jean Hugo.

xxix This happened during the Ballets Russes premiere of *Romeo and Juliet* at the Théâtre du Châtelet in May 1926, with music by Constant Lambert and set design by Max Ernst and Miro. It was the best organized Surrealist scandal: the noise of the whistles with which the Surrealists demonstrated their disapproval was so loud that Constant Lambert, who was conducting his own work, was forced to stop, as the musicians could no longer hear each other, and the dancers could only regulate their steps to the rhythm of the music and the dancers could only adjust their steps to the whistles. There would have been two banners flown, one black and one red. On one, *Vive Sade!* on the other, *Vive Lautréamont!* The leaflets thrown from the galleries bore a text entitled 'Protestation', signed by André Breton and Louis Aragon, which had also been published in *Révolution Surréaliste* (no. 7, 15 June 1926).

xxx *Liliom*, by Molnar: 8 June 1923, and *Celui qui reçoit les gifles*, by Léonid Andréiev (revival), 26 December 1923, at the Comédie des Champs-Élysées; *Les Ratés*, by H.R. Lenormand, 22 May 1920, Théâtre des Arts; *Le Baladin du Monde occidental*, by John Millington Synge, was first performed by the Pitoëffs on 10 April 1919, at the Salle communale de Plainpalais in Geneva, and it is possible that Artaud attended a performance during his stay in Switzerland; *La Puissance des ténèbres*, by Tolstoï, 26 February 1921, at the Théâtre Moncey; Chekhov's *Oncle Vanya*, 15 April 1921, at the Théâtre du Vieux-Colombier, on loan from Jacques Copeau. *R.U.R.*, by Karel Tchapek, directed by Komisarjevski, 26 March 1924, Comédie des Champs-Élysées. *R.U.R.* stands for *Rossum's Universal Robots.*

xxxi There is an obvious error in the Spanish text, the literal translation of which is: 'in a scenic arrangement by Poe'. It is quite possible

that Artaud, as was his wont, dictated the text of his lecture in
Mexico City and that the person transcribing made an error in
hearing Poe where Antonin Artaud should have said Copeau.
Indeed, Maeterlinck's *Pelléas et Mélisande* had been premiered by
Lugné-Poe on 17 May 1893 at the Théâtre des Bouffes-Parisiens,
the premiere that led to the founding of l'Œuvre by Lugné-Poe,
Camille Mauclair and Édouard Vuillard, Maeterlinck's drama was
subsequently staged by Jacques Copeau on 10 February 1919, at
the Garrick Theatre in New York, in the fixed but adaptable scenic
setting established by Louis Jouvet and Jacques Copeau, realized by
them in 1917, at the start of their stay in the United States, and
reconstructed in Paris in 1919, when the Vieux-Colombier
reopened.

xxxii Alexandre de Salzmann gravitated towards Gurdjieff, where René
Daumal had met him. His influence was instrumental in the split
between Daumal and Roger Gilbert-Lecomte. Daumal's
conversations with Salzmann form the theme of *La Grande
Beuverie* (Paris: Gallimard, 1938).

xxxiii Ferdinand Bruckner's *Les Criminels* was first performed by Pitoëff
at the Théâtre des Arts November 1929; *Le Mal de la jeunesse*, first
performed in French by Raymond Rouleau at the Théâtre du
Marais in Brussels on 20 April 1931, was revived by him at the
Théâtre de l'Œuvre on 28 December 1931.

xxxiv Letter published in *El Nacional* on 19 May 1936, under the title
'Cana abiena a los Gobernadores de los Estados'. Republished
in the *Revista de la Universidad de México* 22 (no. 6, February
1968).

xxxv Text published in *El Nacional*, 28 May 1936, under the title, 'Bases
universales de la cultura'.

xxxvi Allusion to Keyserling's *Psychoanalysis of America*, translated from
the original English by Germain d'Hangest (Paris: Stock, 1930).

xxxvii Text published in *El Nacional*, 3 June 1936, under the title, 'Primer
Contacta con la Revolucion Mexicana'. We thought that this text
might be the conference that Artaud was to give to the Ligue des
écrivains et artistes révolutionnaires, a conference that he
announced to Jean Paulhan in a letter dated 26 March 1936,
specifying that he would speak against Marxism and in favour of
the Indian Revolution. According to the recollections of Luis
Cardosa y Aragón, this conference never took place. This does not
mean that the text was not prepared.

xxxviii To our knowledge, 'Un athlétisme affectif' was not published in
this journal. As for the paper Artaud gave at the Congrès de Théâtre

d'Enfants, he most probably read the 'Théâtre de Séraphin' there, the corrected text of which was sent to Jean Paulhan in Mexico at the end of March 1936.

xxxix Text published in *El Nacional*, on 7 June 1936, under the title, 'Una Medea sin fuego', on the occasion of the performances at the Palacio de Bellas Artes in Mexico City by the Margarita Xirgu Spanish Theatre Company of Medea, a Spanish adaptation of Seneca's tragedy by Miguel de Unamuno. Margarita Xirgu was born in Catalonia in 1888 and died in Montevideo. She began her career performing in Catalan, and always paid close attention to elements of native culture. She left Spain in 1936 and had a considerable influence on the development of theatre in South America, both as an actress and as a director.

xl   Text published in *El Nacional*, 17 June 1936, under the title, 'Pintura francesa joven y la tradicion'.

xli   Text published in *El Nacional*, 28 June 1936, under the title, 'El teatro francés busca un mito'.

xlii   The group *Octobre* (The October Group) was formed in 1932 from a split in the Prémices troupe, which was made up of amateur actors (mostly workers, employees, etc.), whose shows were usually performed at events organized by trade union federations or workers' groups. Supported by Vaillant-Couturier and Léon Moussinac, the part of the troupe that wanted a more topical and combative approach called on Jacques Prévert. It took the symbolic name of *Octobre*. Between March 1932 and May 1935, the October group staged the following shows: *Vive la presse*, by Jacques Prévert, with the collaboration of Jean-Paul Le Chanois; *Choeur parlé sur la Commune*, by Jacques Prévert; *Choeur parlé sur les Nègres de Scotsborough*, by Lou Tchimoukow; *La Bataille de Fontenoy*, by Jacques Prévert; *Choeur 'Actualités'* (Hitler's seizure of power), by Jacqùes Prévert (another chorus by Jacques Prévert called on all those who still had their heads on their shoulders to come to the defence of Dimitrov, Thaelman and their comrades who were on trial), *Choeur contre la guerre*, by Lou Tchimoukow, and *Choeur 'Citroën'* (relating to the 1933 strike), by Jacques Prévert; *Les Fantômes*, by Jacques Prévert; *La Famille Tuyau de Poêle*, by Jacques Prévert; *Rien ne vaut le cuir*, by Lou Tchimoukow; *Un brave homme*, by Pierre Prévert and Lou Tchimoukow, *Choeur* 'Actualités', by Jacques Prévert, and *Vie de famille*, by Jacques Prévert; *Choeur sur les gueules noires et les gueules cassées*, by Lou Tchimoukow, and *Choeur 'Yen a qui . . .'* by Lou Tchimoukow; *Choeur 'Il ne faut pas rire avec ces gens-là . . .'*, by Jacques Prévert, and *Marche ou crève*, by Jacques Prévert; *le Palais des Mirages*, by Jacques Prévert; *Mange ta soupe et tais-toi*, montage by Jacques Prévert; *Réveillon tragique*, by Jacques Prévert; *Chorus on the Common Demands of Workers and Peasants*, by Lou Tchimoukow; *Suivez le druide*, revue bretonne by Jacques Prévert. Lou Tchimoukow directed all of these shows. There were also choreographic interludes by the dancer Pomiès based on material by Jacques Prévert. Among the actors in the troupe were: Suzanne Montel, Gisèle Prévert, Agnès Capri, Ida Lods, Sylvia Bataille, Germaine Pontabry, Gazelle Duhamel, Raymonde Leduc, Bussières, Brunius, Guy Decomble, Yves Allégret, Jean Ferry, Marcel Duhamel, Max Morise, Marcel Jean, J.-A. Boiffard, Paul Grimault, Maurice Baquet, Maurice Hiléro, Henri Leduc, Fabien Loris, Roger Blin, Mouloudji, Gilles Margaritis and others. At the time, and this was a rare occurrence for a theatre company, none of these names appeared on a poster or in a programme. In 1933, the October Group had been crowned best amateur troupe at the Moscow Theatre Olympiad, to which the Workers' Theatre Federations of many countries had sent their representatives. The play Antonin Artaud is referring to here is *La Famille Tuyau de Poêle*, by Jacques Prévert. The *Tableau des Merveilles*, adapted by Jacques Prévert from Cervantes, was revived in May 1936 adapted by Jacques Prévert from Cervantes, which had been staged by Jean-Louis Barrault in 1935, with members of the October Group. This was their last show.

xliii We know that Artaud praised the first show directed by Jean-Louis Barrault: *Autour d'une mère*, a play by Jean-Louis Barrault based on William Faulkner's novel *Tandis que j'agonise*. Decoration and costumes by Félix Labisse. Songs by Tata Nacho. Performed by France Igné, Marthe Herlin, Génica Athanasiou, Dina Germain, Georges Lenoir, Paul Higonenc, Jean Dasté, Baby Guy, Yves Gladine, Leblanc, Michel François, Régis, Arsène Arcadelt and Jean-Louis Barrault. Performed at the Théâtre Montmartre (Salle de l'Atelier) on 4, 5, 6 and 7 June 1935.

xliv Published in *El Nacional*, 5 July 1936, under the title, 'Lo que vine a hacer a México'.

xlv Published in *El Nacional*, 13 July 1936, under the title, 'La Cultura eterna de México'.

xlvi Published in *El Nacional* 25 July 1936, under the title, 'La Falsa Superioridad de las elites'.

xlvii Text published in *El Nacional*, 1 August 1936, under the title 'Secretos eternos de la cultura'.

xlviii Published in *El Nacional*, 9 August 1936, under the title, 'Las Fuerzas ocultas de México'.

xlix Here Artaud is refering to 'First Contact with the Mexican Revolution'.

l This title has been literally transcribed from Spanish. But the Spanish translation was certainly an approximation, as we are not aware of any work translated from German with a title of this kind. We thought it might be Sigmund Freud's *Totem and Taboo*, which bears the subtitle: *Interprétaiion par la psychanalse de la vie sociale des peuples primitifs*, and one of its chapters is entitled, 'Animisme, magie et toute puissance des idées', but the first French-language edition dates from 1924, which contradicts the 'current' edition and, it seems, Artaud would have named the author and not just indicated a German book, as if it were about an author whose name he had forgotten or whose fame was not yet considerable.

li Published in *El Nacional*, 18 August 1936, under the title, 'La Anarquia social del arte'.

lii This text was found in 1975 by Alberto Ruz Lhuillier, currently director of the National Museum of Anthropology in Mexico City and sent to Thévenin on 2 December 1975 by Luis Cardosa y Aragón, who intends to add it to a forthcoming reprint of *México*. The copy sent to Thévenin has the following title: 'Conferencia de Antonin Artaud en México' (1936) / (diccada a Alberto Ruz enfrancès y craducida par éste al castellano). The translation was simultaneous: Alberto Ruz Lhuillier clearly remembers working at home and transcribing directly into Castilian the text that Artaud dictated to him in French, probably from notes, which may explain why the original French text has not been preserved.

As for the conference in question, Alberto Ruz Lhuilier, like Luis Cardosa y Aragón, has no precise memory of it. Neither of them remembers whether it was given anywhere at the time or whether the Spanish text was published in the Mexican press. Many lectures were planned during Antonin Artaud's stay in Mexico, but never came to fruition. For example, in a letter dated 21 May 1936 and addressed to Jean Paulhan, mention is made of a series of lectures. *In addition, a group of Israelites has asked me for a series of lectures on the old magical cultures of Mexico, where I will unite their strength with the Kabbalistic culture of the Jews, which modern Jews have betrayed.* Did this project come to fruition? Would this conference be part of this series? We don't know. In any case, there is no mention of the Kabbalah.

liii Apart from 'Franz Hals', a text about a Flemish painter, which Artaud was led to write in Mexico by chance, and above all because he needed to make a bit of money, the texts gathered here are about Mexican artists.

liv This text appeared in *Boletin mensual Carta blanca* 3, no. 5, July 1936), an advertising bulletin distributed by Brasserie Cuauhtemoc, S.A., opposite a portrait by Franz Hals. This portrait, which probably depicts a man drinking beer, once belonged to the Pani collection, acquired almost entirely by the Mexican government, and is now probably in the Mexico City Museum (information supplied by Luis Cardosa y Aragón) – text reprinted in *México*.

lv This text was written during Antonin Artaud's stay in Mexico and given by him to the sculptor Ortiz Monasterio. Enrique O. Henriquez's translation was not published at the time; it was only published in 1968 in *Revista de la Universidad de México* 22, no. 6 (February 1968).

lvi Text published in *Revista de Revistas* August 1936 under the title 'La Pintura de Maria Jzquierdo'. Republished in *Revista de la Universidad de México* 17, no. 12 (August 1963) by researcher Luis Mario Schneider. In 1954, through the journalist Pierre Joffroy, who had visited her at our request during a report he was doing in Mexico, Maria Izquierdo had sent Thévenin two typed copies drawn up in 1936, bearing two successive versions of the translation. We have taken into account the first version (which differs in places from the published version, which is identical to the second version) because it must be a more literal translation, following more closely the original French text. This text was written for an exhibition of Maria Izquierdo's paintings and Eleanor Boudin's sculptures held at the Wells Fargo Building (Madera 14, Mexico City) from 10 August 1936.

lvii A typed copy of the Spanish translation of this short note was sent to Thévenin by Maria Izquierdo via Pierre Joffroy. It was probably published on the occasion of the exhibition held in the Wells Fargo Building in one of the daily newspapers in Mexico City, but Maria Izquierdo did not give us a precise reference for it.

lviii Sentence published in the catalogue of the exhibition held on 10 August 1936 in the Wells Fargo Building. Maria Izquierdo had sent Thévenin, through Pierre Joffroy, a typed copy of the original French text (reproduced here) and its Spanish translation.

lix Original French text. Written by Antonin Artaud on a strip from the newspaper *El Nacional* kept by Maria Izquierdo. Recopied by Pierre Joffroy from the original.

lx   On his return from Mexico, Antonin Artaud worried about finding a gallery to organize an exhibition of the gouaches by Maria Izquierdo that he had brought back to Paris. To give this project a better chance, he wrote this text, which was published in *L'Amour de l'art*, no. 8 (October 1937), a review then edited by René Huyghe. The text, which appeared in the section, 'Peintres contemporains étrangers', was illustrated with four reproductions of Maria Izquierdo's gouaches: *Cimetière* (1936), *Danse magique* (1936), *Prosternation* (1936) and *Architecture* (1937). The exhibition took place in January 1937 at the Galerie van der Berg, 120, boulevard du Montparnasse.

lxi   Paraphrase of this passage from *Une saison en enfer*, in 'Alchimie du Verbe':

> *It seemed to me that everyone should have had several other lives as well. This gentleman doesn't know what he's doing: he's an angel. That family is a litter of puppy dogs. With some men, I often talked out loud with a moment from one of their other lives. – That's how I happened to love a pig.*

lxii   These five texts were rediscovered and published in a variety of Cuban journals, including *Cartles* and *Grafos*. See n. lxii and Introduction, 'Artaud's Messages'.

lxiii   On his way to Mexico, Artaud had made a stopover of about a week in Havana, arriving there on 30 January 1936, and arriving only on 7 February in Mexico, in La Vera Cruz. We knew from Alejo Carpentier that he had given several articles to Cuban periodicals: *Carteles* and *Grofos* [Thévenin was led to believe this was spelt *Grapos*], in order to make some money. The fact was also confirmed by a letter found in the archives of Gallimard editions (V, letter of 27 June 1936, to Gaston Gallimard, 207). The steps taken to find these texts met with considerable difficulty. The only one for which Thévenin obtained a result appeared in *Carteles* on 1 November 1936, under the title, 'La Eterna Traición de los Blancos'. A first copy, typed by the Biblioteca nacional José Martí, and was communicated to Thévenin in 1971, when the first edition of this volume had already appeared. A transcription was given as an addendum to the 1973 reissue. Subsequently, the Biblioteca nacional José Martí was kind enough to send a photograph of the *Carteles* columns reserved for the article. We were then able to observe that slight errors had occurred in the typed report. The transcription in this volume has been revised from the photographed document.

lxiv   Text originally published as, 'El Teatro en Mexico', *Grafos*,
       Havana, June 1936.

lxv   Text originally published as, 'La Corrida de Toros y los sacrificios
       humanos', *Grafos*, Havana, July 1936.

lxvi   Text originally published as, 'Pintura roja', *Grafos*, Havana,
       September 1936.

lxvii Text originally published as, 'Los indios y la Metafísica', *Grafos*,
       Havana, December 1936.

lxviii A succession of fortunate events enabled Thévenin to find this text
       by Antonin Artaud, which appeared in the *Bête noire: Artistique et
       littéraire* published on the 1st of each month (no. 6, 1 November
       [1935]). Thévenin had already examined the most complete
       collection of this journal, edited by Maurice Raynal and Tériade,
       which is available for public consultation, at the Bibliothèque
       littéraire Jacques Doucet, but it contains only four issues. However,
       La Bête noire seems to have appeared eight times. Thévenin then
       learned by chance that Madame Ballard had deposited the archives
       of Cahiers du Sud to the Archives of the city of Marseille. There
       are very few documents relating to the relationship between
       Antonin Artaud and Cahiers du Sud, but it is fortunate that the
       letter of 15 December 1935 to Jean Ballard (VIII, 416) survived. It
       is through this letter that we came to know of the existence of 'Le
       Réveil de Oiseau-Tonnerre' ... A second chance event occurred; a
       friend of Artaud kept eight issues of *Bête noire*. Without him, this
       text would probably have been irretrievably lost.
          We have respected the many subtitles it contains. They are
       surely by Artaud, who conceived of this text, as he wrote to Jean
       Ballard, as a *programme*.

lxix   The last words of this sentence and the following two sentences
       are taken from what Thévenin assumed to be a fragment of a
       letter to the Minister of National Education (VIII, 293, and 396
       n. 1). This does not invalidate our hypothesis: insofar as Antonin
       Artaud wrote to the minister to obtain a mission order, he had
       undoubtedly conceived his letter as a program.

lxx   The last words of this text are also taken from the last preserved
       paragraph of this same fragment of a letter (VIII, 295).

lxxi   Manuscript of ten numbered pages which were part of the
       documents found by Mr Berna (VIII 352 n. 1). The text was
       published by him in *Vie et Mort de Satan le Feu* (Arcanes, 1953),
       then taken up in the *Tarahumaras* (Éditions 'l'Arbalète', Marc
       Barbezat, Décines, Isère, 20 November 1955). If the end of this
       text is only barely sketched, the beginning was worked on by

Artaud: it has many erasures; entire passages have been deleted. The Arcane edition takes absolutely no account of the passages deleted by Artaud. For the long crossed-out passage reproduced in the note below, Mr Berna inserted it into the body of the text, justifying his intervention with the following note, which is as fanciful as it is embarrassing: all this passage, from 'If I speak' to 'to a . . . universal symbols' seems crossed out, then restored, then crossed out and restored again. It has been included. The same goes for the deleted passage, reproduced and inserted in the text, accompanied by this note: The passage from 'No year' to 'two European countries' is contradictorily scrubbed out and reinstated. On the other hand, the last paragraph was arbitrarily discarded by Mr Berna, who also discarded the end of the manuscript. This edition comprising of no notes, adopted the following approach: it published the crossed-out passages in a smaller font, prefacing them with the indication that Artaud had deleted them; it also discarded the end of the manuscript. Despite this, it was not for nothing that Artaud had renounced certain passages of his text, passages which he perhaps intended to take up later in another form. The text gains considerably in force and intensity with their deletion, which we have respected. The manuscript, which was put on the bookstore market almost immediately, had at one time Louis Broder as a buyer, and thanks to his kindness, we were then able to collate our copy with the autograph Artaud was thinking, even before his departure, of the lectures he intended to give in Mexico City (letter of 6 August 1935, to Jean Paulhan, VIII, 288) and very probably written in Paris some of those which he then delivered, days after his arrival. This text is undoubtedly a first conference project.

lxxii 2. Two paragraphs preceding this have been crossed out:

> *It is justice to today's France, to us all, that we have never been as concerned with culture as we have in the last months that have just passed.*
> *The word, in any case, obsesses us, proof, no doubt, that the thing is beginning to be terribly lacking.*

lxxiii *materially* replaces *actually* or *really* ('actuellement'), crossed out.

lxxiv There are two paragraphs that follow, crossed out:

> *If I speak to a Frenchman about fire, he will evoke in his mind the image of a Swedish match, a gas fire, or if he has any imagination[a], that of a factory fire, of a ship burning at sea. Talking to him about the fire from heaven will be tantamount to making him believe that*

I have read holy history and that I burn with an anachronistic and backwards-looking fire as far as antiquities are concerned. He will find it hard to imagine that fire from heaven can be called lightning. But to make him pass from the concrete to the abstract, and to make him suddenly admit the notion of a kind of higher flame which corresponds to the idea of a more precious and rarefied thunderbolt, is an effort that goes beyond his understanding. Ordinary or extraordinary, and in the most favourable case, he will baptize with the name of a hypothesis impossible to verify; my notion, however very classic, of a kind of elementary Akara, *of primordial substance inflamed and which participates at the same time in the spirit of fire and of the soul of light.*

But let's move on. I mean by this that, having emerged from its psychological particularism, it is impossible to interest the great French masses, who nevertheless claim to be educated, in an idea that is even slightly abstract, in one of those abstract and collective ideas through which all true culture begins and without which it cannot last. What I want to affirm is that there is no valid civilization and culture without the accepted idea of a myth which continues to vivify the organisms by allowing them a constant magnetic confrontation[(b)] *with universal symbols.*

(a) It is precisely *imagination* that we find in the manuscript.

(b) *constant* replaces *powerful*, previously crossed out.

lxxv   These three lines replace this, crossed out:

Mercury,   sulphur,   salt
movement   energy   masse

lxxvi   This manuscript is obviously a first draft, an abandoned project, certain elements of which will be used in the 'Eternal Culture of Mexico'. The corrections must have been made during the writing itself and not during proofreading, which would explain the especially elliptical shape of this paragraph where one can suppose that a word was forgotten at the end of the sentence, a verb that would have the meaning of *predominate*.

lxxvii   *gains us measurable deserts* replaces *gains us spread out space*, crossed out.

lxxviii There follow, crossed out, five paragraphs, one of which has just been sketched out:

No year has been richer in disasters, unforeseeable catastrophes, which our disorders seemed to call for. Disorders or excess. False rigor. Order-disorder. Social abuse. Latent madness.

It is abusively and only verbally that one can dare talk about civilization in Europe again.

However excessive it may seem, all true civilization has its bases in astrology, and it knows how to limit its catastrophes and its crimes to a minimum: for truly civilized people, there is no fatality, no destiny, and the destiny not only of individuals but of peoples is written entirely in the sky. It is not for nothing that the Mayas of Mexico keep the secrets of destiny buried in their hieroglyphs, where modern science has found the bases of marvelous astronomy.

The sky has never been able to overwhelm the truly civilized, those who have always known how to make allowance for celestial catastrophes and who also knew how to set about locate (limit) and foresee them.

It is not insignificant, among other things, to note that the 2 European countries [. . .]

lxxxix Following this, crossed out: *And we would look for. And one would search in vain here, in France, for the myths of the masses around which [. . .]*

lxxx This crossed-out sentence follows: *And these bonds are detached on the day when strength is exhausted.*

lxxxi We find '*for*' ('pour') in the manuscript; either Antonin Artaud forgot to trace the last letters of 'pour[ra]', or he failed to repeat the verb . . . *as it is reborn, reborn to teach us again* . . .

lxxxii *true* ('vrai') replaces truly ('veritable'), crossed out.

lxxxiii *extinct* replaces *muffled*, crossed out.

lxxxiv *difficult* replaces *hard*, crossed out.

lxxxv *from the thing to word* replaces from *word to the thing*, crossed out.

lxxxvi The use, on several occasions, of *over there*, which designates Mexico, clearly indicates that this text was written in Paris.

lxxxvii The last lines of the manuscript, in a writing that is increasingly difficult to read, which we transcribe as it is, clearly show that Artaud did not consider this text to be finished and that he reserved the right to develop it, which he thus noted in abbreviated form. The mention, *all the paper here* could even suggest that he had already written another text that he wanted to use as the end of this text.

lxxxviii Louis Massignon's papers have been kindly searched by his son; no letter from Antonin Artaud has been found.

lxxxix A green folder originally intended to contain the manuscript of the *Cenci* is part of the Guy Lévis Mano bequest to the Bibliothèque nationale, Reserve des imprimés. On the first page, we read Antonin Artaud's handwriting, which he crossed out with zigzag pencil lines *Les Cenci ou le crépuscule de la famille* 4 acts, 10 tableaux by Antonin Artaud after Shelley. We have yet to find any mention of this subtitle anywhere else. The folder was later reused to store a file relating to the Mexican period, consisting mainly of newspaper cuttings articles by Antonin Artaud published in Spanish during his stay in Mexico, his presence there and his various public events. Plus, three handwritten sheets, the contents of which we published here. We do not know why the folder was given to Guy Lévis Mano. We can suppose that Antonin Artaud, wishing to bring these texts together under the general title of *Messages révolutionnaires*, was unable to complete the project in Mexico City, thought it might be of interest to him and entrusted him with this file, so that he could form an opinion. Three handwritten sheets are attached. Those bearing the 'Force du Mexique', Artaud must have had them with him during his expedition to the Tarahumaras. In addition to the text, the first page contains notes written in all directions, in the upper, lateral and lower margins, sometimes the page, and generally wherever space had been left blank. Various violet, black and blue inks are used, as well as pencil. One gets the feeling of notes taken, in the moment, for memory. Some of these notes, will be used in the texts about the Tarahumaras. Here are the most characteristic:

> *Rake fire thunder / rain mix souls / inversion fire.*
> *Death that does not want the child / Laocoon / man at the window.*
> *Insexual principle of reproduction.*
> *Division of sound.*
> *man with lance – yellow green cross / his wife yellow braid / green pendants.*
> *Arachnaean death before the Elephant of Nature.*
> *The other side of and the place of Mexican magic / New forms of theatre in France / The Indians did not suffer in vain* [**no doubt draft articles or conferences**].
> *When this world did not exist Nature still existed; it already existed / everything came from God and is with Him; when God withdraws, Nature disappears.*

xc These few lines are written on the back of page 1 of the 'Force du Mexique'. They are all crossed out with horizontal lines.

xci   Still written on the verso of page 1 of the 'Force du Mexique', but
       on the page turned over and between the crossed-out lines of the
       previous fragment.

xcii   Written across the margin (bottom half) of page 2 of the 'Force du
       Mexique'.

xciii Certain elements of this text are reminiscent of 'La numération
       kabbalistique du souffle', 'Le cri par la colère', 'Un athlétisme
       affectif' or 'Le Théâtre de Séraphin' and may be contemporary
       with them. But it may also date from when Artaud was preparing
       his lecture entitled 'Le Théâtre et les dieux'. What is certain is that
       he had the leaflet bearing its name in Mexico City because he used
       the back of it to write the first page of a draft letter to the Mexican
       Minister of National Education of Mexico, M. Vella on 11
       February 1936.

BIBLIOGRAPHY

Works in French by Antonin Artaud

Artaud, Antonin. *L'Arve et l'aume suivi de 24 lettres à Marc Barbezat*. Paris: L'Arbalète, 1989.

Artaud, Antonin. *Cahiers d'Ivry: Volumes 1 and 2*, edited by Évelyne Grossman. Paris: Gallimard, 2011.

Artaud, Antonin. *Les Cenci*. Paris: Gallimard, 2011.

Artaud, Antonin. *Héliogabale ou l'anarchiste couronné*. Paris: Gallimard, 1979.

Artaud, Antonin. *Messages révolutionnaires*. Paris: Gallimard, 1971.

Artaud, Antonin. *Le Moine (de Lewis)*. Paris: Gallimard, 1966.

Artaud, Antonin. *Nouveaux écrits de Rodez*. Paris: Gallimard, 1977.

Artaud, Antonin. *Œuvres*, edited by Évelyne Grossman. Paris: Gallimard, 2004.

Artaud, Antonin. *Œuvres complètes*, Volumes I–XXVI. New edition revised and augmented, edited by Paule Thévenin. Paris: Gallimard, 1984–2011.

Artaud, Antonin. *L'Ombilic des Limbes suivi de Le Pèse-nerfs et autres textes*. Paris: Gallimard, 1968.

Artaud, Antonin. *Pour en finir avec le jugement de dieu*. Paris: Gallimard, 2003.

Artaud, Antonin. *Suppôts et Suppliciations*. Paris: Gallimard, 1978.

Artaud, Antonin. *Le Théâtre et son double*. Paris: Gallimard, 1964.

Artaud, Antonin. *Les Tarahumaras*, edited by Paule Thévenin. Paris: Gallimard, 1971.

Artaud, Antonin. *Van Gogh: Le suicidé de la société*. Paris: Gallimard, 2001.

Translated Works by Antonin Artaud

Artaud, Antonin. *Anthology*, edited and translated by Jack Hirschman. San Francisco, CA: City Lights, 1965.

Artaud, Antonin. *Antonin Artaud: Selected Writings*, edited and with notes and introduction by Susan Sontag and translated by Helen Weaver. Berkeley and Los Angeles, CA: University of California Press, 1976.

Artaud, Antonin. *Artaud 1937 Apocalypse: Letters from Ireland*. Translated by Stephen Barber. London: Diaphanes, 2019.

Artaud, Antonin. *Artaud the Mômo*. Translated by Clayton Eshleman. Zürich: Diaphanes, 2019.

Artaud, Antonin. *Artaud on Theatre*, edited by Claude Schumacher with Brian Singleton. London: Methuen Drama, 2001.

Artaud, Antonin. *Collected Works: Volumes 1–4*. Translated by Victor Corti. London: John Calder, 1968–1999.

Artaud, Antonin. *Heliogabalus or, the Crowned Anarchist*. Translated by Alexis Lykiard. London: Infinity Land Press, 2019.

Artaud, Antonin. *'Here Lies' preceded by 'The Indian Culture'*. Translated by Clayton Eshleman. Zürich: Diaphanes, 2020.

Artaud, Antonin. *The Human Face and Other Writings on His Drawings*. Translated by Clayton Eshleman. Zürich: Diaphanes, 2022.

Artaud, Antonin. *Radio Works: 1946–48*. Translated by Clayton Eshleman. Zürich: Diaphanes, 2021.

Artaud, Antonin. *A Sinister Assassin: Antonin Artaud's Last Writings, Ivry-sur-Seine, September 1947 to March 1948*. Translated by Stephen Barber. London: Infinity Land Press, 2022.

Artaud, Antonin. *Succubations & Incubations: Selected Letters of Antonin Artaud (1945–1947)*. Translated by Peter Valente and Cole Heinowitz. London: Infinity Land Press, 2020.

Artaud, Antonin. *The Theatre and Its Double*. Translated by Mark Taylor-Batty. London: Bloomsbury, 2024.

Artaud, Antonin. *The True Story of Jesus-Christ: Three Notebooks from Ivry (August 1947) by Antonin Artaud*. Translated by Peter Valente. London: Infinity Land Press, 2023.

Artaud, Antonin. 'To Have Done with the Judgment of God, a radio play (1947)'. In *Antonin Artaud: Selected Writings*. Edited and with notes and introduction by Susan Sontag and translated by Helen Weaver. Berkeley and Los Angeles, CA: University of California Press, 1976.

Artaud, Antonin. *Van Gogh, the man suicided by society*. Translated by Paul Buck and Catherine Petit. London: Vauxhall&Company, 2019.

Artaud, Antonin. *Watchfiends & Rack Screams: Work from the Final Period*, edited and translated by Clayton Eshleman with Bernard Bador. Boston, MA: Exact Change, 1995.

Works Cited

Artaud, Antonin. *Antonin Artaud to Alexis Carrel, 15 April 1936*, GULLACC, box 70, section 18–5, file 11–1.

Artaud, Antonin. *Messaggi rivoluzionari.* Translated by Marcello Galluci. Milan: Jaca Books, 2021.

Artaud, Antonin. *Mexíco*, edited by Luis Cardosa y Aragón. Collection 'Poemas y ensayos'. Mexíco: Universidad nacional autónoma de México, 1962.

Artaud, Antonin. Bibliotèque natiuonale de France (BnF), Paris, Collection Serge Malausséna, 'Sort à Hitler'.

Bakunin. Mikhail. *Statism and Anarchy.* Translated by Marshall S. Shatz. Cambridge: Cambridge University Press, 1990.

Bataille, George. 'Le Surréalisme au jour le jour'. In *Œuvres complètes Vol. VIII.* Paris: Gallimard, 1976.

Benjamin, Walter. 'The Work of Art in the Age of Mechanical Reproduction.' In *Illuminations*, edited by Hannah Arendt, translated by Harry Zohn. New York: Schocken Books, 1969.

Bergson, Henri. *L'Évolution créatrice.* Paris: Presses Universitaires de France, 1941.

Boaventura de Sousa Santos. *Epistemologies of the South: Justice against Epistemicide.* Boulder, CO: Paradigm Publishers, 2014.

Bonnet, Marguerite, ed. *Archives du surréalisme 3, 'Adhérer au Parti communiste?'* Paris: Gallimard, 1992.

Bradu, Fabienne. *Artaud, Todavía.* Mexico City: Fondo de Cultura Económica, 2008.

Cardosa y Aragón, Luis. *Luna Park.* Translated by Anthony Seidman. Phoenix, AZ: Phoenix Cardboard House Press, 2016.

Carrel, Alexis. *Man, the Unknown.* New York: Harper & Brothers, 1935.

Derrida, Jacques. 'L'Écriture et le théâtre: Mallarmé/Artaud'. Unpublished manuscript, 1968–1969, typescript.

Evola, Julius. *Revolt against the Modern World.* Translated by Guido Stucco. Rochester, VT: Inner Traditions International, 1995.

Fabre d'Olivet, Antoine. *L'Histoire philosophique du genre humain* I. Paris: Éditions Tranditionelles, 1989.

Ferreira da Silva, Denise. *Toward a Global Idea of Race.* Minneapolis, MN: University of Minnesota Press, 2007.

Glissant, Eduard. *Traité du Tout-monde.* Paris: Gallimard, 1997.

Goodall, Jane. *Artaud and the Gnostic Drama.* London: Scarlet Imprint, 2020.

Hegel, G. W. F. 'Force and Understanding'. In *Phenomenology of Spirit.* Translated. A. V. Miller. Oxford: Oxford University Press, 1979.

Ivan, Lindsay. *The History of Loot and Stolen Art: From Antiquity until the Present Day*. London: Andrews UK Limited, 2014.

Jannarone, Kimberly. *Artaud and His Doubles*. Ann Arbor, MI: University of Michigan Press, 2012.

Kräme, Hans Joachim. *Arete bei Platon und Aristoteles*. Heidelberg: C. Winter, 1959.

Kristeva, Julia. 'Le sujet en procès'. In *Artaud*, edited by Phillipe Sollers. Paris: 10/18, 1973.

Lukacs, Georg. 'Realism in the Balance'. In *Aesthetics and Politics*. Translated by Rodney Livingstone. London: Verso, 2007.

Manifiesto Sinarquista (1937). https://www.memoriapoliticademexico. org/Textos/6Revolucion/1937MCO.html (accessed 10 March 2023).

Naville, Pierre. *La Révolution et les intellectuels*. Paris: Gallimard, 1975.

Pym, Michael. 'Saint-Yves d'Alveydre'. *Advocate of Peace through Justice* 88, no. 11 (November 1926): 609–614.

Said, Edward W. *Orientalism*. New York: Pantheon Books, 1978.

Saint-Yves d'Alveydre, Joseph Alexandre. *Les Clefs de l'Orient*. Paris: Librairie académique, Didier et Cie, éditeurs, 1877.

Seghers, Pierre, ed. *Poètes maudits d'aujourd'hui: 1946–1970*. Paris: Seghers, 1972.

Shiva, Vandana. *Monocultures of the Mind: Biodiversity, Biotechnology and Agriculture*. New Delhi: Zed Press, 1993.

Sollers, Phillipe. 'L'État d'Artaud'. In *Artaud*, edited by Phillipe Sollers. Paris: 10/18, 1973.

Thévenin, Paule, ed. *Archives du surréalisme* 1, '*Cahier de la perméance*'. Paris: Gallimard, 1988.

Thomas, Hugh. *Conquest: Montezuma, Cortés, and the Fall of Old Mexico*. New York: Simon and Schuster, 1993.

Rousselet, Laurine. *Correspondance avec Bernard Noël Artaud à La Havane*. Paris: L'Harmattan, 2021.

White, Joel. *Of Logomachy: Thermodynamics of Sense*. Forthcoming.

White, Joel. 'Outline to an Architectonics of Thermodynamics: Life's Entropic Indeterminacy'. In *Contingency and Plasticity in Everyday Technologies*, edited by Natasha Lushetich, Iain Campbell and Dominic Smith. London: Rowman and Littlefield, 2023.

INDEX